What the hell, her morning already sucked, so she might as well return her creepy co-worker's call…

"Kevin, it's Eileen Ryan."

"Good morning, Detective Ryan," Detective Hickey said, in an annoying, telemarketer-type voice.

"What's up?"

"Are you anywhere in the vicinity of East 235 and Katonah Avenue?"

"No. Why?"

"Well, I've uncovered a piece of…how shall we say?...um…"

"Evidence?"

"Your choice of words, not mine."

"What did you find?"

"With all due respect, Detective, it's kind of a sensitive matter."

She rolled her eyes. Much more of this and she would be retching again. "I'm a big girl, Hickey. I can take it."

"I think it might be best if we discussed this in person. Say, about two o'clock, Romero's restaurant?"

What a shithead. Was he still trying to snag a second date? Where did he think this was going to lead?

"That's not going to work for me. Just spill it."

"Okay—is anyone around?"

Ryan looked up at the sprawling brick building atop the hillside. "No, nobody's around. Just tell me what you found."

"I found some hair fibers at the scene of Declan's murder."

"Yeah, and…"

"The fibers match…"

"Match what?"

"The hair fibers of one…um…Detective Eileen Ryan."

"What are you talking about, Hickey?"

"That's why I wanted to discuss this in person."

"Okay, fuck. Two o'clock, Romero's."

In a neighborhood full of secrets, everyone's a suspect.

Hard-living Detective Eileen Ryan is called to investigate the murder of a popular bartender in her hometown, a tight-knit Irish enclave in The Bronx, New York. But she can't quite remember the night of the murder and has to fight off the advances of a creepy forensics officer who places her at the scene of the crime. Ryan discovers secret societies and double lives, as she moves back into her childhood home to care for her father, a retired police officer who suffered a stroke, and comforts her confidante, the hardened Lieutenant Barry Durkin, another neighborhood alum who's binge drinking through an impending divorce. Will caring for family and friends prevent Ryan from catching the killer—or becoming the next victim?

KUDOS for *The Pot O'Gold Murder*

"A great thriller! Coen brings into vivid focus not only his characters but an entire neighborhood. You'll read this in one sitting—guaranteed!" ~ Number One International Best-Selling Author Jeffery Deaver

"In this gripping, gritty tale, centered on a murder investigation, Shaun Coen brings the bars, back alleys, and unbreakable bonds between family and friends of the Woodlawn section of The Bronx to life. The finely drawn complex characters suck you in, the plot is dead-on, and the details and dialogue make each page crackle and buzz with electric authenticity...this is a killer debut crime novel you won't soon forget." ~ John Roche, Author of *Bronx Bound*

"Shaun Coen's novel of Bronx Irish murder and sex and mayhem is terrifically entertaining: funny, bawdy, fast-paced and explosive. Like all great crime stories it's an outline of a particular society at a particular moment: and Coen's is one at that interesting historical junction when an unchanging way of life is finally, reluctantly, in some cases tragically, changing." ~ Vince Passaro, Author of *Violence, Nudity, Adult Content*

"Gritty and atmospheric, Coen's The Pot O'Gold Murder combines the best of noir with a tough realism. This book is not to be missed and I can't wait to see what Coen does next." ~ Maggie Barbieri, Author of *Once Upon a Lie* and the *Murder 101* series

"If your mother told you, 'Nothing good ever happens after three am,' she was right! Hard drinking, hard living, and murder are on tap in the lurid bars at the northern edge of Shaun Coen's gritty New York. It's Raymond Chandler with an Irish sense of gallows humor." ~ Susan Konig, Author of *Teenagers & Toddlers Are Trying to Kill Me!*

ACKNOWLEDGEMENTS

Thanks to my parents, master storytellers and mimics, for all the love, support, and laughter, and for raising me in the right neighborhood.

Thanks to my family and friends for listening and sharing their stories.

To the good folks at Black Opal Books, my appreciation, and to the men and women of the NYPD, my respect.

The

Pot O'Gold

Murder

Shaun Coen

A Black Opal Books Publication

DEDICATION

To the most wonderful children one could possibly be blessed with: Jack, Dan, and Jenn, who continue to amaze and enlighten. I am so fortunate to have you and am eternally grateful to the woman responsible for bringing you into this wacky world and making you who you are. Rose and kids, I love you and look forward to the next chapter.

Prologue

Tommy "Slats" Slattery was hauling garbage bags down the alleyway between The Pot O'Gold and The Shanty at 6:15 a.m. when he found Declan McManus face down on the concrete, the barrel of a Coors Light protruding from his neck. Dark crimson blood, still wet, streaked down the alley toward a drain. Slats, the mildly retarded porter, often found drunks and fighters passed out in the alley, victims of the previous night's debauchery and inevitable dust-ups. He would either cover them with a jacket or some garbage bags and drag them out of sight of the parishioners who were heading off to early masses and the commuters going to the bakery for coffee and a scone before boarding the number thirty-four bus to the number four subway. Declan, the good-looking, well-liked bartender of the new neighborhood hot spot, The Pot O'Gold, liked to play gags on the waitresses and the bar backs, and Slats was an easy mark. But this seemed different. It was too elaborate a prank, even for Declan. His black Rockport shoes were still polished, his white button-down shirt wasn't overly wrinkled, and not a dark hair on his gelled head was out of place. Declan was a joker and a lover; he wasn't a fighter.

"Come on, get up, Declan," Slats said, as he flung a garbage bag into the metal Dumpster. "That's not funny, man."

Slats scanned the alleyway and looked across the street at Hooligans and MacGuffin's, two of the other eight bars that lined Katonah Avenue. At some point or other, he had worked at all of them. He'd seen some crazy shit at this hour of the morning—naked men and women in various sexual positions, post-coital, mid-coital, and passed out drunk. People he'd never imagine. Mothers and fathers, nurses and lawyers, old women and teenagers, and one time a priest, still in collar with a raspberry on his forehead and an empty wallet beside him. He'd seen tattoos in sensitive places and people defecating in planters, in garbage cans, and even right on the sidewalk. "Nothing good ever happens after three a.m.," his mother always used to say. Except that was when Slats went to work, and he liked to work. It gave him a sense of purpose. Even though he still took abuse from a few obnoxious drunks, it was nothing like the ribbing he used to take from neighborhood kids. Working these hours, he didn't see many kids anymore, which was fine by him. He might have been the only one in Woodlawn who was happy there were thirty-two bars within walking distance and that each of them at one time or another was willing to hire him to take the garbage out for minimum wage. Despite his disability, he'd been able to earn enough to pay the rent on his tiny basement studio apartment and even save some money. He long ago came to the realization that he'd never be able to drive a car or a motorcycle. His eyesight was awful. But he'd really like to ride one of those motorized scooters or wheelchairs to work. Those didn't require a license or good eyesight.

Slats reached out his right leg and, with an unlaced New Balance, the only sneaker wide enough for his feet, attempted to roll Declan over. The body nudged a bit and settled back into place. *So that's what dead weight means*, Slats realized, staring at the smudge his sneaker left on Declan's shoulder. Holding onto the Dumpster for leverage, he placed a foot under Declan's shoulder and lifted again, this time hard enough to roll him onto his back.

Declan's eyes were wide open, as if in shock, and his shirt was covered in blood. It wasn't bright red, or the color of ketchup, like it was in the movies, but a much darker shade. Maroon. Like the stuff kids paint on their faces when they pretend to be Dracula for Halloween. Only this stuff didn't look fake. Slats hoped that Declan would start laughing, or that Orla the waitress would jump out from behind the Dumpster and take a picture with her cell phone camera, but everything was silent and still. He looked around the alley for any sign of life but saw none. Slowly kneeling down, he closed Declan's eyes. Slats grabbed the bottleneck and yanked it, removing it from Declan's throat with a moist smack. A geyser of blood sprayed over both of them.

"Declan?" Slats asked. "Declan?"

He tapped his face a few times but Declan didn't respond. He threw the bottleneck against the brick wall. Broken shards of glass rained down on them.

"Declan! Get up!"

Slats kicked Declan's side in anger.

"Get up, Declan!"

His screams echoed off the brick walls of the alley until a light went on in an apartment above The Pot O'Gold.

Chapter 1

Eileen Ryan's cell phone blared from the nightstand, but at first she didn't budge. When she felt a pair of hairy legs under the sheets, she bolted upright and was somewhat embarrassed that she had downloaded the Neko Case "People Got A Lot Of Nerve" ring tone. Its chorus of "I'm a man, man, man, man, man, man, man eater. But still you're surprised…prised…prised when I eat ya" was catchy enough but not the sort of thing she wanted her nubile young bedmate to hear first thing the morning after. God, he was cute. What was his name again? She looked at the faint white initials she had carved into her wrist with a fingernail at the bar last night to remember but they had already faded. Looked like a D and a P. Or maybe it was DD? BB? No, definitely a D. DB. Before the chorus of her ring tone repeated, she picked up the phone.

"Why?"

"Rough night, iRye?" answered the gruff voice.

"Morning's usually rougher. What's up?"

"Got a stiff one for you," Durkin said.

"I'm flattered, Durk, but you're married."

"I mean a cold one."

"Little early for a beer, but I could use a little hair of the dog."

"Let me know when you're done with the comedy routine."

She reached for the Alka-Seltzer and Vitamin Water she always laid out on the nightstand when she knew her head would be banging in the morning and dropped two tablets into the plastic bottle.

"Okay, I'm listening," she said, watching the bubbles rise.

"I need you to investigate a homicide."

"Aren't there any morning people on the squad who can handle it?"

"This one's got your name written all over it," Durkin said.

"Why's that?"

"Word on the street is that the guy was gorgeous, well-off, liked to drink and gamble."

"Only the good die young."

"Yeah. A real lady killer, too."

"And one of these ladies exacted revenge?"

"That's what I need you to find out. Nobody has a bad word to say about this guy. It's weird."

"Nobody ever says anything bad about serial killers, either. They're always the quiet guys who kept to themselves."

The body next to her began to stir under the covers. *What a way to wake up*, Ryan thought. *Poor guy probably thinks he fell asleep watching* Law & Order *again. But he'll be happy to discover he's in bed with a naked woman.* He probably didn't remember much from last night, either. They were both pretty drunk.

"This is different, though," Durkin said. "A lot of people knew him. Nobody had a grudge."

"Where'd they find him?"

"In an alley with a beer bottle in his throat. He was a bartender in Woodlawn."

"Which bar?"

"The Pot O'Gold."

"Oh, shit."

"What?"

"Declan is dead?"

"Yeah. You knew him?"

Knew him? Ryan thought. *I blew him.* "Be right there, Durk."

Chapter 2

"Always happens right as the shift's about to end," Officer Keegan said to his partner, Alvarez.

"I can use the OT this week," Alvarez answered.

"I can use a drink," Keegan said.

"I'll never get used to working nights," Alvarez said. "Even though I put in eight hours, come eight o'clock in the morning, I just can't drink a beer. I need coffee."

"Coffee keeps me up," Keegan said. "I need a couple pops to go to sleep."

"So nights don't agree with you, either?"

"The job doesn't agree with me anymore."

"Who else would hire you? And give you a gun?"

They parked the cruiser in front of The Pot O'Gold, facing the ambulance, and surveyed the scene before getting out. There were already some weathered-looking Irish men and women, their heads covered in tweed caps, hairnets and scarves, gathered around looking down at the EMTs unraveling a white sheet in the alley, talking in hushed tones with hands covering their mouths. Slats was banging his fists on the brick wall.

"I'll disperse the crowd, you take the retard," Keegan said.

"Don't call him that," Alvarez said.

"That's how I roll. I call spades 'spades' and retards 'retards.'"

"Why do you always get to disperse the crowd?"

"I've got seniority. And you're good with the retards."

Alvarez reluctantly put his hat on and turned down the volume knob on his police radio. Keegan strolled toward the small crowd with a nonchalance that suggested he might just waltz right past them and enter the pub for a drink.

"Yo, Slats," Officer Alvarez called out. "Slats!...Hey, Tommy, man, what's up?"

"No!" Slats cried, as he continued hitting the wall. "No!"

"Okay, okay, ease up on the wall, bro," Alvarez said. "You'll break your hands."

"They killed my friend," Slats cried, charging at Alvarez.

Alvarez was stocky, five-foot-seven-inches and about 180, but he was no match for Slats, who was five-foot-ten-inches and at least 225. Bracing himself low to the ground, the way he was taught to block when he was a high school fullback on a passing play, Alvarez managed to keep his footing, standing Slats upright before embracing him in a bear hug. Keegan raced over to help secure him and push him against the wall.

"Relax, Tommy," Alvarez said. "Relax. Who killed your friend?"

"I don't know."

"Should we cuff him?" Keegan asked.

"No!" Alvarez said. "I got him. You work the crowd."

Keegan gave Slats a searing glance and then walked back toward the crowd.

"I'm going to have to ask you guys to clear out of here," Keegan said. "This is a crime scene."

Keegan saw the white News 12 truck coming down Katonah Avenue and wondered how they got the information so fast.

"What happened?" Bridie McCann, the owner of The Traditional Irish Bakery across the street asked, her red, bloodshot eyes nearly popping out of her pasty white face.

"Don't know yet," Keegan answered. "Watch the news tonight and find out."

A Ford Taurus rolled to a stop and Kevin Hickey got out, dressed in his signature blue jeans, black Reeboks, white V-neck T-shirt, satin blazer, and three-day stubble. He'd been wearing the same outfit for twenty years now, since he was a kid listening to Jan Hammer.

"Hey, Miami Vice," Keegan teased him.

"Keegan," Hickey said, walking past him, a roll of yellow crime scene tape in hand.

Keegan hated Hickey since high school. Hickey was better looking, with clear skin, and in much better shape. He would stay home on Friday nights, watch *Miami Vice* and rest up before baseball games while Keegan would hit the three or four bars in Woodlawn that served minors and get shitfaced. Keegan watched from the bench as Hickey took over his starting centerfield job, even though he knew he was more talented. But Hickey put the time in the weight room and the batting cage while Keegan was riding the pine in Muldoon's and O'Shea's, knocking back shots like an all-star. Then Hickey got Keegan's girl, Maryjean McNeil, on prom night, while Keegan was passed out drunk in the limousine. And now Keegan watched as Hickey took over the crime scene and went to work dusting for prints while he and Alvarez brought Slats in for questioning.

Chapter 3

Katonah Avenue was abuzz all morning and afternoon. The Irish enclave in the Northwest section of The Bronx was usually a sleepy town, as odd as that would seem, being that there were thirty-two bars within walking distance. Compared with the rest of The Bronx, Woodlawn was a quiet pocket without a subway or elevated train tracks passing through its tree-lined streets that were crammed with narrow one and two-family, wood frame, three-story houses on twenty-five-by-seventy-five-foot lots. A well-placed match could set the entire community ablaze within hours, now that the New York Fire Department had closed its Woodlawn engine. A garage or a sizeable backyard was a luxury and a bonus not many enjoyed. Its four square miles had boundaries on every side, some natural, some manmade.

On one end was the Woodlawn Cemetery, which ran the length of East 233rd Street and was flanked by The Bronx River Parkway on one end and the expansive Van Cortlandt Park and Major Deegan Expressway on the other. Katonah Avenue cut through the heart of Woodlawn, from East 233rd Street directly across to the city of Yonkers, which didn't have a subway or an elevated train either. Many believed that the lack of easy access to a subway into Manhattan was what kept Woodlawn somewhat exclusive. If you wanted to work in the city, you had to pay two fares each way—a bus to take you to the subway and back again—or you had to ride the expensive Metro North, which abutted The Bronx River Parkway.

Many of the Irish transplants were long retired now, their social life consisting of having a few drinks in one of the pubs in the afternoon, sitting in at one of the bakeries or diners for a cup of tea and a card game, or attending a wake at Dunphy's Funeral Home and a funeral at St. Sebastian's. The first and second generation Irish and the newer wave of immigrants took over the pubs at night. Each pub had its own clientele. Some catered to sports crowds, broadcasting soccer matches from around the world at all hours of the day, or the Gaelic games from Ireland, hurling and Irish football, and others to music crowds, many of them offering live, traditional music. And yet others catered to hardcore drunks, legless men who stumbled into the darkness for a drink or a nap on the bar. Woodlawners looked the other way, thankful it wasn't them and hoping it wasn't a relative, while outsiders wondered how it was possible or even legal to allow it.

The Pot O'Gold was the newest pub on the avenue, having only been opened for six months. It caused a bit of a stir in the local press but most residents shrugged it off, with one old timer telling a News 12 reporter that "Sure, it's good for the community. There's no place to go for a quiet drink anymore."

The Pot O'Gold didn't offer live music, nor was it a sports hub. Its main attraction was that it was new, and that Declan McManus, the dark-haired, silver-tongued Irishman from County Mayo, was manning the stick. The girls thought he was gorgeous, the guys thought he was one of them. He had a sharp wit and a high tolerance for drunks and alcohol. Guys could spend a night drinking with Declan, and girls would swoon, showering him with tips and anything else he wanted. He didn't go home alone on many nights, but now he would be going home in a box, back to his family in Knock, County Mayo.

Chapter 4

Ryan jumped out of bed and dragged a brush through her shoulder length bleached blonde hair. She pounded the vitamin seltzer combo and briefly thought about marketing it as a hangover relief while she pulled on some jeans and a T-shirt, strapped on her holster and then nudged the shape under the covers. Who was that again? Started with a "D."

"David?...David?...Come on, get up. You gotta go. It's late. I have to go to work."

Definitely wasn't David. It was something Irish.

"Dermot?...Dermot!" she yelled. "Let's go!"

She nearly tripped over a pair of Timberland boots and sweatpants as she flipped on the overhead light switch. She went into the bathroom, gargled with Listerine, brushed her teeth with Gleem, then blew some breath into her cupped hands and inhaled. Still smelled like tequila. *Got to cut back on the shots*, she told herself. She grabbed her make-up kit and poked her head out the doorway.

"Donal?...Come on, Donal, get up!"

She applied some rouge to her cheeks and started with the eyeliner when she was startled by the sudden appearance of her young naked conquest in the mirror. Ordinarily, she'd have been frightened, but his chiseled six-pack abs and morning glory erection had her intrigued. Was there time for a quickie?

"It's Danny," he said.

Shit. Danny, of course. She had etched the initials D B into her wrist at the bar to remember it was Danny. Danny…Brady? Boyle? Burke? Looking into his navy blue eyes, she now remembered they were singing *Danny Boy* and pawing at each other while singing off key to the jukebox in the back room of The Shamrock until the patrons playing pool told them to shut the fuck up and get a room. Now she remembered. Danny Boy. Said he worked in a meat packing plant. She watched him pee and wondered if the meat packing remark was a sexual reference or a pick-up line. Certainly was apropos. As tempting as it was, she decided she had to go see Durkin.

"Sorry, Danny Boy," she said. "Party's over. Time to go home."

Chapter 5

O fficers Keegan and Alvarez led Slats into the station and straight back into a dark room with an overhead light and sat him on a wooden stool before a metal table.

"You want something to drink?" Alvarez asked.

"I'll have a Fanta," Slats said.

"Fanta? I don't think we have Fanta. How 'bout some water?"

"You have Fanta," Slats said. "I saw it in the soda machine in the hallway. I want Fanta."

Alvarez looked up at his partner and flicked his neck in the direction of the door. Keegan went into the hall to fetch the Fanta.

"I know you're upset, Slats, but see if you can remember everything that happened this morning that may help us understand why Declan McManus is dead," Alvarez said.

"I got up, same as I always do, at two o'clock in the morning, and went to work," Slats said.

"You woke up and went straight to work?"

"Yep."

"And you're still living in that basement apartment on McLean Avenue?"

"Yes. I live at 921 McLean Avenue, Yonkers, New York, 10704."

"Okay. Did anybody see you go to work?"

"Sheila."

"Who's Sheila?"

"Sheila's the best waitress in the world. She works at The Comfy Corner."

"Did you go into The Comfy Corner?"

"Yeah. I had scrambled eggs with cheese and toast, just like I do every morning."

"So you didn't wake up and go straight to work. You stopped off for breakfast."

"Yes, same as I always do."

"Okay, Slats? It's really important that you think hard and give us honest answers."

"I am honest!"

"But you said you woke up and went to work but you really woke up and went to the diner and then went to work."

"A man's gotta eat."

"I hear ya. It's just that you can't leave out any details. Nothing. Okay?"

"I'm telling the truth!"

"Okay, just relax. We want to help you remember all the events that led up to Declan's death."

"I don't know the events. I just found him."

"I understand that. I just need to hear how you found him."

"On the ground. Dead—where's my Fanta?"

Alvarez rubbed his face. Why did this shit always happen right before he was ready to punch out? Yeah, the OT was nice, and he sure could use it, as he was saving up to buy a nice little pontoon boat he had seen for sale on City Island. Working the night shift wasn't so bad, he told himself, as long as he was catching stripers in the Long Island Sound by eight-thirty each morning.

"Let me check on that," Alvarez said.

He poured some crappy coffee into a Styrofoam cup and wondered if the department would ever go green or at least switch to paper cups. If he went out of his way to buy fair trade coffee, couldn't New York's Finest buy some recyclable cups? He heard an officer typing out a complaint report and realized if the department hadn't yet switched over to computers from typewriters and carbon paper, he could forget about drinking from a paper cup, unless he went to Costco and bought them himself. He saw Keegan talking with Lieutenant Durkin by the soda machine.

"Keegs, where's the Fanta?" he shouted.

"We ain't got no Fanta. There's some Welch's, though. See if the retard likes grape soda."

Alvarez walked over to them. "I asked you not to call him that."

"Why not? The fuckin' dude's retarded."

"Slats is a good guy. He's just a little slow."

"He's been stalking Woodlawn for years, terrorizing little girls and scaring old ladies," Keegan said. "That retard is dangerous."

"Lieutenant, are you going to reprimand him, or what?" Alvarez said.

Durkin, who stood six-foot-four and had thinning red hair and layers of bags under his eyes, looked down at Alvarez and remembered he had a retarded sister, or one with Down Syndrome or something. Whatever it was, he always threw Alvarez fifty bucks around Memorial Day, when he supposedly walked or biked for a cure for something his sister had. Durkin suspected he was partially financing Alvarez's annual Bar-B-Q but as long as he wasn't invited, he was happy to contribute without feeling obligated to go.

"He's right, Keegs," Durkin said. "You gotta be a little more sensitive."

"C'mon, Durk. The dude's retarded. Why can't we just say it?"

"Because we just can't anymore, okay?" Durkin shook his head. "Why did I ever let you work nights?"

"Take me off of nights, please," Keegan said.

"You'll miss the differential," Durkin said. "It's paying your alimony."

"That differential comes with a price. It's tough to get laid when you're working nights. Not many joints hopping at eight in the morning."

"Join a gym," Durkin said. "Lots of lonely housewives hit the gym in the morning. My wife does."

"No offense, Durk. But I'm not interested in seeing your wife in spandex."

"You'll never get off nights, Keegan."

"I never get off anymore period."

"'Scuse me," Alvarez said, stepping between the two of them and sliding a dollar into the soda machine. Though the red light indicated that there was no Fanta left, he punched the plastic tab and out rolled a bright orange can.

"Look at that," Keegan said. "You got the touch. You oughtta play the number tonight."

"Are you going to help me get a statement from the witness?" Alvarez asked.

"You mean the suspect," Keegan said.

"Slats? A suspect?" Alvarez said. "Are you joking?"

"He's got blood all over him and his prints are all over the scene," Keegan said.

"How do they know that already?" Alvarez said.

"Forensics ran the prints through the laptop," Durkin said.

"Can you believe that forensics faggot Hickey has got a friggin' laptop in his cruiser?" Keegan said. "I bet that prick is watching porn all night on it. When are we getting laptops in our car, Durk?"

"Never," Durkin said.

"You really think Slats is a suspect, Lieutenant?" Alvarez asked.

Durkin shrugged. Nothing surprised him anymore. He had fourteen months until he could retire with a full, non-taxable pension of $140,000, and he intended to make it without a shred of guilt. The sleepless nights of thinking over cases, the long hours sitting in courtrooms waiting to testify, the crappy coffee, the mutants of The Bronx—he couldn't wait to say goodbye to all of it. He just wanted to bang out and get some solid sleep while the wife was at the gym.

"We'll launch an investigation, see what shakes out," Durkin said.

"There's no way Slats could've done this," Alvarez said.

"Why not?" Keegan said. "He's got a record. We've picked him up several times."

"Only when he defends himself from the kids that harass him," Alvarez said.

"And what about the Cheryl Lind case? He just mistakenly entered her apartment one night and put his hands on her?" Keegan said.

"Cheryl Lind has had half the hands of Woodlawn on her," Alvarez said. "Including yours. Let's not forget she has a record, too. And a history of lying to the police."

"Slats's prints are on the beer bottle and the Dumpster, his shoe marks are on Declan's shirt, and Declan's blood is on his shirt," Keegan said. "What more do you want?"

"How about a motive?" Alvarez said.

"Who the fuck knows?" Keegan said. "In case you haven't noticed, Declan's not talking. I think the retard just ran wild."

"Don't call him a retard!" Alvarez said. "Slats wouldn't hurt a fly."

A loud bang echoed through the station house. They turned in the direction of the interview room and through the small rectangular window saw the metal table upturned and Slats flinging his wooden chair against the wall.

"Then again, maybe he would," Keegan said. "If it went after his Fanta."

Chapter 6

Ryan had forgotten that Danny Boy lived in Brooklyn. Despite what she told him last night in the bar, she had no intention of driving him home. She dropped him off at the number four train, grabbed a MetroCard from the stack behind her sun visor—for those nights when she drank responsibly, parked the car, and took the subway home—and told him that she had an emergency. He asked if he'd see her again, and she shrugged. That's when he pulled a CD in a plastic, slim line jewel case out of his back pocket and dropped it on the passenger seat. She could see it had a phone number on it, written in a red Sharpie, along with two words in quotations: "The Man." He asked for her phone number and she made one up—it was actually the old number to Nico's pizzeria, etched into her brain since childhood when her family abstained from meat on Fridays, fish for the parents, pizza for the kids—gunned the engine, and sped off.

She entered the precinct with a twenty-two-ounce coffee and marched straight into Durkin's office. He was at his computer, poring over the CompStat numbers, which showed concentrated pockets of the precinct where crimes were being committed. There was an uptick in burglaries in the Bainbridge section and the usual late night assaults in Woodlawn, on Katonah Avenue and on East 242 Street, spilling over from the bars on McLean Avenue, which fell under Yonkers cops' jurisdiction.

He wondered if the Yonkers police stationed outside of

Paddy Doyle's, the biggest bar on McLean Avenue, directed patrons to take their fights into The Bronx so they wouldn't have to deal with them. Maybe he'd order Alvarez and Keegan to sweep East 242nd from midnight to four, when most of the fights broke out.

"Morning, Durk," Ryan said.

"Yes, it is," Durkin said, looking at his watch. "Three more hours to go."

He meant until noon, when he could go home. Pointing to her coffee cup, he directed with a wag of his index finger for her to dump some into the mug on the desk.

"I take it black," she said.

"That what she said," Durkin said.

"You never use that right, do you?" Ryan said, pouring some of her coffee into his mug.

"That's what she said," Durkin said.

"Okay, that works."

She glanced at his computer screen. "Burglaries are up, surprise, surprise. So is heroin."

"Yeah, doesn't take a rocket scientist to figure that out. Economy tanks, people start using and stealing. Idle minds—"

"Can't wait for the graffiti artists to come back."

"Well, if we're going to revert to the '70s in this city, at least I hope the music comes back, too."

"You like disco?" Ryan asked.

"No, all the other stuff. Stones, Zeppelin, Steely Dan, Elton John…"

"Classic rock."

"Yeah, and the progressive stuff. Pink Floyd, Yes, jam bands like the Allman Brothers."

"Got news for you, Durk. There's a classic rock station on the radio. Plays nothing but. If you were to turn that box on your desk on and tune it to 104.3, you'd think you were in a time warp. They don't play anything after 1981."

"I'm not allowed to play the radio anymore. Certain members of the force didn't want to be subjected to my musical tastes. Complained to the white shirts."

"That's ridiculous."

"It is—but, there's only two hours and fifty-six minutes left."

"You used to count down the years."

"Now I take it day by day, hour by hour, minute by minute." He launched into the chorus of The Doobie Brothers' "Minute by Minute."

Ryan stopped him before he got to his embarrassing Michael McDonald falsetto impersonation. "So, what's the deal with Declan?" she asked.

"The porter found him in the alley with a bottle in his neck. We picked him up for questioning."

"Hulkhead?"

"Pardon?"

"The porter. They call him Hulkhead. Don't you remember Hulkhead?"

"No," Durkin said.

Ryan was reminded that Durkin was a few years her senior. Once she turned eighteen, she considered everyone the same age, but Durkin probably wouldn't remember Hulkhead patrolling the neighborhood with his Sony Walkman and long overcoat, collecting empty cans and bottles from garbage bins.

"He's been answering to Tommy," Durkin said.

"Right, Tommy. But everyone, well, all of the mean kids, anyway, used to call him Hulkhead."

"I thought his nickname was Slats."

"One of many. Trust me, Tommy Slats was, is, Hulkhead."

Everyone had a nickname in Woodlawn, sometimes more than one. Could make it tough for police officers and outsiders to keep track.

"You were one of the mean kids?" Durk asked.

"So were you."

"You must have me confused with one of my brothers."

That was easy to do. There were ten Durkins, all boys, each born a year apart. If you graduated from St. Sebastian elementary school from 1977-1987, you had a Durkin in your class. If you went to church that decade, a Durkin served your mass. The old pastor, Father Doyle, used to joke about them at the early masses, during the Prayer for the Faithful. The lector would recite the specific causes and the congregation would sleepily respond, "Let us pray," and then Father Doyle would end with, "And for poor Mrs. Durkin..." and again, the congregation would robotically reply, "Let us pray."

Ryan thought back to elementary school, remembered that Eddie and Marty Durkin were on the seventh and eighth grade boys basketball team, and that Barry was older than both of them. He used to come watch their games and in later years, collect them from the bars when it got too late. Maybe Barry wasn't one of the mean kids. He always had a job, either a paper route or bagging groceries in the supermarket, and didn't spend all his nights on Katonah Avenue harassing girls, drinking beer, and smoking pot. Years ago, this all seemed legal, and cops were never on foot patrol. Teenagers would congregate on street corners with boom boxes and blast Peter Gabriel, Kiss, and Black Sabbath; smoke cigarettes and joints; drink quarts of Bud from plastic cups or nips in brown paper bags; sit on the hoods of cars; and intimidate anyone who walked by. Ryan remembered buying a quart of milk from the corner deli for her mother one night—she couldn't have been more than nine or ten—and having to pass by the group of teens in jean jackets and Pro-Keds. Her heart was pounding. She heard one of them make kissing and sucking noises at her, and she ran home as fast as she could. That was the first time she thought about being a cop. She initially thought about being a vigilante, like Charles Bronson in the *Death Wish* movie that her father loved. It seemed to be on Channel 9 almost every week, and she'd occasionally watch the black and white set with the rabbit ears along with her dad, as the mustachioed guy in a knit cap casually walked up to gang members and sprayed them with bullets. That's what she wanted to do to those guys on Katonah Avenue. But *Death Wish* ended with the widowed Paul Kersey on the lam. She wanted to come home to a family every night, not be out on her own. Oh, well. Not every wish could come true. As her father used to tell her and her three siblings whenever they voiced their desires, "We can't all play centerfield for the Yankees."

She never knew what he meant by that when she would ask

Santa Claus for a bicycle for Christmas, but it started to sink in when she hit her teen years. When her older sister Maureen wanted to go to Vassar College and study philosophy, Ryan remembered hearing, "We can't all play centerfield for the Yankees," and when her brother Brendan voiced his desire to go to San Francisco to form a band, she remembered thinking to herself, "We can't all play centerfield for the Yankees." By the time Ryan told her father that she wanted to be a cop, all he said was, "Jesus, Mary and Joseph, not a cop. Please."

"He's in the back," Durkin said.

"Who?" Ryan answered, snapping to.

"Tommy. Slats. Hulkhead. Whatever you call him."

"Why? Is he a suspect?"

Durkin shrugged. "His prints are all over the crime scene. They're on the bottles, the Dumpster, the garbage bags."

"Why wouldn't the porter's prints be all over the scene? He worked there."

"True. But his sneaker mark is on the deceased's shirt, too. He said he kicked the body to roll it over, to make sure he was really dead."

"The Hulkhead I remember wasn't capable of killing someone, I don't think."

"Anyone's capable of murder in the right circumstances."

"What would be his motive?"

"Who knows? Did Declan stiff him? Steal his girlfriend?"

"Hulkhead has a girlfriend?"

"He may *think* he has a girlfriend."

"You mean, he may covet someone that Declan dated."

"Dated, laid, whatever."

"Any idea who?"

"Not yet. From what we hear, this Declan guy got around."

"Oh? Really?"

"Yeah. Why? Is this news to you, Ryan?"

"Ah, no, I guess not. He was attractive. And bartenders have been known to get lucky on occasion."

She couldn't believe she was jealous. It was just a one-night-only deal with Declan. That was the way they both wanted it. Still, her competitive nature got the best of her. *Oh, well. We can't all play centerfield for the Yankees.*

"Well, this guy got lucky a lot. And one of the broads he got lucky with may be the one that Tommy wanted to get lucky with. You know The Comfy Corner diner?"

Didn't everyone? It was a rite of passage if you grew up in Woodlawn to finish off a late night of boozing with an Irish breakfast at The Comfy.

"Of course."

"You know this waitress, Sheila?"

"I haven't been there in years. I wouldn't remember any names."

"Find out what you can about her. It's the only name he's mentioned."

"Who's doing the questioning?"

"Just Alvarez and Keegan so far."

"I'm sure you have your reasons, Durk, but why am I being asked to investigate this murder?"

"'Cause, you're a good detective and they're only beat walkers. The most they can do is secure a scene and 'tween you, me, and the lamppost, they're barely capable of that. Keegan's on the spectrum and Alvarez—he's a good kid, but a little too...gung-ho or something. Heart's in the right place, but I'm afraid he's gonna be one of the guys you read about in the paper, and it won't be on the sports page."

Ryan slugged some coffee.

"And," Durkin continued, "I got a hunch there's more to this than it seems. People have been drinking in Woodlawn bars for a long time. A fair share of them have drinking to blame for their premature deaths, but they don't just die in the alley after a rough night."

Durkin swirled his coffee and fought it down. "How can you drink this shit black?"

"Once you try black, you never go back."

"You're talking about the coffee, I presume."

"Shouldn't make presumptions in your line of work."

"I'm not supposed to say this, either, Ryan, but you got the best legs and biggest...eyes...on the force, and a better chance of getting to the bottom of this murder than anyone else."

"I don't want to step on anyone's toes, Durk."

"I need Keegan and Alvarez to patrol the streets, look into this rash of burglaries, and break-up fights, and I need you to solve a murder case. If those guys give you any shit, let me know."

"That shouldn't be a problem."

"Yeah, and this Declan kid should be home sleeping it off right now instead of getting pumped with formaldehyde."

Right, thought Ryan. *We can't all play centerfield for the Yankees.*

Chapter 7

Ryan peeked into the interview room and saw Keegan standing in the corner under the window fiddling with his iPhone and Alvarez sitting across the table from Slats, who had two cans of Fanta before him. She knocked on the door and thought she heard Keegan mumble "Easy Eileen."

Alvarez got up and opened the door.

"You say something, Keegan?" she asked.

"No."

"I thought I heard my name."

"Oh, yeah, I just said, 'Easy, Eileen' when you knocked on the door. I didn't want you to startle the witness."

Ryan stared him down. She knew Keegan from years ago, before he was on the job, when he patrolled Woodlawn's bars instead of its streets. He was always getting into fights. Cute kid, with a small dose of acne and a bad case of little man complex that got the best of him when he drank. Back in those days, Ryan had been branded with the unfortunate handle of "Easy Eileen," because she fooled around with a couple loudmouthed boys who exaggerated their conquests. The fact that every jukebox in Woodlawn had a copy of the one-hit-wonder band Dexy's Midnight Runners single "Come On, Eileen" didn't help, either. Some asshole would always put it on and the jokes would start.

That was why she stopped hanging out in Woodlawn. A small town could be hell for a sexually confident female who was hitting her stride.

She motioned for Alvarez to enter the hall with her. "I'm taking over the questioning in this case."

"Oh? Really?"

"Yeah. You don't like it, talk to Durkin."

"I will."

He looked her up and down and stormed off to Durkin's office.

"Keegan? You can leave now."

"Says who?"

"Durkin has some assignments for you and Alvarez."

Keegan slid the iPhone into his shirt pocket and waltzed passed her. He looked back at Slats and whispered into her ear, "If the retard gives you any trouble, call me."

"Funny," she said. "Durkin said the same thing about you."

Keegan held his tongue. He had already been reprimanded for his politically incorrect rumblings, and the force had seen a rash of sexual harassment lawsuits. Like most of the veterans, Keegan was clockwatching to his pension now, too. He had an older brother of forty-five already retired from the force collecting his pension in Florida, working part-time as a security guard for the Tampa Bay Devil Rays. It was a life model he intended to follow.

Ryan shut the door and smiled at Slats.

"Hi, Tommy, I'm Detective Ryan."

"Hello."

"You want to get out of here?"

"Yes."

"Come with me."

As they passed Durkin's office, she could hear Alvarez pleading his case for remaining on the investigation and Durkin calmly responding that the matter was out of his hands. He had done his job, Durkin assured him. Arrived at the scene, kept the crowds from contaminating any evidence, and brought in a distraught witness and possible suspect. Now it was time for the detectives to take over. The conversation brought back memories of her early years on the force as an overzealous foot soldier.

છૂબ્છ

She cut her teeth around Yankee Stadium, stationed outside 161st Street and River Avenue, first in uniform helping with crowd control, then as a plain-clothes detective arresting ticket scalpers hawking counterfeit ducats and Red Sox fans who liked to do shots and smoke weed in the parking lots. Collars came quick and easy and she worked her way up the ranks. Most times, if the people seemed in control, just catching a buzz before paying exorbitant prices for watered down swill inside the Stadium, she looked the other way. If guys were obnoxious and likely to ruin the experience for the kids in attendance, then she'd move in, confiscate their beer or drugs, and if they got testy, she'd run them in and let them sleep it off in the drunk tank.

Most games weren't a problem. Tuesday night games in May against Kansas City didn't bring the riff-raff that a Boston series on a hot summer weekend would. Those fuckers were arrogant. "Massholes" her colleagues had dubbed them. Even though she wasn't much of a baseball fan when she took the job, she had pride in her hometown and fond memories of the Yankees' World Series wins in the '70's, when it seemed like everything around them was ready to collapse or burn to the ground. Even her father, who preferred rooting for their perennial underdog crosstown rivals, the Mets, took pleasure in watching Reggie Jackson smack three home runs on three consecutive swings. Love him or hate him, who couldn't admire that feat?

Her assignment to the area coincided with the arrival of good-looking homegrown talent Derek Jeter, Mariano Rivera, Bernie Williams, Jorge Posada, and Andy Pettitte, which peaked her interest not only in the team but also in its history and the neighborhood. Being stationed in and around the stadium for four World Series wins cemented a place in her heart for those teams and her job. She knew she was seeing something special and liked nothing better than arresting one of those Massholes with the funny accents who thought they were going to walk into her office, the hallowed ground at Yankee Stadium, and spray paint their name or piss on The House That Ruth Built. Not on her watch.

Her superiors noticed her skill and professionalism. Even after 9/11, when security at the Stadium was tight and nerves were on edge, Ryan was the epitome of cool professionalism. She never let assholes interfere with other peoples' good time, but she gave them the opportunity to redeem themselves. The chance to cease and desist and, if necessary, apologize was always offered before the cuffs came out. As professional as she was on the job, she was something of a legend off the clock as well. She could drink with any of her co-workers and had a reputation as a party girl—two things she made no attempt to hide. With two older brothers and one older sister, she could handle herself in a street fight as well as a catfight. She didn't take losing lightly so she made a point of not losing at all. From darts to target practice to drinking games to hooking up, she usually came out on top. Unless, of course, she wanted to be on the bottom.

She did a stint as an undercover detective, too, dressing in garish make-up and gold lame shorts and patrolling Lexington Avenue in the Twenties, near the armory, and then up in the Hunt's Point section of The Bronx. It was more unpleasant than dangerous. She wore a wire, had a pistol at the ready in her purse, and backup was always nearby. In just a few hours each night, she'd rack up dozens of arrests. What she couldn't understand was why these guys just didn't go to a bar. It may cost a couple dollars more and the success rate wasn't as high, but at least it didn't go on your record that you struck out and your wife and children didn't have to find out about it. What surprised her most was that the majority of her prospective johns were married guys looking for quick blowjobs. No wonder half of all marriages ended in divorce. A few months on streetwalking patrol was turning her off of men completely. She asked for a change of scenery and the department obliged, and now she filled her days investigating murders, rapes, drug trafficking, the dissemination of kiddie porn, and the occasional abduction.

As her Jeep rolled passed The Pot O'Gold, she assured Slats that the windows were tinted and that nobody could see in.

There were still some old-timers standing around, pointing down the alley and sipping coffee from paper cups.

"I didn't do it," Slats said.

"I know you didn't, Tommy," she said. "We'll find out who did."

"How come you believe me and the other cops don't?"

"It's not that they don't believe you, but they don't know you. I remember you, Tommy. I grew up in Woodlawn."

"You did?"

"Yep. Not too far from your apartment. I used to eat at The Comfy Corner all the time, too."

"You did?"

"Sure. There was always a nice waitress working there."

"Was it Sheila?"

"I don't know."

"Sheila's the best."

"Yeah? You like Sheila?"

"She takes care of me."

"How so?"

"She brings me my breakfast every morning. Most important meal of the day."

"Yeah, it is," Ryan said, remembering that so far she had swallowed nothing but an Alka-Seltzer and Vitamin Water cocktail and a quart of coffee, which she needed after the six tequila shooters and half dozen beers last night. That couldn't be good for the stomach or the liver or any vital organ, for that matter. "Should we go visit Sheila?"

"Okay," Slats said.

Chapter 8

They slid into a window booth at The Comfy Corner and watched as Sheila, the trim, toned waitress with the Dorothy Hamill haircut tended to the late breakfast crowd. Ryan thought back to her days as a teenager waitressing at Francesco's restaurant. The money was good and the owners were nice, but the bar crowd on weekends was disturbing. A bunch of paunchy, middle-aged Italian guys with slick hair-dos, pinky rings, and ankle holsters would drink Absolut and cranberry, get coked up, trade insults, and hit on the help. Ryan believed that the waitress costume, a button down blouse and tight black slacks, was an asshole magnet. She couldn't wait to trade it in for a gun and a badge. As she watched Sheila coasting from station to station, she realized that working the morning shift was much better for a waitress's self-esteem and faith in humanity. The old-timers smiled and said, "Good Morning" and "Thank You." True, the fifteen percent tip on an egg sandwich and tea only amounted to pennies, but when you factored in the harassment that went along with a three-course, five-drink dinner tab, at least you exited your shift with dignity intact, even if you were a little lighter in the wallet.

"You okay, Tommy?" Sheila said, sliding him an orange fountain soda and a straw.

"Now I am. The cops arrested me."

"You weren't arrested," Ryan said.

"That's all anyone's talking about this morning," Sheila said. "You and Declan."

"Declan is dead," Slats said. "When I found him he was dead."

"Oh, Tommy, I'm so sorry," Sheila said. "That's awful."

"I didn't do it."

"Course you didn't," Sheila said, grabbing his hand. "You poor thing—and poor Declan. God, I can't believe something like that happened here."

"It happens everywhere, Sheila," Slats said. "That's what the cops said."

"Well, sure you read about it in the papers and see it on the news, but it's still a shock when it happens to someone you know. Such a nice guy, too."

"You knew Declan?" Ryan asked.

"Sure I did," Sheila said. "Who's your friend, Tommy?"

"This is Detective Ryan," he said.

"Oh?" Sheila said, looking her over. She looked familiar but the hair was different.

Ryan held out her hand. "Eileen."

"Sheila," she said, taking her hand in a firm grasp. "Can I get you something to eat?"

"Yeah, I'll have the Irish breakfast and do you have Vitamin Water?"

"No. Coke, Sprite, ginger, and orange."

"Just coffee then. Do you have any little packets of Tylenol or aspirin?"

"No. But I may have something in my purse." Sheila turned to Slats. "You ready for lunch, Tommy?"

"Um…"

"Tuna salad on rye?"

"Cheeseburger."

"You had the cheeseburger yesterday. Have the tuna. It's fresh."

"Okay."

"Be right back," Sheila said, as she refilled a few coffee cups before retreating into the kitchen.

"She takes good care of you, that Sheila," Ryan said.

"Yeah."

"Does she work every day?"

"She's off Sundays and Mondays."

"Where does she live?"

"Hart Avenue."

"In Yonkers?"

"Yeah."

"Have you been to her house?"

"Never inside. But I walked her home a few times."

"Oh?"

"Sometimes she gets nervous if there's creepy guys hanging around."

"I see."

"Does she have a boyfriend?"

"That's personal. And you're not supposed to ask personal questions."

"I didn't mean anything by it. It's just, she's very pretty, don't you think?"

"She's beautiful, but she doesn't like if you ask her if she has a boyfriend."

"Have you asked her?"

Tommy blushed and fidgeted with his hands.

"Have you asked her to be *your* girlfriend?" Ryan asked.

"That's personal," Slats said. "And you're not supposed to ask personal questions."

He drained his orange soda and made sucking noises with his straw while Ryan looked around the diner. Place hadn't changed a bit. Same décor, same clientele. Red booths, Formica counter, Irish immigrants.

Quite a different crowd from the four a.m. set trying to stave off a hangover by scarfing down a bacon burger—as if an enormous fat and caloric intake pre-dawn would miraculously absorb and negate the effects of the alcohol—but everything else was the same.

Sheila returned with coffee and two yellow, oval tablets.

"This'll cure ya," Sheila said.

"What is it?"

"Solpadeine."

"What's that?" Ryan asked.

"A mild narcotic."

"Perfect," Ryan said. "Thank you. Where did you score these?"

"Brought 'em back with me the last time I was home. They're legal across the pond."

"You're joking."

"No. Go into any pharmacy and the first thing to greet you will be a stack of these boxes."

Maybe that's why the Irish drink so much. If there's no hangover to deal with, party on. Couple of these to get you back on your feet and a couple of drinks to knock you back on your ass. It's like exercise for the addictive personalities. Ryan swallowed the pills, whatever they were, and the promise of their effect made her feel instantly better. The power of suggestion. If only non-alcoholic beer had the same effect. Or better taste.

"What part are you from?" she asked.

"Galway," Sheila answered.

"Oh, that's where my grandparents are from," Ryan said.

"Is that right? Small world," Sheila said.

It sure is, Ryan thought, *which makes my job easier.* "What part was Declan from?"

"Mayo, I think," Sheila said. "But he'd been living in a flat in Dublin with a bunch of lads before coming out here." She sighed. "I still can't believe he's gone. He was the nicest guy. How could anyone do that?"

"It's strange," Ryan said. "It almost seems like a random act of violence but…do you know if he had any enemies?"

"Did you come in for the coffee or to interrogate?" Sheila said.

"I'm sorry, Shelia," Ryan said. "I don't mean to sound insensitive, but at the same time, I'd like to know who did this to a guy that everybody seemed to like."

"Not everybody liked him," Slats said.

Sheila and Ryan both looked at Slats, who continued fidgeting with his meaty hands, which were in dire need of a washing and a manicure.

"Oh no?" Sheila said.

"Who didn't like him, Tommy?" Ryan asked.

"Some members of the club didn't care for him. Jealous, I guess."

"What club?" Ryan followed up.

"The Five O'Clock Club."

"What's the Five O'Clock Club?"

"I'm not supposed to talk about it," he said, putting his head down and rocking in his seat.

"Tommy, if you know anything about this, you really should tell the police," Sheila said.

He covered his ears and continued rocking.

"It may not mean anything, Tommy," Ryan said, "but if you think you know something that may help us find who did this, you should let us know so we can check it out."

He looked at both and them and rubbed his face.

"It's okay, Tommy," Sheila said.

"Don't be afraid," Ryan added.

"Damn it, Sheila!" he screamed. "Can you just bring me my sandwich?"

"Shh!" Sheila scolded him with a finger and then spun around toward the counter.

"And another orange soda! Please!" he said.

Chapter 9

Ryan checked her cell phone and saw that she had some text messages from Durkin and one from Kevin Hickey. She closed her phone. Too early in the morning for Hickey.

Tommy ate his tuna sandwich in silence, and Sheila went back to taking care of her customers. Ryan looked down at her plate of Irish sausages, blood pudding, white pudding, two scrambled eggs, bacon, and two slices of buttered toast and tried to tally up the calories. It was pointless. Just open the gums and throw it down, cholesterol be damned. Her mother used to make breakfasts like this every Sunday morning, and she managed to live into her mid-seventies, which was more than enough in Ryan's opinion. If you still had some teeth, hair, and faculties, you were ahead of the game. In fact, you won. Game over.

She'd watched her father hanging on through a heart attack and a stroke, struggling to get words out, and unable to dress himself and prayed that she wouldn't ever have to live that way. Not that she was much of a believer in prayer, but it couldn't hurt, even if it didn't help. She surprised herself by finishing everything but the bacon and pushed her plate away. What day was today? Wednesday? She wouldn't need a meal again until Friday.

She grabbed the eighteen-dollar check and left a seven-dollar tip. Slats didn't make an offer to pay, but she wouldn't have let him anyway. Talk about a rough morning. Go into work and find a co-worker dead. Although she'd fantasized about that on occasion, she never actually meant for it to happen. "There's an asshole everywhere you go," her father always used to tell her. Turned out he was right about a lot of things. But the assholes on her job never did anything to deserve a bottle in the jugular. What was it that would make someone want to do in Declan?

Much of their night together had been a blur, as those nights so often were. She remembered his gorgeous, navy, blue eyes. Movie star eyes—Paul Newman's, to be exact. And she remembered his strong jawline and dark black hair, and that killer smile. The devil's smile. She remembered looking across the bar to order a drink and seeing that smile.

"What'll ya have?" he asked, in that lilting brogue, and she couldn't get any words out. She just smiled right back at him.

"I don't get off until four, so what'll you have in the meantime?" he replied.

On a less attractive guy, his confidence would've could across as ugly arrogance. Maybe it was the brogue, but with Declan it seemed cute and playful, just like him. The rest of the night was sketchy. Her friend Karen was with her, of course, flirting and fighting off all comers. They drank a lot, Ryan remembered. Mostly Coronas, but then they switched over to some fruity concoction that Declan claimed to have created called the Devil's Punch. It was red, sweet, and she knew he poured cranberry juice and some clear liquor into it. Gin, vodka, maybe poteen? She didn't know. Whatever it was, it worked. They got wasted. Karen paired off with a laborer they called Miami Steve. He was short, with red hair slicked up in a giant pompadour like Bryan Setzer, in a sleeveless denim shirt and ropey gold chain with a crucifix. Cute, but not Ryan's type. Too much of a poseur. Karen went for that thing in small doses but he was nobody she'd ever be serious about. Declan was more Ryan's type: classically handsome, high cheekbones, well-built but not overly muscular. And he was witty, which was even more important to her. *We're all going to lose our looks*, she figured, *but a sense of humor never goes away.*

It was a Thursday night, she remembered. They closed the bar, got a quick bite to eat at the Irish Cafe...or was that with Kieran, the bartender from the Five Corners?...went back to her apartment, and made quick work of it. A little too quick for her liking but not bad. She remembered him leaving early, while she was still sleepy and drunk, and not much else, other than that he was definitely not circumcised. No information that would be useful in this investigation. And that was that. He never called and she hadn't been back to The Pot O'Gold. She had made a conscious effort to avoid the Woodlawn bar scene and preferred going out in Manhattan, but on that particular night Karen had wanted to scour the old stomping grounds, either out of nostalgia or because of the easier commute home, and Ryan had willingly obliged. What are BFFs for?

❧❧❧

Ryan took Slats back to his apartment to make sure he was okay. He said his head hurt but he refused to take anything for it. He said no to drugs, he told her.

The apartment was a wreck. Upturned milk crates served as furniture, and discarded fast food wrappers littered the floor. She noticed a stack of porn magazines by the mattress on the floor and saw the flickering blue screen light of an old television set that had been left on without sound in the kitchen area.

"This place could use a woman's touch," she said.

"What's that supposed to mean?"

"It's filthy, Tommy."

"I spend all day cleaning at work. I don't like to clean when I come home."

She noticed a burger wrapper on top of a dresser next to a Hellmann's jar that was half-filled with what looked like watered down mayonnaise.

"Shouldn't this mayonnaise be left in the refrigerator?" she asked.

"Don't touch that!" he yelled, lunging at her.

She evaded his grasp and instinctively backed up to the door, not taking her eyes off him.

"That's mine," he said, clutching the jar.

When she realized it wasn't mayonnaise and considered what it might be, she felt the blood pudding rising up her esophagus.

There was no way in hell she was using his bathroom. Covering her mouth with one hand, she threw open the front door with the other and made a run for it. She got as far as the alleyway, to the base of the steps that led up to McLean Avenue, where she launched an Irish breakfast to the curb.

Chapter 10

Ryan drove her cherry red Jeep Liberty to the corner of East 235th and Katonah and parked across from the C-Town Supermarket. Before getting out of the car, she swallowed some Tic Tacs and checked herself in the mirror. The bags under her eyes were getting a little darker and the crow's feet a little longer. She'd have to take it easy this week, maybe hit the gym, get some sleep. She brought a pair of binoculars from under the seat up to her eyes and looked across at The Pot O'Gold. A weird feeling rumbled through her stomach. Not nausea, but the kind of anxiety one experienced when you knew you'd forgotten something important but you couldn't remember what. There were two Irish guys in about their sixties, she guessed, standing outside the pub, gesturing down the alley. The News 12 truck was still stationed in front, and she watched a technician come out of Seamus's Deli with coffee and a sandwich and climb back into the passenger seat. Too early to go snooping around, and she didn't want to wind up on the news, either. Putting down the binoculars, she whipped her bleached-blonde locks up into a ponytail and pulled a Yankees cap tight over her head, slipping the tail out the hole in the back. Then she opened the door, in need of air and more coffee to stave off the inevitable headache. Solpadeine worked miracles but nothing lasted forever. No wonder people got addicted.

She ducked into the Traditional Irish Bakery on the corner, a popular pick-up spot for day laborers. Now that the Celtic

Tiger had gone into hibernation in Ireland, a new wave of immigrants had recently descended on Woodlawn looking for work. As bad as things were in the States, they were worse in Ireland. Unemployment rates fluctuated between the mid-to-high teens, and many children were being raised without fathers, who had left on vacation visas for the States, where they planned to work illegally. But there wasn't much work to go around, and competition was fierce. Connections and persistence were necessary and, when neither of those won out, what little money they had tended to be spent in the pubs, where leads were pursued but only a buzz usually found. Americans didn't even enter certain pubs in Woodlawn because they felt unwelcome. They'd get looks as if they were CIA operatives crashing IRA meetings. Some pubs didn't have televisions, and one didn't even have windows. A dark, black hole built into the ground floor of an apartment building, its main lighting source was the neon glowing from a jukebox that played a steady rotation of Wolfe Tones and other rebel songs. When the door swung open and sunlight streamed in for a brief second, patrons would cower or shield their eyes. The bakery had a somewhat similar feeling, though not as intimidating. There was an eerie quietness to what used to be a bustling breakfast spot. Maybe they were all in shock over Declan's death. Ryan didn't make eye contact with any of the guys sitting at the corner, talking in thick brogues, walking straight past the glass cases of raisin scones and soda bread to the coffee urns, pouring herself a large cup of black. As she stood at the counter to pay, she could feel eyes on her ass. She managed a quick turn of her head to catch them, but they made no effort to conceal their stares. One guy with a ruddy face and red hair even smiled at her, like a sadistic Leprechaun.

"Top o' the morning to you, Eileen," he said. "Didn't expect to see you up so early."

She looked intensely at him but didn't speak. Who the hell was he?

"I almost didn't recognize you under the cap," he said.

Ryan felt trapped in a bizarre dream. Or a David Lynch movie. Or a bizarre dream sequence in a David Lynch movie.

"Have you lost your voice?" the man persisted. "Not used to all that singing, I guess."

Singing? He must have me confused with someone else. "I'm sorry...do I know you?" she asked.

The other men at the table laughed.

"Jaysus, we were grand pals last night, so we were," he said. "We sang half the feckin' jukebox at Finian's Rainbow."

Oh shit. No memory of that at all.

"You've got quite a voice," the man said.

Ryan rubbed her face and took off her sunglasses to get a better look, hoping that something would jar her memory.

"I've never heard a woman sing Van Morrison like that. And the Sinead stuff as well."

Sinead? Ryan hated Sinead O'Connor, and not because she ripped up a picture of the Pope on *Saturday Night Live.*

"Oh...ah...thanks," she said.

"Are you all right?" the man asked, rising from his seat and walking toward her.

He was actually much better looking up close. His cheeks had a rosy glow, the result of either sunburn, high blood pressure, or too much whiskey, but he had the most interesting green eyes, like a cat's. He had a bit of a beer gut but broad shoulders and the legs of a runner.

"I don't...I'm sorry...it's...just...I've just heard some disturbing news..."

"About Declan?" the man asked.

She nodded.

"'Tis awful, isn't it?"

"Yes, it is," Ryan said.

"We were probably the last ones to see him alive," the man said.

"What?" Ryan said.

"They say it happened shortly after five o'clock. I'd imagine it's only a matter of time before the cops get 'round to asking us about it."

Why the hell would they be asking *us*, Ryan wondered. Was she a part of *us*, or was this guy confused? Some of his information was wrong. Slats said he found the body at 6:15.

But then again, he could be mistaken. He wasn't all there, either. Who was?

"What was your name again?" Ryan asked.

The men at the table roared with laughter.

"Jaysus. I thought for sure you'd remember me. You gave me your number and all, said to ring you this week."

Okay, I have a drinking problem, she thought. She put the sunglasses back on and stormed out with her coffee.

"Eileen, wait."

The man walked after her, following her to the Jeep.

"I didn't mean anything by that," he said.

She turned and looked into his green eyes.

"I'm not judging, you know," he said. "I was pretty loaded myself last night. I mean, fuck, we've all been loaded, right?"

"Where did I meet you?" Ryan said.

"Finian's Rainbow."

"And where did we go after Finian's Rainbow?"

"We did the crawl up and down the avenues—The Turntable, Beckett's, Fibber's, Hooligans, The Pot O'Gold."

None of it registered. She opened the door of her Jeep and closed it behind her.

"Wait, Eileen—please," the man said.

She turned the engine and put the Jeep into gear.

"Can I still call you? Please?"

She thought he looked a bit like the Lucky Charms leprechaun and imagined him plying her to eat marshmallow hearts, moons, clovers, and stars. She nodded yes, if for no other reason than she might need him to piece together the final hours of last night. He might be a witness or an accomplice to the murder, for all she knew. Or maybe a potential boyfriend.

A sadistic smile stretched across his face. "My name's Conor," he said.

Chapter 11

To avoid passing the News 12 camera crews shooting B roll of the crime scene, she made an illegal U-turn, drove down East 233rd Street, and entered The Bronx River Parkway North, exiting at the Kensico Dam.

She parked the car in the shady lot and started walking the footpath, punching Karen's work number into her cell phone.

It rang until her voicemail took over.

She called Karen's cell.

"What happened last night?" Karen answered.

"You tell me."

"I don't remember."

"That makes two of us."

"Oh, shit. Are you serious?"

"Why aren't you at work?

"I just got home. I woke up in some disgusting crash pad in the middle of a bunch of guys. And apparently none of them work, 'cause they were all sleeping when I left. I called in sick. I had to come home and shower for like an hour. I feel so dirty."

"Oh, shit."

"What?"

"Karen, do you think we were drugged?"

"Oh, God. I hope not—I mean, we were drinking a lot."

"Enough for both of us to black out?"

"I don't know…maybe."

"Declan is dead."

"What? Oh, shit—Wait, which one was Declan?"

"The bartender from The Pot O'Gold. They found him with a broken bottle in this throat."

"No."

"Yes."

"Oh, shit—"

"Yeah. And I just found out that I was there last night and I don't remember it."

"Really? Was I there?"

"I don't know."

"Wow, I can't believe it—He was gorgeous."

"Yeah, and now he's a beautiful corpse."

"Didn't you hook up with him once?"

"Yeah, and now I have to find out who killed him."

"Can't you just call in sick, like me?"

"I wish I could. I feel like shit."

"Where are you?"

"Walking it off in Kensico Plaza. You wanna join me?"

"I can't get out of bed. I'm going back to sleep."

"How can you sleep?"

"I have faith in our police department to find out what happened."

"Please, Karen?"

"Why don't you come over when you're done walking? Bring some ice cream. And pizza."

"Why? Are you pregnant?"

"You know that's impossible. I've been on the pill since ninth grade and I still insist on condoms."

Ryan was distracted by a shirtless man in headphones who was jogging down the path with a black Labrador. A thin layer of sweat glazed his hairless chest and perfectly chiseled, rock-hard abs.

"You there, Eileen?"

"No."

"No?"

As the jogger got closer, Ryan took off her sunglasses and offered her most flirtatious smile. The jogger didn't notice.

"I must look like shit," Ryan said. "Some hot guy just

jogged passed me and I gave him my best fuck-me eyes and he didn't even notice."

"He's probably gay."

"Thanks. That makes me feel better."

"What are friends for?"

Ryan clicked off the phone and made a sharp turn toward her Jeep. Before she climbed in, she felt a familiar rising in her throat. *Oh, God. Not again.* She ducked down behind the opened door and hurled another round of Irish breakfast and coffee.

Chapter 12

The Jeep rolled to a stop in the parking lot amidst the bucolic grounds of the Browne Rehabilitation Facility in White Plains. Before Ryan exited, she listened to her voicemail messages. There were two from Durkin saying he may have leads for her to check out and one from Kevin Hickey.

"Detective Ryan, this is Kevin Hickey from forensics. Please give me a call at your earliest convenience regarding the investigation of the murder of Declan McManus, and...about some other things, too, so...ah, just give me a call."

What a dick. He must've had his television permanently tuned to the '70s Cop Show Channel. Every incident involving Hickey sounded scripted by the writers of *Hawaii Five-O*, *Cannon*, *Kojak*, *The Mod Squad*, or *The Streets of San Francisco*, and he overacted like Jack Klugman from *Quincy, M.E.* She had made the mistake of accepting a dinner invitation from Hickey six years ago, and he'd been calling for a second date ever since, even though he was married to a Mexican woman he met while vacationing at a Sandals resort in Cancun. Rumor had it she was the cleaning lady and, in lieu of a tip, he left a marriage proposal and she accepted. Nobody on the force liked Hickey. And worse, nobody trusted him. The prevailing thought in every precinct was that Hickey would throw anyone under a bus to advance his career. A lot of guys imitated him but, in this case, it wasn't flattery. It was pure hatred, and in Keegan's case, jealousy and hatred. Keegan always used to say, "I'm Kevin Hickey, not only would I like to play a police officer on TV, but I like to play police officer in real life, too." It wouldn't have surprised Ryan one bit if Hickey had approached her when she was streetwalking undercover. But, what the hell, her morning already sucked. She hit send.

"Kevin, it's Eileen Ryan."

"Good morning, Detective Ryan," Hickey said, in an annoying, telemarketer-type voice.

"What's up?"

"Are you anywhere in the vicinity of East 235 and Katonah Avenue?"

"No. Why?"

"Well, I've uncovered a piece of…how shall we say?…um…"

"Evidence?"

"Your choice of words, not mine."

"What did you find?"

"With all due respect, Detective, it's kind of a sensitive matter."

She rolled her eyes. Much more of this and she would be retching again.

"I'm a big girl, Hickey. I can take it."

"I think it might be best if we discussed this in person. Say, about two o'clock, Romero's restaurant?"

What a shithead. Was he still trying to snag a second date? Where did he think this was going to lead?

"That's not going to work for me. Just spill it."

"Okay—is anyone around?"

Ryan looked up at the sprawling brick building atop the hillside. A few patients in wheelchairs were sitting in the courtyard with their relatives, most of them with their heads down in some degree of vegetative or sleep state.

"No, nobody's around. Just tell me what you found."

"I found some hair fibers at the scene of Declan's murder."

"Yeah, and…"

"The fibers match…"

"Match what?"

"The hair fibers of one…um…Detective Eileen Ryan."

"What are you talking about, Hickey?"

"That's why I wanted to discuss this in person."

"Okay, fuck. Two o'clock, Romero's."

That would give her two hours to meet with her father and try to figure out what the hell was going on. At least it was Romero's, her favorite Italian restaurant on Arthur Avenue. And Hickey would be picking up the tab.

Chapter 13

The nurses all smiled as Ryan made her way past their station and tiptoed to her father's room. She didn't want to disturb him if he was resting. He had made a lot of progress since being transferred from Montefiore Hospital to Browne, which had a reputation as being the best rehabilitation facility in the area. It took her father a while to warm up to the staff, but he had taken a shine to one particular physical therapist who was his stubborn match. Her aggressive method of therapy involved throwing tennis balls full force at him. After the first two bounced off his chest, his athletic pride kicked in. He managed to deflect the third and fourth and he caught the fifth. It was the first time he had lifted his right arm since suffering the stroke eight weeks earlier.

He was sitting in a wheelchair, looking beyond the *Family Feud* game show on television, out toward the parking lot.

"Tha' you, Eineen?" he said, his speech still sounding like his tongue was swollen from a bee sting.

"Yeah, it's me, Dad."

She sat on the bed to face him. His flannel shirt was buttoned wrong but she thought it was a minor miracle that it was buttoned at all.

"You put your own shirt on?" she asked.

He looked down and what now constituted a smile spread across his face. Not all the muscles on the left side of his face had regained full elasticity but the glint in his hazel eyes was there.

"Dad! That's great!"

His laugh quickly gave way to tears. The nurses had warned her that the patients tended to get emotional during their recovery. When the little things like combing hair and brushing teeth and shaving and buttoning shirts could make a man cry—a man as tough and somber as her father—it was powerful stuff. *And still, we take our health for granted,* she thought, even though it had been a monumental task and a major accomplishment to tie her own shoes today.

"Pretty soon, you'll be outta here," she said, grabbing a tissue to dab at his tears. He reached up and took the tissue from her and did it himself. "Show off," she said.

"How's the job?" he managed to say.

She sighed. "Sometimes I think I should've listened to you a little more. You told me not to be a cop."

He looked up at her but the glint was gone. This didn't sound like her.

"I got a disturbing call this morning," she said. "A murder in Woodlawn."

"Woodlawn?" her father said. "Wow."

"Yeah. The times they are a-changing, Dad. We never heard of anyone getting killed in Woodlawn when we were growing up."

There were accidents, of course, and domestic disputes. Some kids were killed in automobile crashes, and an elderly woman died from carbon monoxide poisoning, but murder? If it had ever happened, she wasn't aware of it.

He shook his head slowly from side to side.

"A bartender. Irish guy. So far no leads, no suspects. I'm sure it'll be on the news later."

He gave a flick of his head in the direction of the television. Other than baseball or basketball games, he didn't much care for what was on it unless it starred Charles Bronson or Clint Eastwood.

"You don't want to watch it?"

He shook his head no. She turned off the television.

"The nurses," he said. "They like to watch."

His speech had come a long way, too, but she was afraid

that if she told him so he'd be reduced to tears again.

"You look great, Dad. You got a nice shave, and they clipped your eyebrows. You look ten years younger. And ten pounds lighter."

"The foo sucks," he said.

"The food?"

He nodded.

"Ah, well. Once you get home you can go back to your own diet. Minus the red meat, fat, and cholesterol, of course...which leaves you with oatmeal and low sodium soup, I guess."

He sighed.

"It was fun while it lasted, Dad. Most people wouldn't live through what you have so far."

He waved that thought away. "I can't walk," he said.

"You will," she said.

He shook his head from side to side.

"Sure you will. You're talking again, you're using your right arm again. You may not be able to drive, but you'll walk."

"No, I won't," he said, and the tears started falling again.

Oh, well, Ryan thought. *We can't all play centerfield for the Yankees.*

Chapter 14

On the ride down to Romero's, she called Durkin's cell but it went right to voicemail. She imagined him escaping into his man cave in the basement to catch a nap while his wife was swimming at the gym or doing the shopping. What an odd pair they were. She was a total gym rat, a sculpted physical fitness buff, and Durkin was lanky but pudgy and shook like Jell-O when he laughed. He was a cerebral guy, never wanted to lift a finger if it weren't absolutely necessary, and despite downing gallons of coffee a day, seemed on the brink of sleep at all times while she raced around like a rabbit on steroids. Whatever lead Durkin had for her was going to have to wait.

She stopped to check in on Karen, forgetting to bring the pizza and ice cream, but she did bring a bottle of Vitamin Water and an Alka-Seltzer packet. It wasn't Solpadeine but it was the best legal hangover remedy she had discovered in this country, short of a Bloody Mary, and she didn't have time to stop off for celery stalks and tomato juice. If straight vodka worked, Karen was sure to have a bottle stashed under the bed. She claimed she kept it within reach in the event that one of her guests got out of line, but Ryan knew it was for those mornings when Karen couldn't even make it to the bathroom or the kitchen without a little hair of the dog. It was sad, but still, kind of funny. At least no kids were being hurt, Karen always used to say.

Despite several rings, Karen wasn't answering the doorbell,

so Ryan let herself in with her spare key. She hated doing it, worried that someday she'd find Karen dead, or, like the last time, in bed with a guy. The television was blaring in the living room, tuned to News 12, but Karen wasn't watching it. A middle-aged anchor with comically dyed red hair was recapping a gruesome discovery outside a local watering hole and turned over the live feed to a beautiful Latin girl with full lips who looked like she was going to swallow the microphone. Lolita Hernandez repeated that it was indeed a gruesome discovery between the suddenly Spanish sounding pubs, *De Pot O'Gold* and *De Shandee*, and a mystery that had the locals stumped, as the victim was well-liked and after saving up some hard-earned money had planned on returning to Ireland to help his wife raise their two children.

"Wife and children? He didn't mention anything about a wife and children!" Ryan screamed. "Sonofabitch!"

Karen came running out of the bedroom, her blonde tresses a tangled mess. A hungover Medusa. "Oh, my God! You scared the shit out of me."

"That scumbag was married. With children!"

"The guy you were with last night?"

"No, the guy they found dead this morning."

"Oh."

Karen took the Vitamin Water and chugged from the bottle.

"I can't believe it," Ryan said. "That slimeball."

"Wow. Sucks for his wife and kids."

Ryan thought about that for a second, took back the Vitamin Water, and had a sip.

"Yeah, it does. I should've known."

"How would you know?"

"He wore a locket. I bet it had pictures of his wife and kids in it."

"He wore a locket? That's kind of gay."

"He definitely wasn't gay. Unless he was a Method actor who didn't suffer stage fright."

"What's a Method actor?" Karen asked.

"They attempt to actually become the part they're playing."

"Isn't that what all actors are supposed to do?"

"Yeah, but this way teachers can charge more money for teaching the Method."

"Ah, gotcha. It's like gaining entry into a club or something."

"Right." Ryan sipped more water. "Did you ever hear of the Five O'Clock Club?"

"Is that like the Four-twenty Club?"

"What's that?"

"People who leave work and get high at four-twenty in the afternoon."

"Really?"

"You're a detective and you don't know that a lot of people get high?"

"Tell you the truth, we're not that concerned about people smoking a little herb. Got bigger issues. How do you know about this club?"

"I work in an office. With other people. We have access to the Internet and email."

"Are you a member?"

"I haven't smoked pot since high school. And the only club that's ever wanted me as a member is the Mile High Club."

"And if my memory serves me correctly, you were a more than willing participant to gain entry. I was on that trip to Cancun."

"God, I miss Spring Break. Don't you?"

"No. Problem is, I *never* missed a spring break. Maybe if I skipped them and studied instead, I could've been something other than a cop."

"You can get out in six years and do something else."

Six years? Ryan didn't think she'd make it. By then she'd be forty-three, with her full twenty years in on the job. The pension probably wouldn't be enough to live on comfortably for the rest of her life, not if she wanted to travel a lot and keep a place in New York. She could go back to school and get a degree. But in what? She thought about being an elementary school teacher, maybe somewhere with a warmer climate. San Diego? Miami? Summers and holidays off would be nice. Then again, she'd have to deal with kids. She didn't have the patience for kids. Maybe high school? Or college professor? No, she wasn't cut out for that. Wasn't intellectual enough and didn't have the discipline. Maybe she'd just go back to waitressing. By then she'd be too old to be hit on. Or maybe she'd waitress in Florida, slinging blue plate specials for the blue-haired customers and marry an old geezer for his money.

"You think this was a crime of passion?" Karen asked, as Lolita Hernandez's brow furrowed in confusion while she tried to decipher an old Irish woman's answer to her question. It was a Northern Irish brogue, a rising lilt with every answer sounding as if it were in the form of a question. The interview was beginning to sound like a comical episode of *Jeopardy*. The young reporter was too rattled to follow-up so she kicked it back to the studio anchor.

"I bet some jealous bitch he was screwing found out he was married and waited for him outside and killed him," Karen surmised.

"I don't know, Karen," Ryan said, gulping some Vitamin Water. "I don't have a friggin' clue anymore. Now I know how Durkin feels."

"Durkin?"

"Lieutenant Durkin at the four-seven. He can't wait until he retires. He's counting the hours."

"At least you guys can retire. I'll be a secretary for the MTA for the rest of my life. If they don't fire me, that is. This is my third sick day this month."

"You gotta be careful, Karen."

"I know. I'm a little worried that I can't remember most of last night."

"Me, too. Everything after The Shamrock is a blur."

"That's where I left you. Me and Aidan went to Paddy Doyle's for a drink, then The Dubliner, but then…I don't even want to know."

"I think I may have closed The Pot O'Gold."

"Really?"

"That's what some guy told me on Katonah Avenue this morning."

"Oh, shit. How are you still walking?"

"A waitress gave me some narcotics. And this helps," she said, holding up the Vitamin Water.

Karen took the Vitamin Water and drank. "This stuff's good."

"Yeah," Ryan said. "Great for a hangover. It's got B12 or B6 or something. You may want to get your own bottle, though. I've been puking all morning."

"Eww."

"Sorry. I gotta go meet Hickey for lunch."

"You've been puking and you're going to eat again?"

"You know what's even worse? Once I start feeling better, I'm afraid I'll start drinking again."

Chapter 15

Hickey loved this, Ryan could tell—sitting in the back of the restaurant up against the exposed brick wall, swirling a glass of Chianti the size of a fish bowl with one hand, the other slung over the empty chair next to him, striking his best Tony Montana pose. His poor wife. Life must be hell for a Mexican maid at a Sandals resort if coming home to a self-absorbed asshole like Hickey every night seemed like a good proposition.

She sat across from him without returning his smile. "Make it quick."

The waiter, a rail-thin kid with a pencil mustache, approached and asked what the lady would like to drink.

"Water," Ryan replied.

"Are you sure?" Hickey asked.

"Yes, I'm sure."

"The wine list is excellent. They have some nice Barolos and Super Tuscans by the glass."

"That's great. I'm having water. Tell me about these fibers."

Hickey looked up to make sure the waiter was out of earshot. "Well, when I arrived at the crime scene, I began cordoning off the area—"

"I know the procedure. Tell me about the fibers."

"Easy, Eileen, I'm getting to it."

"Say that again and I'll put a bottle in *your* neck."

"What?"

"I mean it, Hickey. I don't have time for your bullshit."

"What bullshit? Eileen, I'm trying to help you out here. Your hair was found at a murder scene."

"Where?"

"On the brick wall near the Dumpster...and..."

"And where?"

"On the deceased's body."

"You're full of shit."

"No, I'm not. And I'm not judging, either, but I thought you should know. This guy wore a locket around his neck, and inside was a bunch of hair. We ran them and one was a match. Yours."

Ryan's mouth fell open, but no words came out. The image of the locket was so palpable she felt as if she could reach out and touch it, the way she did the night she slept with Declan. It was a gold bar with a Claddagh design. He told her it was something his mother gave him before he left Ireland, and that she had worn it when she came to the States. It was supposed to help him find his true love and return home safely, the way it had for her. She met his father at a ceili dance at the Irish Arts Center and moved back to Ireland with him three years later.

Something about Declan's story seemed strange. She'd been lied to by many men, and she almost always knew when. There were so many tells: the averted gaze, a facial tick, a sniffle, an involuntary lurch of the eyebrows, a swishing of the lips to cleanse the palate of the untruth. Was this guy that good a liar? And did he really carry around wisps of hair from his conquests? Her job was to uncover the truth. Too often, she found that it carried over into her personal life.

"How do you know it's mine?" Ryan said, the lump rising in her throat again.

"All detectives' fingerprints and hair samples are on record, you know that," Hickey said. "It helps differentiate the good guys from the bad guys at the crime scene."

"Unless they're one and the same."

"I don't think you're a crook, Ryan."

"Oh, thank you, Hickey. I'm relieved I'm not a suspect in

the case that I'm investigating. Let's not forget protocol here."

"I know all about protocol, but I also know for sure that the fibers found at the scene are yours."

He took a sip of his wine, peering over the rim of the glass at her. "You sure you don't want a glass?" he asked. "This is a very complex Chianti."

"I'm sure."

"Do you remember that time we went to dinner?"

"Yeah. It was six years ago. And it wasn't Romero's. It was some pizza joint with a kids' birthday party going on."

"I didn't know about the party."

"Whatever. We've both moved on."

"Right. Well, after I drove you home—"

"You tried to put the moves on me."

"I did not try to put the moves on you."

"You started petting me like I was a dog."

"What are you talking about?"

"You were stroking my hair. It was creepy."

He took another sip of his wine. "I don't remember anything like that."

"Selective memory."

"What I do remember is that you left behind some hair that night, too."

"What?"

"It was stuck to the headrest of the car. Just a strand. And, you know, out of curiosity, I scanned it."

"You what?"

"It's what I do. It's fascinating to me."

"You're a weirdo, Hickey. And perverted."

"There's nothing weird or perverted about it. It's just…science."

"No. That's weird. So is Declan's hair collection. I've come across a lot of weird shit on this job but this is just a little too much for me right now."

The waiter appeared and asked if they were ready to order.

"I'll take the chicken parm over ziti," Ryan said.

"Veal scaloppini over penne," Hickey said.

"Wrap mine to go, please," Ryan added.

Chapter 16

She nibbled on some Italian bread from Romero's as she drove back to her apartment. So much had happened in the past eighteen hours that she couldn't digest it. She couldn't even digest her food. It was all being regurgitated. All she knew was that Declan was dead, she may have been at the scene, he was carrying a strand of her hair and so was Hickey, whom she went out with once six years ago.

"Men," she sighed. "Fuckin' weirdoes. No wonder I haven't married one."

The underground garage was a little nerve-wracking at night, but she never felt nervous during the daytime. But there was that gnawing wrench in her gut. She'd been having it all day. Whatever she drank last night did not agree with her. Probably an ulcer mixed with nerves. She tried to talk herself out of it. What was to be nervous about? She had a piece on her. Something about underground garages just freaked her out. Even in shopping malls, she hated them. Dark, smelly, scary places. But it was better than dealing with the alternate side of the street parking on Johnson Avenue, and at least she was anonymous in this building. Nobody knew who she was or what she did and that was the way she liked it. Just before reaching the elevator, she turned sideways to walk between two parked cars, a black Audi wagon and a silver BMW SUV, when she thought she heard footsteps. Then she felt hot breath on her neck. She whirled around and came face to face with a white Bichon Frise, scratching at the barely cracked window of the BMW passenger seat. Drawing her pistol, she nearly shot it dead through the glass and probably would've if it weren't for the fact that the marinara sauce from her take-out bag was now dripping onto the hood of the car. The lid remained in place, however, though the bag was totaled. She looked around and decided to leave it right there on the hood. Wiping the excess sauce from the side of the take-out tin, she dropped the napkins in a garbage can and rang for the elevator. Fucking dog. *What idiot leaves a dog locked in a car? Probably a man. Weirdoes. Both of them. Men and dogs.* She was glad she didn't share her apartment with either species. Maybe someday she'd get a pet. When she retired. But not a dog. Nothing that you needed to walk or scratch. An aloof cat might be fun. But then it would be hard to travel. Forget the pet. Couldn't you just rent those now when you need an instant companion? She boarded the elevator and pressed twelve.

She put her lunch in the fridge, hoping she'd be able to hold it down later that evening, kicked off her sneakers, dropped her coat, and unbuttoned her pants. She was getting a little paunchy. Rubbing her gut, she called out to Mother Time, "Play nice, you old bitch."

The site of the tangled bed sheets reminded her of Danny Boy. That was fun. At least, she assumed it was fun. She couldn't quite remember the details. He certainly was gorgeous. And strong. What did he do for a living again? She pictured him as a mechanic, working under a car on a lift, in a white tank top, his sweat mixing with the grease, a cigarette dangling from the corner of his mouth. *Yeah, that's it. I had sex with James Dean or The Fonz last night.*

Taking a long look down the Hudson toward the George Washington Bridge and New York City beckoning beyond it in the distance, she thought of how lucky she was to live in an apartment like this. Sure, the dishwasher never worked and it needed a paint job, the hot water always ran out between eight and eight-thirty in the morning, but the views were staggering: the GW Bridge and Manhattan skyline to the south and to the north and west, the Palisades. She'd leave the blinds open, lay on her back, and look out at the window right before she was about to climax and feel like a movie star, on top of the world. But now she closed them shut, grabbed a wastebasket, dragged it to the bedside just in case, and crawled back under the covers. She was exhausted.

She awoke at 4:15 a.m. with cottonmouth, reached for a Vitamin Water that wasn't there, and ambled into the kitchen. The coffee hadn't been made, as usual, so she opened the fridge, drank a Vitamin Water, and made a batch. Her stomach still felt queasy but she remembered the chicken parm from Romero's. She placed it in the microwave and hopped in the shower. By the time she got out, she didn't feel like coffee or chicken. *What the hell was I thinking? Chicken at four-thirty in the morning?* She peeled off a hunk of still soft Romero's bread, grabbed the Vitamin Water, her phone, and keys, and left.

Durkin had left another message, wanting to know if she had anything yet and asked her to call back, but she needed some time to wake up. *I should really stop drinking,* she thought, clutching her stomach with her right hand and steering with her left. She drove down McLean Avenue and saw the last of the stragglers leaving Paddy Doyle's, a few of them legless. A taxi rolled to a stop before her and called out to the staggering trio. Two of them accepted the offer. The third one waved them off and zigzagged in the direction of The Comfy Corner. She turned onto Kimball and headed toward Katonah Avenue. Malarkey's was dark, as was Beckett's, MacGuffin's, and Hooligans, but there was a light on in The Pot O'Gold. She pulled over and reached for her binoculars. Through the window on the door, she could see a lone overhead light in the middle of the bar, shining down on amber liquid in a half-full rock glass. Or was it half-empty? There was no place for optimism at this hour on a weekday morning. As far as she could tell, no one was in the place. Maybe it was a tribute to Declan, leaving the light on above his favorite drink, blackberry brandy.

She banged a U-turn and headed back up toward McLean Avenue, when she noticed a familiar gait on the sidewalk. It was Slats, overdressed in a sweatshirt jacket and jeans, with a large set of orange earphones clamped onto his head, the kind worn by road crews operating jackhammers. She wondered if he even listened to music or just wore them to drown out the insults that mean kids had been hurling at him for most of his life. *Kids are cruel*, she thought. *I was cruel.* She remembered being in elementary school and how she and her clique made fun of the nerds and the girls who didn't shower every day. *God, we were mean. Good thing we grow out of that. Or at least some of us do.* Otherwise, she wouldn't be patrolling Katonah Avenue at five in the morning, looking for clues to help solve a murder.

When she saw Slats cut down the alleyway between the hardware store and MacGuffin's, she pulled over to the curb. She cut the engine, checked for her piece, turned her phone to vibrate, and exited the car. Her sneakers squeaked on the wet concrete sidewalk, but Slats was wearing those headphones. He wouldn't have heard a jumbo jet, never mind her Nikes. She peered around the brick wall down the alley. Empty. She quietly strode down to the end of the alley and stopped when she heard a familiar sucking sound. Then moaning. Just beyond the hardware store, up against the wall of the dentist's office, someone was getting a blowjob. Maybe that's why Slats wore the headphones.

She was going to call out "Get a room," but if they were that desperate, drunk, or passionate, it wouldn't matter. *Been there, done that*, she thought. Just the other night, as a matter of fact. With Danny Boy. That would explain her hair fibers on the alley wall near the Dumpster, but she didn't want to tell Hickey that. The stench of the Dumpster suddenly filled her nose, jarring her memory. The rank smell of the Dumpster was the reason they left the alleyway and went back to her apartment. Shit, she wondered, was Declan already dead in the alley while she and Danny Boy dry humped in the darkness beside him? She recalled coming out of the restroom and finding no one left in the bar except for…Conor. He was the one who told her Danny Boy went outside for a smoke and she went to look for him.

The quickening moans brought her back to the moment and

she tiptoed past whoever was in the throes of drunken ecstasy, confident that her rustling wouldn't discourage them.

She heard a succession of knocks. Five quick raps. Then there was a five-second pause and five more knocks. Her watched beeped. Five o'clock. The backdoor of MacGuffin's opened, throwing a sliver of light across the concrete patio. The sucking stopped. Slats entered the saloon and the door closed again. The sucking and moaning started up again. So this was the Five O'Clock Club.

Chapter 17

There were no windows on this side of the saloon so she went back out onto Katonah Avenue and passed the front door to MacGuffin's, careful to duck beneath the windows, then cut down the narrow alley between the saloon and Iggy's barber shop. Turning sideways to fit between the fence and the wall, she sidestepped until she came to the basement window. She knelt down and cupped her eyes with her hands, cursing herself for not bringing the binoculars. Slats waltzed by, the earphones still wedged onto his head, rolling a plastic garbage can full of empty beer bottles. She watched him stack the bottles into cardboard cases and place them on a hand truck. There was a walk-in freezer behind him, and a door to another room, slightly ajar. Cigarette smoke wafted out into the hall. She could see a pair of legs in jeans, and another in black slacks, seated around a table. Her guess was a card game was in progress but she couldn't be sure. She shimmied farther down the alley, toward a second window that might supply a better view, knelt down, and peered in.

The unmistakable, pungent aroma of marijuana struck her nostrils like a swift jab. Sweet stuff, not the harsh, throat-scratching, expectorant that she sampled back in high school. The door to the room leading into the rest of the cellar was closed. In the corner, she noticed a head bobbing. She pressed her face against the glass and saw the white shock of hair and the thick, square black eyeglass frames of Father McLanahan. His eyes were shut as he leaned back against the wall and thrust his pelvis forward. His hands were clasped around long locks of brown hair bobbing before him. Ryan couldn't make out if it belonged to a man or a woman. A rush of sickness overwhelmed her. She backed out of the alley and vomited on the sidewalk.

She heard the wheels of a car rolling to a stop and picked her head up. Great. The cops. Keegan was behind the wheel, with Alvarez riding shotgun.

"You okay, Ryan?" Keegan asked.

She nodded and waved him off.

"You need a lift?"

She shook her head no and motioned for him to keep going.

"You're not driving, are you?"

Why couldn't some guys take a hint? And Durkin was worried he'd read about Alvarez in the paper? She had an inkling that Keegan would wind up dead, the victim of an inside job. Someone on the force wouldn't be able to tolerate his stupidity anymore and would just end him, citing impatience.

"I'm on the job!" Ryan said.

Keegan laughed. "Whaddya, undercover as a drunken bimbo?"

Alvarez shook his head, embarrassed for both of them.

"You are retarded, Keegan," she said.

Even Alvarez didn't object.

"Isn't there a Dunkin' Donuts that needs monitoring?" Ryan asked.

"Durk wants us to patrol the pub crawl strip, be on the lookout for possible thefts, assaults, drunken bimbos...one for three with a walk will get you in the Hall of Fame."

Alvarez didn't get the baseball analogy but Ryan did. Her father would tell her brothers on the baseball field that the difference between hitting .333 and .250 was going one for three with a walk instead of one for four. Moral of the story? Don't swing at bad pitches. Be patient and make the pitcher throw you a strike, something you can hit hard, the way she wanted to hit Keegan's smiling, pock-marked face and Dippity-Do gelled head at that moment.

He fancied himself a Ray Liotta-type tough guy. There was

enough of his ilk on the job to fill a Scorsese movie, *Wannabes*.

Keegan's expression suddenly changed as he looked beyond Ryan, towards the alley.

"Friends of yours, Ryan?"

She whirled and saw a young man and a woman walking past the hardware store. Must've been the couple down the alley.

"No," Ryan said. "Young lovers in need of a room, that's all."

Slats followed closely after them, dragging garbage cans to the curbside for collection—the sight, sound, and smell of which probably chased off the late night lovebirds.

"The retard works at MacGuffin's, too?" Keegan said.

"Don't call him that," Alvarez demanded.

Ryan envied Tommy's headphones at that moment and imagined that Alvarez would be willing to pay a hefty sum for them, too. Poor guy. What did he do to deserve nights with Keegan?

After making sure the lids were secure and impenetrable to raccoons, Slats looked in their direction.

"You following me?" he shouted.

"No, we're not following you, Tommy," Ryan said.

"What?"

Ryan motioned for him to take off his headphones. He obliged, reaching down to his belt and pressing a button on his Walkman. *My God, a Walkman.* She'd assumed it was an iPod or an MP3 player. She hadn't seen a Walkman in years. Her father had given her one for Christmas when she was in seventh grade, when she still bought cassettes. Van Halen and Michael Jackson and Bruce Springsteen and Sting and Brian Adams. Did any of those tapes exist anymore? Several had melted on the dashboard of her brother's Gran Torino on a spur of the moment trip to Long Beach one hot summer day in high school. Others came undone, could no longer be rewound with a pencil, and had to be trashed. She wondered whatever happened to her Walkman.

"What?" Slats repeated.

"We're not following you," Ryan said. "We're working. Just like you."

He stood silently for a couple seconds, couldn't think of a comeback, put his headphones back on, and retreated down the alley.

"Regular hotspot of activity that alley, huh?" Keegan said.

"You don't know the half of it," Ryan said.

"Oh no? What else going on down there?"

"I can't even say it."

"That bad?"

"Something illegal?" Alvarez said.

"Depends on your religion, I guess," Ryan said.

"What? They sacrificing lambs or something?" Keegan said.

"Something like that," Ryan said.

Nausea was overcoming her again.

"I'd love to chat, but I gotta run," she said, bolting for her Jeep without waiting for a reply.

Chapter 18

Private name and number came up on her cell phone. That would be Durkin.

"What's up, Durk?"

"You are, apparently. Keegan tells me you've had another rough night."

"It's not what you think."

"I think you might need some help, iRye. Maybe you should go up the river for a couple weeks and dry out."

"Thanks for the offer, Durk, but I really don't think that's necessary right now."

"It would be strictly confidential. You'd receive full pay and benefits. It's covered, you know."

"I appreciate the coverage and I'll be sure to contribute to the PBA this Christmas but that's not going to happen."

"You sound sober."

"I am."

"So, is Keegan lying?"

"Durk, have you ever seen me puke from drinking too much?"

"No."

"And I assure you, neither has Keegan. I either got some rotten bread at Romero's, some bad Irish narcotics, or the sight of Father McLanahan getting a pre-dawn hummer is enough to make me vomit."

"I lost you after the bread."

"You heard me."

"You went to Romero's and didn't invite me? You know that's my favorite restaurant."

"You can't even think about it because it'll make you sick, too. How many times have you received communion from those hands?"

"What's an Irish narcotic? Jameson and Guinness? Isn't that called a car bomb or something?"

"Solpadeine. It's like the Irish version of OxyContin. Friend to hunchbacks, hangovers, and housewives."

"Got it."

"You got McLanahan, too, didn't you?"

"Yeah. Maybe *I* should go away for a few weeks."

Ryan saw Slats making his way down the street, off to his next job, The Pot O'Gold.

"Shit," Ryan said.

"What?"

"I can't talk. Slats is coming."

She thumbed off her phone and ducked down under the dashboard. Counting silently to herself, she got to sixty seconds and rose up. She looked out the passenger window. No sight of him. Whirling around, she screamed when she came face to face with him, his big head blocking the driver's side window. His scraggily beard was in desperate need of a trim, his chipped teeth in need of a cleaning and his breath in need of Listerine. His beady eyes looked larger through his bottle-thick glasses.

"Tommy! You scared me!"

"Don't follow me!" he yelled, banging on the glass.

"I'm not following you!"

"I'm innocent!" he yelled.

"I know you are. I'm just doing my job."

He banged on the glass again. "Leave me alone!"

"Tommy, who are those men down there?"

He banged on her window with both fists. "Go away!"

"Is that the Five O'Clock Club?"

He kept punching her window.

"Tommy, stop it. You're going to hurt yourself. Just tell me what those men are doing down there. I saw them, you know."

He kept punching without answering. She couldn't help but think—and knew it was mean—*Hulkhead mad.*

"Tommy, can you hear me? *Tommy can you hear me!*" she pleaded like Pete Townsend, her voice cracking. "Take off those headphones. Tell me what's going on."

He just banged away. Ryan was actually relieved when Keegan and Alvarez rolled to a stop across from her. Keegan got out of the car and strode purposely, tapping Slats on the shoulder. Slats spun around and swung at him but Keegan ducked down, grabbed him by the waist, and pushed him up against Ryan's Jeep.

"Assaulting a police officer, retard?" Keegan said. "Now you're going to jail."

Alvarez reluctantly got out of the car to help him contain Slats. Keegan slapped the cuffs on Slats and shot a fierce look of determination through the window at Ryan. He wanted a "thank you" but Ryan couldn't bear to give it to him. Slats still didn't deserve to go to jail but at least this would effectively put an end to Keegan's night. By the time he was done finger-printing and filling out paper work, it'd be time to punch out. With Slats in the backseat, Keegan looked at Ryan one last time before gunning the engine and speeding off to the pre-cinct. She breathed a sigh of relief, knowing Keegan would be off the streets for a few hours, and then called Durkin.

"They're bringing him back," she said.

"Who?"

"Keegan's got Slats in cuffs for attempting to assault a po-lice officer."

"Did he?"

"Technically, yeah, I guess. But he didn't know it was a cop."

"Why do I work nights?"

"I don't know. I nearly assaulted Keegan myself and I know he's a cop."

"Believe me, I restrain myself almost every day. Should I give him a commendation?"

"Who? Keegan or Slats?"

"Maybe Keegan will break a fingernail or stub a toe and

have to go out on disability for a month."

A white van made its way down Katonah Avenue and came to a stop outside MacGuffin's. Two men emerged from the shadows of the alleyway, each of them carrying a pillowcase, opened the back door of the van, and got in, closing the doors behind them. Then the van sped off up Katonah Avenue.

"That was interesting," Ryan said.

"What?"

"Two guys with pillowcases just left MacGuffin's and entered the back door of a van that pulled up."

"Slumber party somewhere?"

"Not likely."

"Any writing on the van?"

"Negative."

"You want to follow it?"

At that moment another figure emerged from the shadows and started walking north on Katonah Avenue, toward Yonkers. She recognized the unmistakable shock of white hair.

"I can't. I've got to go to church."

℥℥℥

Durkin stared at the phone receiver for a couple seconds, wondering if he heard her correctly before radioing in to Keegan. "I need you guys to go back to Katonah Avenue and look for a white van."

Keegan rolled his eyes then picked up the radio.

"Can't right now, Durk. We've got a perp in custody and we're bringing him in."

"Put Alvarez on the horn."

Alvarez picked up the radio. "Yes, Durk?"

"Spin the car around and find me a white van in the vicinity of Katonah and McLean, will you?"

"Yes, sir."

Keegan grabbed the radio. "Durk, with all due respect, I don't mean to question your authority or anything, but this perpetrator attempted to assault a police officer. I *am* bringing him in."

"Keegan, drop the perp where you found him and find me the white van. Now."

Durkin didn't wait for a response. He dropped the receiver and got up to make a crappy cup of coffee. DeValia—the short, rotund black woman who favored curly-tressed wigs, long purple fingernails, and five-inch spiked heels—was dumping sugar cubes into her Styrofoam cup, making whistling and exploding noises as each one hit the liquid, sending droplets splashing onto the counter. When she wasn't fixing shitty coffee, she processed the complaints in the precinct.

"Why do we work nights?" Durkin asked her.

"Because it's better than working days at Midtown South," DeValia said.

"That's true," Durkin said. He put in seven years at Midtown South, a non-stop carnival freak show on the west side of Manhattan. From ticket scalpers at the Garden to habitual flashers to raving lunatics to belligerent homeless men to domestic disputes to murder, rape, arson, child abuse and abductions, Midtown South had it all. Everything to make you lose faith in humanity and make you glad that you carried a gun. Dealing with Keegan on a daily basis was nothing compared to the Jesus freak who regularly stopped into Midtown South with clocks and fake dynamite strapped to his robe, threatening to bring them all down. Durkin put in for a transfer right after 9/11, when he became fearful that the next threat would be real. DeValia followed right behind him. Compared to Midtown South, the gig at the 4-7 was like supervising a daycare center, except that along with the domestic disputes and petit larceny there were occasional rapes and murders. There was no perfect precinct to retire in, it was still, after all, The Bronx, the poorest borough of New York City, but the 4-7's coverage of Woodlawn, Wakefield, Williamsbridge, Baychester, Edenwald, Olinville, and Fishbay was about as cozy as it got for the NYPD.

Chapter 19

Ryan was surprised to find the church doors open so early. The first Mass wouldn't start for another twenty-five minutes but there were already several blue-haired ladies kneeling and trembling over their rosary beads. They fingered the chains with bony hands covered in liver spots while their mouths moved without making any sound, their heads shaking involuntarily. Despite the low hum of the organ playing "Here I Am Lord," Ryan heard Roger Daltry's voice singing "Hope I die before I get old."

A few men strolled in, all of them dressed impeccably. The type of guys who used to put on a suit and fedora to attend a Yankees game. *Funny how some traditions change.* She remembered watching clips of old Yankees games during rain-outs, when the men in the stands—and it was mostly men back then—were decked out in suits and hats covering hair slicked back with Brylcreem. They'd smoke cigarettes and yell through rolled up newspapers at Maris, Mantle, DiMaggio, and Yogi. When she attended a game as a kid with her older brothers in the eighties, guys in cut-off blue jeans shorts sat in front of them, removed their shirts, drank draft Budweiser from waxy paper cups with plastic cling wrap lids, and passed joints to one another. Some groups were probably nostalgic for both days, but not her. She wasn't nostalgic for the church, either.

St. Sebastian's had recently been given a six-million dollar spit shine, according to the weekly bulletin left on the seat next to her. A new coat of paint had been applied, the bricks were pointed, and a new, twelve-passenger, handicapped-accessible elevator had been installed at sidewalk level to accommodate the increasingly elderly population who could no longer climb the ten steps into the chapel. New carpets had been laid, tabernacles purchased, statues commissioned, gold-plated ceiling trim installed. The roof had been torn off down to the studs, with a new, slate shingle replica of the original replacing it. Incredibly realistic and bloody hand sculpted and painted renditions of the Stations of the Cross—inspired, perhaps, by Mel Gibson's *The Passion of the Christ*?—had been mounted along the walls between the refurbished stained glass windows that were sure to scare the bejesus out of any toddlers along for the show with their parents. The early morning sun bouncing through the stained glass windows gave the painted red blood a bluish tint on station number nine, Jesus falls for the third time, under which Ryan sat. There was enough to look at in the facility to take your attention away from what was being spoken in it but the benches were still hard and uncomfortable. There was more leg room and softer cushioning on the kneelers but, still, not a seat one would want to have when subjected to one of McLanahan's patented twenty-minute sermons where he would reiterate that if we didn't step up our games, we were all going to hell.

A lone altar boy emerged from the sacristy in a cassock and surplus and lit the candles. They always used to serve mass in pairs. Her two brothers, Patrick and Brendan, were an altar boy tag team. They only did it to serve an occasional wedding and receive a tip and if they got the nod to serve a funeral during the week, they missed an hour of school. It was better than sitting out in the congregation they told her. If girls had been allowed to serve back in her day, she imagined she'd rather be up there on the comfortable chairs than sitting in the hard pews, too, and she'd probably take sips from the cruets of wine, just like her brothers did. They even managed to smuggle a bottle of wine out of the sacristy before the eighth grade dance but were caught red-handed and purple-lipped in the bathroom by Father McLanahan, who promised them they would be going to hell. For most fourteen year-olds, it was the type of promise that would serve as an impetus to turn their lives around but her brothers interpreted it as carte blanche to do whatever they wanted for the rest of their teenaged years and beyond without worrying about the consequences, since they were destined to go to hell anyway, or so they told their mother every time they got in trouble. Ryan sided with them. If you were going to blame the church, why not go big?

She hadn't been in St. Sebastian's church since her mother's funeral. It was the last time she had seen Father McLanahan before this morning, too. Something about him turned her off. She was never fully convinced that he was genuine. He reminded her of the stories her father had told her—which he heard from his father—about priests in Ireland, men who opted for a lifetime of free food and clothing and a guaranteed roof over their heads rather than relentless hours in the field trying to bring in a profit from a turnip crop. "No priests ever starved during the famine," her father always used to say, and he'd point out that every priest who ever served the parish looked as if he'd never missed a meal, either. Her mother was more of a holy roller, but she had doubts about her faith, too. She always put her envelopes in the collection basket every Sunday, "just in case," as she used to say. It was the same approach she took to praying before bedtime and meals. Did it help? Couldn't hurt.

About two-dozen people, all but one of them over seventy, had shuffled in by 6:30, when Father McLanahan promptly appeared from the sacristy and stood behind the altar. He didn't bother marching up from the center aisle for the early mass, just motioned with his arms for the congregation to rise, which was no easy task for most of them. Speeding through the first two readings, a letter from Paul to the Corinthians and something else Ryan couldn't hear, he kept his head down, forgoing eye contact with the congregation. Ryan cased them instead. Were any of them paying attention? Or were they all there just for show—just in case, like her mother? They were nodding and speaking to themselves and patting their breasts with hands wrapped around rosary beads, the same as they did before the mass started. Their movements seemed involuntary, the result of aging or muscle memory, rituals having been drilled into them through repetition over the years. Father McLanahan seemed to be taking advantage of them, going through the motions, knowing that they couldn't really hear him anyway. Maybe they expected nothing more, but he certainly wasn't doing anything to shed light on the meaning of the scriptures. He didn't offer a homily, either. Too early for that, too, she supposed. He raced through the consecration of the gifts, jogged down to the first few pews to hand deliver Communion, and waited impatiently as the last of the patrons approached him for a wafer. When he threw his head back for the final prayer, it was the same look he had when she saw him just an hour earlier with his back to the wall in the basement of MacGuffin's.

"The mass is ended, let us go in peace," Father McLanahan said, before nodding to his altar boy and then half-sprinting down the aisle after him. Either he was showing off how spry he was for a man of his age, or he was in a hurry to get somewhere else. He didn't even bother to greet the parishioners as they filed out of the church, just made a beeline for the side aisle that would take him back into the sacristy.

"Excuse me?" Ryan called out to him.

He ignored her call. She slid across the pew into the aisle and started after him.

"Father! Father McLanahan!"

He spun toward her with a look of bewilderment. Did he know her?

"Father McLanahan…hi, it's Eileen Ryan."

"Eileen Ryan…" he said. "Eileen Ryan…"

He couldn't recall seeing her name on any church envelopes. This was a tithing parish, after all. It said so right on the front of the weekly bulletin.

"I had some older brothers who were altar boys. My mother was Dorothy Ryan…you said her funeral?"

"Oh, yes, yes, yes. Now I remember. Pardon me, but there are a lot of Ryans in the parish."

"Totally understandable." She cleared her throat. "I was wondering if you had a minute to chat?"

He looked her over. Not many women under fifty attended the early masses on a weekday. In fact, she would be the only one in the past fifteen years that he could remember, other than some Dominican home health care aides who took care of elderly members of the parish.

"Is it a confession you'd like to make?"

"Actually, I was wondering if you'd like to make one."

Chapter 20

"The bloody nerve of you, to come into the Lord's house and talk to me like that," Father McLanahan said, as they walked toward Vireo Avenue.

He had agreed to give her a few minutes of his time, as he needed to administer communion to a sick, elderly parishioner who was at death's door. Trading in his vestments for civilian clothes, a beige windbreaker over a crisp Bill Blass white dress shirt, khakis, and topsiders, with a Yankees baseball cap covering his shock of white hair, he was not a man easily mistaken for a priest. And with that salty tongue, he sounded more like the clientele at Yonkers Raceway or could even pass for a major league baseball manager.

"I was taught that we're all sinners," Ryan said.

"Indeed we are," Father McLanahan said. "But there's a time and a place for everything. A church is a place of worship and prayer."

"I seem to recall Jesus getting mad on occasion, even flipping over tables at the Temple," Ryan said.

"Did you want to discuss scripture, Ms. Ryan?"

"No. I'd like to discuss the Five O'Clock Club."

He stopped and looked into her eyes. "What's the Five O'Clock Club?" he asked earnestly.

"You tell me."

"I haven't a clue."

"What goes on in the pubs after hours? Drinking, drugs, sex, gambling, what else?"

"You're asking me what goes on in the pubs? I'm afraid you've got the wrong man."

"Do I?"

He picked up his pace again and began walking briskly down Vireo Avenue.

"May I remind you that I'm a detective and that—"

"Am I under investigation, Ms. Ryan?"

"You might be. How well did you know Declan McManus?"

"Isn't he the young lad who was killed the other morning?"

"That's him."

"I didn't know him at all."

"I don't believe you."

"He may have come to church once in a while but we get a lot of people at church. I wouldn't recognize them all." He turned and glared at her. "How well did *you* know Declan McManus?"

"Not well enough. But I don't know why anyone would want to kill him."

Ryan was seething inside as she answered his question. It sounded as if he were insinuating something. She didn't like when the person she was interrogating had the upper hand, information she lacked.

"Oh no?" Father McLanahan said, almost mockingly.

"No? Why? Do you?"

"If you'd excuse me, Ms. Ryan," he said, turning up the stairs of an apartment building, "I need to administer to my flock. I don't have time for meddling in police investigations."

"But you have time for blowjobs in the basement of Mac-Guffin's before the early mass?"

His face turned red faster than an Irishman at the beach. "May God forgive you," he said. "And cleanse your filthy mouth."

"It's not my mouth you need to worry about, Father."

Chapter 21

The smell of Arturi's Bakery on McLean Avenue brought back pleasant memories of her childhood, buying homemade lemon and cherry Italian ices in a paper cup for a quarter. Now they offered almost a dozen flavors, everything from chocolate to watermelon to cream to pina colada and raspberry.

This place was heaven to a little kid. And dangerous to an adult woman. Just by looking at the cheesecakes through the glass cases she felt like she put on ten pounds.

"Any leads, Detective?" she heard a woman with a brogue say.

She turned to see Sheila, The Comfy Corner waitress, in line behind her.

"Oh, hi," Ryan said. "I'm sorry, I didn't notice you."

"You seemed a bit entranced by those cakes. I don't blame you."

"You on the way to work?"

"Took the day off. But when you're used to waking at three in the morning it's tough to sleep in."

"Yeah, I can imagine. I'd need a few pills or something."

"Oh, I know. But then you need the pills to go to sleep every night."

"That's true. It's a vicious cycle."

"Yeah. Don't want to be a hamster on *that* wheel." Sheila ordered coffee and a crumb bun to go and Ryan followed her out with a cinnamon roll and coffee. "So, do you have any leads?" she repeated.

"Hunches, but no solid leads."

"Did you find out any more about the Five O'Clock Club?"

"Seems to be an after-hours club of some sort. Drinking, gambling, sex."

"Yeah. That's what I figured."

"Detective's instinct?" Ryan asked.

"Waitress instinct. Some of them come in for breakfast. The usual crowd comes in right after the pubs close, four or four-thirty, but then later on, seven, seven-thirty, we get a few more. A lot of the bartenders. Some of the women they pick up."

Ryan had an a-ha moment. Now it made sense. The guys who served the drinks all night and maybe snuck a few along the way unwound after their shift. They got together at one of the pubs for some more drinks and a card game, plied some women with sweet talk or nose candy and, voila, the Five O'Clock Club. But what was Father McLanahan doing there? And would one of these debauched card games result in Declan's death? She thought back to her night with Declan. Didn't they close the bar and have a few nightcaps? Weren't there a few other people in the bar, too? Was there a card game going on? She gulped some coffee. *Holy shit, was I an unknowing, if not an entirely unwilling, participant of this club?*

"Do you know Father McLanahan?" Ryan asked.

"The pastor? I do, yeah."

"Ever see him around? Outside of church? In the pubs or anything?"

"He used to stop into the diner for the occasional cup of coffee but it would turn into work for him. All the old timers would bend his ear. 'Tis a big parish. With lots of elderly. And they're forever seeking out a priest for last rites and house calls, administering to the sick and such."

Ryan sipped more coffee. She had a very different image of him.

"Why?" Sheila asked. "You don't think he's a suspect, do you?"

"I was just curious about him. He's a peculiar man, isn't he?"

"I don't know much about him," Sheila said, ripping the plastic tab off her coffee cup. "But we're all a bit peculiar, aren't we?"

Ryan laughed. "Yeah, you probably think I'm nuts, the little you know about me."

"Not at all. Just trying your best to get by, like the rest of us."

Ryan felt an immediate connection with Sheila. It usually wasn't like this with her girlfriends. Most of them were like Karen, friends from early childhood and elementary school. They bonded through puberty and periods and high school and boyfriends and *General Hospital* and Duran Duran and Rick Springfield. Most of those friends had gotten married and moved away to the suburbs to raise kids so she didn't hang around many single women her age anymore, and she worked with mostly men so she found herself checking out other women's fashion and style and haircuts and mannerisms, trying to figure out who they were and if she should be more like them. With Sheila, what you saw was what you got. She was confident, honest, attractive, and comfortable in her own skin, not trying to fit it with the others and always on guard, afraid of being politically incorrect. Ryan felt as if she had slid into a booth for a cup of coffee and made a friend. She was always envious of those guys, complete strangers, who could walk onto a basketball court, start a pick-up game, compete against one another, and then go off and have a beer together and watch a ballgame. That just didn't happen with women. Maybe that was why she paired off so easily with guys instead...*shit, this is a lot of analyzing for so early in the morning.* She wondered if Sheila felt the same way.

"You want to sit in the park or something?" she asked.

"All right, yeah," Sheila said in a cheery lilt.

As they walked down McLean Avenue toward the benches at Stillwell Park, Ryan felt her stomach flutter. Not the nausea she had been experiencing but the excitement of a budding relationship, like she had just been asked to the senior prom by

Emmitt Dooley, the power forward with the amazing pecs who never noticed her in high school. Probably gay, as Karen would say. *But I've never felt this way with a girlfriend before*, Ryan thought. *Could I be...nah.* Bedding another woman was on her sex bucket list, maybe even as part of a threesome. Also on the list was a black man, but the conversation at Devalia's bachelorette party scared her: "Let me tell you something, sisters, size does matter—but it hurts."

Ryan was also afraid that there was a smidgeon of truth in the old adage that once you tried black, you never go back and she wanted to keep her options open. And she wasn't sure if her father would ever approve, and the guy had already had a stroke, so...

Stillwell Park had also gotten quite a facelift. When she was a kid, there were two swings on one end and a metal slide with rusted steps and peeling paint that baked in the sun on the other. She used to climb those steps with her mother watching nervously, yelling at her to hold on and demanding that she not fall. There were no fond memories of playgrounds from her childhood, only in adolescence, when the teenagers took over the parks after sunset, with boomboxes and cases of beer. They'd pool their money and walk to bodegas on White Plains Road where they wouldn't get carded and buy cases of Schaefer and Budweiser and Stroh's, which they'd guzzle before they got warm rather than kick in another two dollars each for bags of ice and a Styrofoam cooler. And it wasn't because they were environmentally conscious, as evidenced by the shards of glass they left in their wake after a night of boozing on the baseball fields and basketball courts that made sliding a risk and every groundball an adventure. They'd sing along to whatever was on K-Rock and WNEW-FM, which was usually a steady diet of Zeppelin, Stones, Beatles, and Who. Teenage Wasteland indeed.

The parks were now devoid of broken beer bottles and the plastic jungle gyms looked much more enticing and suitable for tumbling on, but still, she couldn't imagine herself sitting on these benches watching her toddler teetering on the monkey bars and making small talk about nap times and rashes and gluten-free crackers with other women she hardly knew. It was enough to try to sleep and eat right herself. She wondered how women did it, the raising of kids and entering into surface relationships with other women just because they shared the violent experience of childbirth and spent a good portion of their days wiping shit off everything.

"Will Tommy be okay now that you've called in sick?" Ryan asked.

"Tommy's well taken care of at the diner, so he is, the poor guy. My heart goes out to him. Can't be an easy life."

"Yeah. Sometimes I used to think it would be easier. To be unaware of what's going on around you, but then you realize he knows exactly what's going on."

"Oh, he does. His mother did a fine job raising him. He works hard and he's pleasant enough to be around, as long as no one instigates him."

"Yeah."

Almost as if she were reading her mind, Sheila said, "You don't think it would be possible for someone to convince him to kill Declan, do you?"

Ryan shook her head. "I don't think so. Unless it was someone who had a lot of control or power over him."

"Like a boss?"

"Yeah."

"Well, he has lots of bosses. He works in all the pubs."

"Yeah, or maybe a priest."

Sheila looked into Ryan's eyes. "Father McLanahan?"

"I don't know. I'm just reaching for straws here."

"As far as I know, Tommy's not very religious."

"It just doesn't make any sense. Unless Declan was involved in drugs, or he owed someone a lot of money, or he had some scorned lover—"

"Knowing Declan, probably all three."

"Yeah?"

"Well, I mean, you're the detective. Why do these things usually happen? Either a crime of passion, a fit of rage, or a calculated execution. I don't think Tommy is capable of any of those things, but I know there are a few lads who are, once they're fueled with the drink and riled up. I know a few women who are capable of murder, as well."

"You'd make a good detective, Sheila."

"Oh, please. I'm not even a good waitress. I can barely butter toast and pour coffee."

"He was married, you know."

"Declan?"

"Yeah."

"Get out!"

"That's what I heard on the news."

"You can't believe everything you hear on the news."

"No, but that would make sense, wouldn't it?"

"More sense than Father McLanahan having Tommy murder him—unless you know something I don't."

Ryan picked at a piece of her cinnamon roll. "I probably shouldn't tell you this—I shouldn't tell anybody this—but, for some reason, I trust you, Sheila. And I have to tell someone. I'm pretty sure I saw Father McLanahan this morning in the basement of a pub on Katonah Avenue getting a blowjob."

"Yeah?"

"You don't sound so shocked."

"Well, I know he's a busy man, but I'd imagine he'd find time for recreation just like anyone else."

"But he's a priest."

"I'd think a Bronx detective would be a little more jaded."

"And I'd think an Irish waitress would be a little more surprised."

"You mean naive?"

"Not naive, but—you are Catholic, right?"

"Haven't been to church in twenty years except for funerals and weddings. Have you?"

"Other than this morning, no, not too often."

"Have you been to Ireland lately?"

"Not in twenty-eight years."

"You'd see a big change now. It's not our parents' Ireland."

"It's not our parents' Woodlawn anymore, either."

"Times change. Whether it's progress or not, I don't know. But you'd be hard pressed to find anyone my age in Ireland who thinks the sun shines out of a clergyman's arse anymore."

"Would anyone think they'd be capable of murder?"

"They're people, just like us. And if people weren't capable of murder, there'd be no Catholic Church at all, would there? There'd be no need for a police force, either, for that matter."

Ryan sipped some more coffee. "What are you doing tonight Sheila?"

"I have a date."

"Oh."

"With Haagen-Dazs and the tele."

Ryan laughed. "I thought you meant—"

"I know what you meant. I just broke off with my boyfriend. The eejit walked right by the window of The Comfy Corner with his arm around some blondie."

"You're kidding."

"I'm not. No offense, the bottle suits you, but here I am just out of bed, slinging coffee and hash browns to some trucker, and there he goes off with some bleached blonde Barbie doll. 'Twas like needles in my eyes. I nearly ran after them with the pot of coffee and dumped it on the two of them. Then I came to my senses." She sighed. "So, I know how these things can happen. Had I a broken bottle in my hand and a few drinks in me, believe me, I was very capable of plunging it into the fucker's neck, so I was."

"You know what I think?"

"What?"

"I think we need to get into the Five O'Clock Club."

"What's this 'we' shit?"

"It beats Haagen-Dazs and the tele."

"Depends what's on."

"Are you up for it?"

"I don't think so."

"Come on, it'll be fun. I'll call my friend Karen and the three of us will go out. We'll have some drinks and some laughs and check out some guys and—"

"Solve a murder?"

"Maybe. What do you say?"

"I don't know. I think *Law & Order* is on."

"Isn't that always on?"

"'Tis, but it's over in an hour and sounds a lot less dangerous."

"Come on, it'll be fun."

"I don't think so."

*This is what it must be like for guys who keep trying to
score dates*, Ryan thought. Only she never played it this hard
to get unless she thought the guy was a complete asshole. *She
must think I'm an asshole.*

"Give it a chance. You may like it."

"Give me your number and I'll ring you if I have a change
of heart," Sheila said, taking out her cell phone. "But don't
wait up for me. No offense, Detective, but I'm leaning toward
the tele."

Chapter 22

Ryan couldn't believe how excited she was. Not to solve the case but to go out with Sheila. She was fascinated by her looks—the high cheekbones, pale skin, full lips, and close cropped, black hair—the kind only a woman confident in her sexuality could get away with wearing without someone thinking she was a lesbian. Then there was her brogue, her sense of humor, her vocabulary. *'I'll ring you.'* Her mannerisms and frankness were a welcome relief, as was her total lack of self-consciousness. Ryan immediately called Karen to tell her about her new friend.

"Sounds like you're in love," Karen teased.

"I know. I think I am."

"I would be so jealous."

Ryan laughed. "You so would not. What do you say? You up for it?"

"If I take another day off, I'll get fired."

"So don't take off."

"I can't go out drinking all night and go to work anymore. Not that I ever could, but I just can't anymore. Not now. Heads are rolling. Opportunities are scarce for secretaries who take a lot of time off."

"Please, Karen?"

"No can do. I am officially on the wagon again. Go with your friend Sheila. I don't want to be the third wheel."

Ryan sighed. "Okay. I'll call you on Friday."

"Good luck, and remember to use protection."

Ryan didn't laugh. All of a sudden she had an extraordinary burst of energy. She had all day to get ready for this potential date and didn't know what to do with herself. The apartment could use a cleaning. What if she brought Sheila home? OMG, she had nothing to wear. She'd have to stop off at the mall, maybe buy a new dress. Something casual. Would that seem weird? Too dressy? Maybe just a new top and some jeans.

Macy's was having a sale so she bought all three, along with some new bras and underwear from Victoria's Secret. Lacey, black, thong underwear and clear strapped bras. God, she was horny. When was the last time she had sex? Oh, right, Danny Boy. Just a couple nights ago. Too bad she was too drunk to remember most of it. *Did I even come?* Couldn't have. She was so wet she nearly masturbated in the dressing room mirror, the paunch be damned.

She threw her packages on the front seat and noticed the CD Danny Boy had dropped on it, now on the floor of the car. He had instructed her to drink some wine and think of him while she listened to it. She scoffed at the hand scrawled title of it: "The Man." She slid it into the CD player as she drove out of the parking lot, the familiar opening horns of "Real, Real Gone" blaring from her speakers. Ah, so the title meant Van "The Man" Morrison and wasn't a reference to himself, thank God. Probably should've told him she was fluent in the catalogue of the Belfast Cowboy, which occupied every jukebox in Woodlawn. Van was one of a handful of artists that both the locals and immigrants could agree on, along with Springsteen, The Beatles, The Stones, U2, and for a time, odd as it seems now, Garth Brooks. But it was Van more than anyone who provided the soundtrack to life in Woodlawn. Passing by any of the pubs at any given hour of the day, one would encounter his familiar growl or farting saxophone. She was thankful the CD didn't start with "Gloria" or "Brown-Eyed Girl," and not because her name was Eileen and she had blue eyes, but because those two songs had been played to death. Never hearing either of them ever again would be perfectly fine with her.

She pulled into a strip mall on Central Avenue, remembering that she really needed to clean the apartment. Loading up

with gloves and detergents and mops and sponges at the supermarket, she then stopped at the liquor store. When she
reached for the Private Selection bottle of Robert Mondavi
Merlot, an easy, inexpensive fallback when overwhelmed with
choices, she noticed a magnum of the same wine for nineteen
dollars. Always in search of a deal, she put back the 750 ml
bottle for $12.99 and bought the 1.75 liter magnum. Back
home, she plopped The Man CD into the Bose system, popped
the cork, squirted some Spic N Span over the kitchen tiles and
set to work. The up tempo "Real, Real Gone" was a great
house cleaning song, perfect for a commercial, she thought, as
the grease and grime disappeared from her kitchen floor tiles
while she vigorously scrubbed. She sang along to "Enlighten-
ment," belting out its chorus of "Don't know what it is," but
found her mind wandering through the next ninety minutes of
ruminations on God and mystics and a "Queen of The Slip-
stream," whatever the hell that was. By the time the saxophone
intro wailed on the last song and The Man inquired "Did Ye
Get Healed?," she found herself answering aloud as she
looked at the nearly empty magnum, "No, I got drunk."

The CD didn't have the effect that her conquest had desired. Not entirely, anyway. She was drunk and wouldn't mind
a roll in the hay, but she was tired. Had he been in the room
with her, great, but she certainly wasn't driving out to Brooklyn to fuck him and if she called and invited him over, she'd be
asleep by the time he arrived. She could hop a taxi over to the
Deuce and pick up a willing Manhattan College coed for an
early afternoon quickie, but he'd hardly measure up to Danny
Boy, and she'd hate herself for it afterward. She wrote him off
as another hopeless and geographically undesirable romantic
with a great body and good taste in music. *If I only had a nickel for every one of those,* she told herself unconvincingly and
collapsed on the bed, still wearing her bright yellow dishwash-
ing gloves.

Chapter 23

When her cell phone rang at 8:30, her heart skipped a beat. Shit. Four-hour power nap. *OMG, is it Sheila?* Ryan was never this nervous about taking a phone call from a guy. *What is going on?*

"Hello?" she answered, like an anxious schoolgirl in the days before the big dance.

"You got anything yet?" Durkin's gruff voice answered.

"Oh, it's you."

"Yeah, I get that a lot," Durkin said. "Sorry to disappoint you. Did the day bring you any surprises or leads?"

Other than that she had feelings for an Irish waitress? "No," Ryan said. "Nothing. Other than McLanahan."

"Yeah, we touched on that already."

"Sickening, isn't it?"

"I'll probably go to hell for saying this, but I never really liked that guy," Durkin said. "He always seemed like a hypocrite to me."

"Bingo. Do as I say not as I do."

"Right."

"Do you still go to church, Durk?"

"You know, I do the big ones—Easter and Christmas, an occasional Palm Sunday. Unless there's a game on."

"Durk, I have brothers. I know they watch games on Christmas. Definitely football, sometimes basketball."

"Okay, you got me. I don't do much church anymore, and every Sunday's Palm Sunday for me."

"You still believe in hell?"

"I think there's gotta be something after this life, whatever it is…hell? I don't know…heaven? I hope so…but there better not be any purgatory, 'cause this right here is purgatory enough for me."

"You'll make it, Durk—to retirement, anyway. I don't know about heaven."

"Well, if I don't, I'll keep a seat warm for you."

"Isn't hell supposed to be hot?"

"Then I'll try to keep the beer cold."

"Are you insinuating that I won't make it into heaven?"

"No, just that I'll die before you."

"I don't know about that."

"Trust me. I will."

"This is getting a little morbid for me, Durk."

"Sorry, don't mean to ruin your night."

"You didn't. I'm going out with a hot Irish waitress."

"That doesn't sound right coming from you. For a second there I thought I was talking to Keegan."

"You don't call Keegan, do you?"

"Only when he's late for work. You don't date women now, do you?"

"I haven't made a habit of it but there's a first time for everything."

"Who I am to judge? Whatever floats your boat, kiddo." He fought down another gulp of awful coffee, sensing it burning a hole in his esophagus as he swallowed. "Did you know that Declan McManus was the first homicide in Woodlawn in twelve years?"

"Really?"

"Yeah. And I'd like to hope there isn't another. Not on my watch, anyway."

"What if it wasn't a homicide?"

"You think it was suicide?"

"Too much of a stretch?"

"From what I hear the guy had a pretty good life—"

"Or lives—"

"—looks, money, women—"

"—wife, kids, debt."

Durkin sighed. "Did I catch you at a bad time, Ryan?"

"No, it's just, don't you think that a guy like that would be depressed? He left a wife and kids, had a bunch of empty sexual relationships—"

"My heart's breaking for the guy."

"—was involved with drinking, drugs and gambling."

"It's not exactly Vegas."

"Don't you think he was searching for something?"

"Aren't we all?"

"Well, yeah, but—"

"Sounds like he found it."

"You don't mean that."

"Maybe he *thought* he found it. Or maybe he didn't. I didn't know the guy. But regardless of how empty he felt his life was or wasn't, I don't think you end your shift, walk outside your office, and stab yourself in the throat with a beer bottle."

"No."

"That's why you're getting paid to find out what did happen."

"That's all you got for me, Durk?"

"I get paid to deal with Keegan."

"Any advice for me?"

"Don't fall in love with the waitress. I made that mistake once and I'm still paying for it."

"If your wife ever heard what you say about her—"

"Make sure she doesn't."

"Where would I see your wife? I never go to the gym and you never take her out."

"I'm taking her out tonight, as a matter of fact. It's her birthday."

"Oh, nice."

"I'm thinking Romero's."

"That's *your* favorite restaurant. Shouldn't she choose on her birthday?"

"She doesn't even know about it yet. It's a surprise. I could take her to Applebee's and she'd be happy."

"Don't."

"So Romero's it is, then."

"Enjoy."

"You, too. But you're on your own tonight. No phone calls while I'm eating, okay?"

"I better not hear from you, either."

"Deal."

Chapter 24

Ryan rounded the corner of Hart Avenue and saw Sheila standing on the porch, smoking a cigarette, just like Ryan used to when she waited for dates to pick her up. She never let her boyfriends come into the house. None of them would pass muster with her father or brothers. Sometimes it felt like she had three fathers growing up. If her brothers saw her out at the Kent Cinema double feature, or in bars with guys they didn't like, they'd make it clear that they didn't approve with not so subtle gestures such as grabbing them by the shirt collar and telling them to "leave my fuckin' sister alone," and on one occasion, punching a guy in the face and explaining afterward that "my sister doesn't date douchebags."

She didn't realize until much later that they were right about that guy, Denny Dooley, a total dick if ever there was one. "Dool The Tool" became his nickname, though he did have the cutest dimples when he was seventeen, and he had invited her to *Goodfellas*, which she really wanted to see. Had she known her brothers would be sitting three rows behind her and ready to pounce like Joe Pesci when The Tool made his move, she would've chosen another theater.

Sheila saw Ryan's Jeep approaching and stubbed out her cigarette on the porch. She plopped into the passenger seat and said, "Would you believe they didn't have one feckin' pint of Haagen-Dazs at the deli."

"Just my luck," Ryan said.

"This better be good, Detective."

"It'll be fun, I promise," Ryan said, checking out her lip gloss in the rear view mirror and stealing a look over at Sheila's cleavage. The push-up bra was a miraculous invention. If she ever served eggs and coffee in that get-up, she'd be wiping more than crumbs off The Comfy Corner counter. "Where to?"

"You're the detective. You figure it out."

"Do you want to stay in Woodlawn?"

"I don't care. I'm only after a couple drinks and a few laughs. Wherever we can find them."

"Technically, I'm supposed to be working."

"Well, if you can squeeze in solving a murder or gathering a few clues, that'd be all right, too, wouldn't it?"

"Yeah, that would be great."

Sheila lit another cigarette. "Do you mind?"

"No," Ryan lied.

She hated cigarette smoke. It nearly killed her father, who once had a two packs a day habit before having a massive coronary when she was getting ready to go to her high school graduation. Neither of them had smoked since.

"Did you know that there are thirty-two bars within walking distance of Woodlawn?" Ryan said, turning onto The Bronx River Parkway heading south.

"One for each county in Ireland," Sheila answered.

Ryan had never thought of that. The images of the ubiquitous bumper stickers that used to plaster the backs of well-worn work trucks and station wagons in the 1970s re-entered her memory: $26 + 6 = 1$. Now she knew what they meant. Twenty-six counties in the south of Ireland plus six in the north would equal one united Ireland. There were lots of IRA supporters in Woodlawn when she was growing up, and they made no effort to hide it. In fact, they were so proud of it, they even advertised it on their cars. There was another popular bumper sticker from that era, as well: *But Who Is Kitty O'Shea?* Maybe Sheila could shed light on that mystery before the night was over, too. Otherwise Kitty's identity would be left in the hands of Google and Wikipedia, two sources Ryan didn't totally trust.

"I doubt you could walk to all of them," Sheila said. "Not

in the same night, anyway. Unless you were only drinking water."

"That's true."

"You're not planning on attempting that tonight, are you? 'Cause you may have to find yourself a new partner."

"No, I'm just curious how many of them are involved in this Five O'Clock Club."

"I'd imagine most of them would be."

"Yeah?"

"Don't pretend like you're some stranger to the after-hours crowd."

"Oh, I've seen my share of after hours," Ryan said. "Not that I'm proud of that."

"No law is going to stop people from doing what they like."

"That's what keeps me in a job."

"You're lucky in that respect. You're recession-proof."

"That's true. Police work is recession-proof."

"But you'd have to be bulletproof, too."

"Never been shot at yet, thank God."

"So you do believe in God?"

"Well, someone's watching over me. They say He loves a drunk, right?"

"That's just the booze talking."

Ryan got off at the East 233rd exit and drove along the Woodlawn Cemetery toward Van Cortlandt Park, stopping at a red light at the intersection of Kepler Avenue.

"Ever been in that place?" Ryan asked.

Sheila looked out the window at a dreary looking pub, The Dungeon. Through the window she could see the flicker of a television screen that resembled the patron sitting below it: old, gray and round.

"Too depressing," Sheila said.

"Their motto hangs above the bar, 'Come on in and have a seat, it's better here than across the street.'"

Sheila looked across the street at the cemetery, then back at The Dungeon, as an elderly pot-bellied man with a red, bulbous nose dressed in a tweed cap and wool overcoat came stumbling out of it.

"Somehow I doubt it," she said.

As the light changed, Ryan rolled on toward Herkimer Place and parked the car. "Ever been to The Red Herring?"

"No, I don't usually come over this far. McLean Avenue is much closer to my house."

"I know, but that's not my jurisdiction. That's Yonkers."

"What if you're work brings you there?"

"Then we're supposed to share in the investigation, possibly turn it over. Gets complicated."

"Well, let's keep things simple tonight. And safe."

"There's nothing to worry about."

"Easy for you to say. You're packing a gun."

"I have an extra one in my ankle holster if you want it."

She always carried her department issued Glock 19 in her waistband when she was on duty and her Smith & Wesson LadySmith 60LS Revolver in the ankle holster. Couldn't be too careful, and the LadySmith's smaller J-frame and shortened trigger to accommodate a woman's fingers made it a cinch to conceal, grab and fire in an emergency. Despite its lightweight twenty-one ounces, it had the power of a .357 magnum, capable of bringing down a brown bear at close range.

"Jaysus. I wouldn't know what to do with it," Sheila said.

"Just point and shoot. Like operating a camera. It's easy. And kind of fun."

"I try to make a habit of never pulling the pistol on a first date," Sheila said, lighting another cigarette and puffing quickly before entering the bar. "I'd like to be thought of as fun. But not necessarily easy."

Everyone's got habits, Ryan thought, *some good, some bad*.

Chapter 25

The Red Herring was dead. A couple of day laborers in work boots, dirty jeans, flannel shirts over thermals, and baseball caps, were sipping draft beers under the lone television on the wall and a dead ringer for Danny Boy was hunched over the pool table sliding a cue between his fingers, an unlit cigarette dangling from his lips. The elderly bartender looked up from *The Racing Form* over his bifocals at the two ladies and went back to his charts.

"Should we even bother?" Ryan said.

"They do serve alcohol, don't they?" Sheila said.

"There's thirty-one more to go," Ryan said.

"I don't care. It's up to you."

"Come on," Ryan said, turning to leave, with Sheila close behind.

"Can I help you, ladies?" the bartender said.

"No, thanks," Ryan said. "Wrong place."

Once outside, Sheila said, "Who's happier that we left, him or us?"

"Really. How can you do business with that attitude?"

Before they reached the Jeep, someone called out, "You looking for something?"

They spun around to see one of the patrons in a flannel shirt and baseball cap exiting the bar, lighting a cigarette. He slowly approached them.

"No, thanks," Ryan said. "Come on, Sheila."

"Why you runnin'?" flannel shirt said. "I ain't gonna bite.

You must be lookin' for something. All dressed up for a night on the town. I got something that can help you have a good time."

"Oh, yeah, what's that?" Sheila asked.

"Come here, I'll show you."

"Sheila, don't."

As flannel shirt approached, Ryan could see that he had dark eyes, a small scar beneath his right eye, and three diamond studs in his left ear. He looked around and reached into his waistband. Ryan did the same. He drew a plastic baggie full of powder. She drew her pistol.

"Whoa, relax, Momma," the man said. "Just being friendly, that's all."

"Get the fuck out of here," Ryan said.

"Just chill. Be cool. It's all good."

"Get back inside the bar before I bust a cap in your ass."

He backpedaled, flashing a sinister smile. "You ladies have a nice night," he said. "I'll see you around."

He ducked back into the bar and they made a run for the Jeep. Ryan gunned it and turned down Van Cortlandt Park East towards McLean Avenue.

"One down, thirty-one to go, is it?" Sheila asked.

"Started out with a bang, didn't we?"

"Almost. 'Bust a cap in your ass'? I thought that was something they only said in the movies, like 'make my day.'"

"Sorry about that," Ryan said, a throaty laugh escaping. "I've actually never said those words before."

"Jaysus. I never thought I'd miss Haagen-Dazs and *Law & Order* as much as I do right now."

"We'll go get a quiet drink and everything will be fine."

"If you're trying to make a good first impression, you're off to a strange feckin' start, I can tell you that," Sheila said, lighting another cigarette.

Chapter 26

Keegan was behind the wheel, singing along to early Bruce Springsteen on the radio when Alvarez grabbed his arm.

"What?"

"Shh."

"C'mon, I let you listen to your merengue shit."

Alvarez killed the radio.

"Look," he said, pointing at a row of cars parked along the dark stretch of road on Van Cortlandt Park East, under the oak trees near Kepler Field.

They belonged to commuters who drove from Yonkers and other points north to catch the bus and the subway to their jobs in Manhattan, and to people who rented apartments in the nearby multi-family houses and buildings. The local residents tended to leave their cars there for long stretches of time, as there weren't any alternate side of the street parking rules in effect other than from six to eight a.m. on Tuesday mornings when the Sanitation Department cleaned the streets. Though the spaces were legal, they were magnets for thieves, as streetlights were few and far between and not always in working order. Despite hundreds of calls to three-one-one, several streetlights on the park side remained broken. The regulars knew this and didn't make a habit of leaving any valuables inside. GPS systems, iPods, cash, cell phones, and chargers had a tendency to disappear and a car would occasionally go missing as well. Some patrons of the nearby bars on McLean

Avenue had started to park along the strip in the early evenings, to avoid the meters that were in effect until eight, and
because Yonkers cops were doing more frequent spot checks
for drunk drivers. This way, drivers left their cars over The
Bronx border and got on the Major Deegan Expressway at the
East 233rd entrance, rather than on the McLean Avenue exit in
Yonkers, bypassing a popular checkpoint. In conjunction with
the recent uptick in crime was a rash of car break-ins along this
strip. Alvarez thought he spotted one in progress.

"Pull over," he demanded.

Keegan obliged, finding a spot at the top of East 240th
Street. Alvarez exited the car, quietly closing the passenger
door. Keegan followed. Slinking along the sidewalk, ducking
behind trees, Alvarez scared the daylights out of an elderly
man out walking a Shih Tzu that was in mid-shit. The little
dog barked and Alvarez held a finger to his lips. The old man
took the hint and yanked the dog's chain, cradling it in his
arms. Alvarez waved him off and the man continued down the
street, leaving the steaming little nuggets behind.

"That was a seventy-five dollar ticket you just let walk
away," Keegan said as he sidled up next to him, careful of
where he stepped.

"There's bigger shit to get off the street," Alvarez said,
flicking his chin down the road.

A broad-shouldered figure in a hooded sweatshirt was de-
liberately circling a red Jeep. It appeared as if he were wiping
the door handles with something. When he walked around to
the sidewalk and ducked down by the back tires, they lost sight
of him. Alvarez jogged across the street and motioned for
Keegan to continue down the opposite side, with the intention
of corralling the perp from both sides so he couldn't escape.

Alvarez moved from car to car, ducking beneath their
hoods. An out of service bus rolled up the road from the depot,
its lights darkened with no passengers, and Keegan ran alongside it, using it as cover to cross the street. He was closing in
fast, with his gun drawn.

Shit, Alvarez thought. No need for that—or was there?
What if this hoodie was armed and pulled a piece? Was this

how the term "hood" originated? What seemed like a ten-minute debate in his head took all of a nanosecond. Alvarez reached for his gun. Better play it safe.

He had never fired his weapon in three years on the force and had only pulled it from its holster in the line of duty twice, both times following Keegan's lead. Twice he had convinced himself that he wouldn't do that anymore, because he knew Keegan would pull his piece if a fly buzzed through the room or a mouse scampered across the floor. But once again he found himself holding the cold metal, which always felt lighter when the adrenaline was pumping, racing to make sure Keegan didn't fire. Though Alvarez was a stellar marksman and practiced weekly, he often wondered how he would perform if the target moved laterally and fired back. The white paper targets with the painted on pistols, black rings, and red bulls-eyes that approached methodically in the well-lit shooting range were easy to hit. He could drill those in his sleep. Would he be able to hit someone who was dodging for cover and firing back, intent on killing him first?

Keegan stopped on the street side of the Jeep and stood in a three-point stance. Again, Alvarez questioned his partner's move. Was this really necessary? Over what? A petty thief stealing an iPod or an EZPass tag? *Maybe we should've kept that cruiser rolling, let Keegan sing his off-key, pitchy Springsteen.*

Alvarez sprinted onto the sidewalk and slipped on a fresh mound of dog shit, piled neatly on the wet leaves. Not the nuggets of a Shih Tzu, but the logs of a Labrador whose owner only fed quality cuts of meat and kibble, Pedigree and Eukanuba. Up in the air Alvarez went—Keegan swore that his whole body was parallel with the roof of the Jeep—and down hard he came, flat on his back. He lost his hat but maintained a grip on his pistol.

The man in the hooded sweatshirt, dusting for prints on the stem of the Jeep's back tire, looked up and saw the fallen figure holding a gun. He reached into his waistband with his right hand and yelled, "Freeze! Police!"

With his left hand, he fumbled for the lanyard that identified him as a forensics officer, but before he could withdraw it from under the zippered sweatshirt, a bullet pierced his middle finger and lodged in his heart.

Chapter 27

"What's your drink?" Ryan asked.

"Anything with vodka."

"Vodka and orange with a splash of cranberry and a Coke, please," Ryan said.

Paddy Doyle's was always a safe bet. Any night of the week there was bound to be a crowd. The weeknights were manageable but on the weekends there would be a line to get in and depending on what band was playing, the cue would run halfway down the block, which was usually good for business at Donny Brook's, too. A long line can be a buzz kill and the need for another drink supersedes the clientele one drinks with. It was still early in the evening by bar standards, at least in Woodlawn. Pubs didn't get packed until eleven or midnight. Didn't anyone get up for work in the morning anymore?

"Did I hear you right?" Sheila asked.

"Yeah. I ordered you the vodka, with some orange juice for the vitamin C, and cranberry juice to stave off urinary tract infections."

"What are you, my friggin' doctor, now?"

"Have you ever tried it? It's good."

"I'll try anything once. What did you get for yourself?"

"Coke."

"You drag me out of the house on a weeknight, bring me around to the drug dealers, and now you're not going to drink with me?"

"I'm on duty." *Oh, and I drank a magnum of wine by my-*

*self this afternoon while cleaning the apartment in case you
came home with me.*

"You're undercover, aren't you?"

"Yeah, but I gotta keep clean."

"Then why the fuck did we park half a mile away?"

"I didn't want any of the beat cops to see my car."

"Well, this'll be a short session if I'm drinking alone, I can
tell you that. Can't you knock off work a bit early? All work
and no play makes Eileen a dull date."

Ryan smiled. "Maybe I can knock off a little early."

"That's the spirit," Sheila said, raising her glass to her lips.
"Knock off early and knock a few back." She took a big swig.
And then another. "That's good. I've never mixed those be-
fore."

"Yeah. That's what my friend Karen and I order when we
want to drink healthy."

"We used to drink Bloody Jesus, Mary, and Joseph back
home. Or Vampire juice."

"What's that?"

"Vodka and V8, with a celery stick."

"That's a good healthy cocktail. Red wine is good, too. You
know, for the antioxidants."

"Oh, sure. Gallon of that each night is great for the heart, so
it is."

"I see you subscribe to the same health plan as I do."

"May as well enjoy what life has to offer. It can all be gone
in an instant."

"That's true."

Ryan thought of her father, once a big, strong, healthy man,
reduced to crying in his wheelchair over three well-balanced,
low-sodium, tasteless meals a day. And her mother, who ate
whatever she wanted and never seemed to gain weight, never
spent a day in a hospital outside of giving birth, and avoided
doctors. She suffered a massive coronary on her way to the
bank to clean out her Christmas Club account. Never made it
to the bank. Dropped dead on Martha Avenue.

"Is it me, or is this place crawling with cops?"

"Hmm?" Ryan said, coming to.

She looked around. A couple of guys did look familiar, but she couldn't place them with any precinct. She'd always run into someone she knew in Paddy Doyle's, either bar regulars or old acquaintances from the neighborhood. Often times there was a wake letting out from Dunphy's across the street and those who came to pay their respects would congregate at the pub after it. Most of the time Ryan didn't want to see the old crowd and relive the glory days. Part of the reason she reached for the bottle, both the bleach and the booze, was to forget about the old days and go unrecognizable amongst her past acquaintances.

"I don't know," Ryan said. "Do you want to go somewhere else?"

"No, no, this is fine. I have a drink and a seat, and a good view of the guys."

"Oh? In the market for another boyfriend, are you?"

"Well, I'm not getting any younger, but I'm not out on the prowl, either. Not like them two, anyway."

They looked over at a pair of forty-somethings in way too much make-up, way too tight jeans, with way too much cleavage popping out of tiger print blouses. The one with black hair wore a black blouse with white stripes, the one with strawberry blonde hair wore orange with black stripes.

Ryan stifled a laugh. "Why not tattoo 'cougar' on your forehead?"

"We don't look that sad, do we?"

"No! God, I hope not. At least you don't."

Ryan reached for her purse and pulled out a compact, checking herself in the mirror.

"Ah, stop it now," Sheila said. "You're getting all paranoid."

"I do look old, though, don't I?"

"Not at all. Not a day over thirty."

Ryan shot her a look.

"Fuck. I meant twenty-five."

Ryan laughed. "And I was attracted to you because I thought you were honest."

"And I thought you'd be a serviceable drinking partner,"

Sheila said, holding up her empty glass. "Come on, Eileen. I can't drink alone."

Ryan looked into her violet eyes and sighed. *Fuck me, I'm weak,* she thought.

Sheila began singing Dexy's Midnight Runners' only hit, "Come on, Eileen."

"Don't," Ryan said.

"Sorry. I'm sure you've heard that enough."

"'Nother one?" the bartender asked, scooping up Sheila's empty glass.

"Make it two," Ryan said, pushing her Coke toward him. "And take this away."

"That's the girl," Sheila said.

"Don't make me regret this in the morning."

"Famous last words."

Chapter 28

You shot Hickey," Keegan said, helping Alvarez to his feet.

He could tell that information didn't register. Alvarez's chest heaved and sweat beaded on his upper lip and forehead. Keegan picked up the fallen hat and placed it on Alvarez's head.

"D—d—d—d—o—o something," Alvarez said.

"I did. I called it in."

"Is he okay?"

"I don't know. He's not talking."

Alvarez started shaking.

"You okay?" Keegan said.

"Help him!" Alvarez yelled. "We've got to help him."

Keegan looked down at Hickey, who was clutching his heart, the blood soaking through his gray hoodie. He knew the man was gone. The Hickey who showed off shagging balls on the high school baseball field with a snatch catch and danced to Michael Jackson's "Beat It" on the Four Provinces's dance floor while everyone else did shots of Alabama Slammers and made fun of his *Miami Vice* fetish, and walked down Katonah Avenue with his first love, Maryjean McNeil, holding hands and kissing her in front of Nico's pizzeria in broad daylight. Gone.

Keegan recalled a conversation he had in the police academy with the other probees about what they'd do if some crack whore or a mass murderer were dying in front of them. Would they perform CPR? Or would they let them die? Keegan never answered the question.

Alvarez dropped to his knees and blew into Hickey's life-less body. He swallowed hard and put his gun back in its holster, while the siren of an approaching ambulance grew louder.

"Eddie?" Keegan said, his voice cracking and barely audible.

Alvarez pumped Hickey's chest, cleared blood from his mouth, and blew into him again.

"Eddie?" Keegan repeated, his throat so dry it didn't register.

Alvarez beat on Hickey's chest with his fists, as if he wanted to hurt him.

"Eduardo!" Keegan called.

Alvarez turned, blood now dripping from his own mouth and spilling through his hands.

"He's gone," Keegan said.

Alvarez looked down at Hickey, back up at Keegan, and began sobbing, his whole body shaking and trembling.

"Fuck," Keegan said, a look of disgust on his face. He reached into his back pocket, producing a handkerchief, and began patting Alvarez's back. Not in a comforting manner, but vigorously wiping. Alvarez looked at him, his red eyes filled with tears, seeking an explanation.

"You got dog shit all over your back," Keegan said.

Chapter 29

Two drinks later Sheila and Ryan made their move to the makeshift dance floor. When the dinner crowd dispersed, tables were pushed against the wall to make room for drunks to shimmy and shake. A few stragglers were finishing off late suppers but that didn't deter them. They shook their booties along with the cougars, knowing they looked pathetic, but they couldn't stop laughing. Ryan leaned in and whispered, "All we need now is for the DJ to play 'It's Raining Men.'"

Sheila nearly fell with laughter. She never danced like this in public. In fact, she never danced at all. "Most people shouldn't drink and drive, but I shouldn't drink and dance," she said.

Shit, Ryan thought. *My car.* She hadn't planned on drinking tonight. But this was getting fun. If she left the car where it was, she knew she'd end up driving. She didn't mind taking a cab home, but she hated waking up in the morning and not having her car. Especially if she woke up in someone else's bed. Karen owed her a favor. She decided to call it in. After setting Sheila up with another healthy cocktail, she went to the bathroom to call Karen.

"Karen, can you do me a huuuuuuge favor?"

"Did you forget your protection again?" Karen asked. "When are you going to take the pill?"

"Two things I'll never do, get flu shots or go on the pill. I just don't trust them."

"You know you make, like, zero sense, right? You've totally confused the things that you should allow into your body with the things that you shouldn't."

"There's nothing entering my body tonight other than vitamins and alcohol."

"The night's still young."

"Karen, I need you to pick up my car."

"Why?"

"I'm afraid I'll drive drunk."

"Hasn't stopped you before."

"I know but I'm trying to be responsible. Can you help me out?"

Karen sighed.

"C'mon, Karen. You said you were trying to be more responsible, too."

"I did? Was I drunk when I said it?"

"Okay, maybe you didn't say it, but you were certainly thinking it."

"Where's your car?"

"On Van Cortlandt Park East. Near 240th Street."

"And what do I do with my car?"

"Can you take a cab over? Then drive my car to my apartment and take a cab home?"

"Um…let me think about that…hmmm…no."

"Please, Karen? I'll pay you."

"I have an idea. Why don't *you* take a cab home and leave your car where it is?"

"But then I'll have to take a cab back to my car."

"Wait—so, it's okay for me to take two cab rides so you can have your car when you wake up in the morning?"

"Please?"

"Ah, that would still be a solid 'no.'"

"Then why don't you sleep at my apartment? Go to work from there."

"Because the last time I did that you forgot about that arrangement and you came home at four in the morning with a guy."

"I promise you that won't happen tonight."

"You know that's a promise you're incapable of keeping if you're drinking."

"Karen, if I bring anyone home tonight, it'll be a woman."

"Is that supposed to encourage me?"

"Aren't you just a little curious?"

"I am way too sober for this conversation."

"That makes two of us. C'mon, what do you say?"

"Where are you?"

"Paddy Doyle's."

Karen sighed. "Okay. Give me an hour."

"An hour?"

"*Law & Order* is on."

Chapter 30

Karen looked stunning. Her blonde hair had been freshly washed and blow-dried and her make-up deftly applied to raise her cheekbones and highlight her green eyes. Ryan jumped off her stool to greet her, wrapping her in a bear hug.

"Oh my God, you look hot," Ryan said.

"You were making me jealous with all that dirty talk," Karen said. "And you never know who you'll run into."

"I wish I was a natural blonde like you," Ryan said.

"Oh, please."

"Really, I do."

"You're drunk. You gonna introduce me to your new friend or what?"

They turned to face Sheila, but she was in mid-conversation with a handsome guy with a buzz cut and multiple piercings. Each ear was dotted with gold studs, several silver hooks protruded from his eyebrows, and the base of his neck was stamped with a cobra tattoo.

"Oh, don't want to interrupt anything," Ryan said, turning back to Karen.

"Isn't that the bartender from Beckett's?" Karen asked.

"I don't know. Haven't been there in ages."

"He used to be, anyway. I remember that tattoo."

"Is that a snake?"

"Yes, he is."

"I meant the tattoo."

"Yeah, that is, too. And let me tell you, when you see it on the ceiling mirror it's so lifelike it's frightening."

Ryan laughed. "You want a drink?"

"You're evil."

"Don't tell me you got all decked out just to drive my car home."

"Well, what did you expect me to do, put a bag over my face?"

"Just one?"

"No, I can't. I have to, have to, *have to* go to work in the morning."

"Soda?"

"Too fattening."

"Water?"

"Too boring."

"What then?"

"Nothing."

"You sure?"

"Oh, twist my friggin' arm, bitch. I so hate you right now."

"Healthy cocktail?"

"Fine. But stop me after one. You don't want me to drive your car around drunk."

"Oh, that's right—maybe you shouldn't have any."

"Make it a double."

They giggled their way through several drinks, surveying the scene. Seemed like more of a blue-collar crowd, which wasn't surprising given that it was a weeknight. Alongside the ranks of the unemployed, there were cops and firemen, some nurses and other professionals who worked odd schedules, blowing off steam on what amounted to their weekend. The recession didn't affect these jobs and it didn't seem to be hurting the bar business, either. If anything, it seemed to be helping it. The Woodlawn definition of "pounding the pavement" apparently meant having a few drinks in the pub each evening and browsing Craigslist each day. Connections were still more important than education and qualifications. Some things, indeed, never changed, and were more pronounced during an economic downturn.

"I better go," Karen finally said, three drinks in and a good buzz on her. "I can't afford to get fired."

"Thanks, Karen. I owe you a solid."

"Right," Karen said, pumping her fist. "A solid."

She wished she could talk like cops. Around her office nobody would know what that meant. They didn't do "solids" in the MTA secretaries' office. They just did time. Punched in every morning, signed out for lunch, signed back in, punched out at night. It was sort of demeaning. They weren't children. As long as all the paperwork was completed on time, everyone received their paychecks, and their insurance claims were all sorted out, who really cared what time anyone arrived or left, or how many hours it took? Had anyone ever timed out that it took exactly forty hours of typing, filing, and answering phones to complete the week's work? She could do a week's worth of work at home, in her jammies, with a laptop and a cell phone, in ten, twelve hours, tops. The other twenty-eight hours of the week were spent bullshitting about co-workers' kids and marriages and husbands and boyfriends and vacation plans and television shows that she didn't watch. *Lost. The Amazing Race. The Voice.* She could care less. What she wanted was a gun for protection, like Ryan had, and for someone to do her a "solid."

She took Ryan's car key and clipped it onto her keychain, which housed her car and apartment keys, a spare key to Ryan's apartment, and a jump drive that backed up her iPod. Walking out of the bar alone was almost worse than the walk of shame the morning after a one-night stand. She could feel the eyes on her and knew what everyone was thinking: Struck out. Loser. Just got her period. Better than slut, whore, ho, and all the other jibes that were lobbed her way when she left some apartments in the daylight, with make-up smeared and hair tousled, but she felt shame nonetheless. She always felt shame when she drank. Usually it was when she drank too much, stayed out too late, hooked up with a guy who turned out to be a jerk, missed work the next day, felt nauseous, or had a headache, but now, she only had a few drinks and a little buzz but she still felt shame. *Why the hell do I keep on doing it?* she wondered. The bouncer didn't even hold the door open for her as he did on her way in. He just smiled, nodded, and looked vaguely uncomfortable that he didn't have any lovely parting gifts to offer her. She felt like screaming, "I wasn't trying to hook up!"

But then again, that wasn't entirely true. She would like to find a companion to settle down with eventually. Not that she wanted kids or a family but she'd like to have someone to eat dinner and take vacations with, and when she was older she'd need someone to drive her to the store and wheel her around to dentist and doctor appointments. For a time her grandmother had lived with her when she was a teenager. It wasn't the grandmother she remembered, the one who bought her butterscotch candy and cashmere sweaters and feety pajamas when she was a little girl. This version of grandmother, confined to a wheelchair with an oxygen tank stuffed into its storage compartment, didn't even seem to know who she was. A tube was permanently attached to her nose and her bony hands were covered in liver spots. Karen's mother, a homecare health aide, used up all of her sick days ferrying this grandmother around to appointments, up until the last one at Velvet Touch, from which she never returned. All these years later, Karen couldn't help but think that her mother dropped off her grandmother at a whorehouse. *Who names a nursing home Velvet Touch?* She did not want to end up like her grandmother and never would've dropped her mother off at a whorehouse had she lived that long.

The strip along Van Cortlandt Park East was as dark and intimidating as she remembered. A popular lovers lane spot at one time, before Son of Sam made them off-limits around these parts in the '70s, it was still a popular dog walking spot, as evidenced by the shimmering logs and steaming pellets caught in the headlights of the occasional passing car. Ten o'clock must be the designated time for dog walkers. Lot of good those pooper-scooper laws did. There must be fifty pounds of fresh dog shit dropped on that sidewalk alone each night, she estimated, as she stepped onto the street to avoid ruining her new Manolo Blahniks, though she could probably spear turds with the four-inch spiked heels all the way to the Jeep, which was two blocks away. A horn honked as a car passed, and she wasn't sure if it was a warning to get out of the way or if it were some teenagers harassing her. *Probably some jerk*, she thought, *though my ass does look good in these jeans.* She stole a quick glance over her shoulder and saw a smoke-filled car of teenagers laughing. What did they know? Assholes. Probably gay.

She continued walking in the street until she arrived at the Jeep, clicked open the lock, and slid into the driver's seat. The engine turned quietly as the dashboard display lit up. Other people's cars always made her feel a little out of sorts. All of the equipment was generally the same and in similar places but she always needed a few minutes to get acclimated. Sitting up on this perch took some getting used to also, though with her new heels she didn't need to move the seat up, she could actually reach the pedals. She was used to riding low in her Toyota Camry and straining to see out over the hood. Up in this chair she could look down at everyone. It felt good. Like she was in control and on top on the situation. She strapped in, turned on the lights, and rolled out, unaware that there was blood splashed on the back passenger side door, and along the back wheel well and tire.

She was extra cautious, not because she had a few drinks in her, but because it wasn't her car. And it was a nice car. Jeeps didn't have the best reputation but this was a new model and Ryan had it tricked out with a top-notch sound system, heated leather seats, and a sunroof. Karen opened the roof, turned up the radio, and blasted the heat. What a bizarre feeling, wind whipping through her hair while her butt cheeks got toasty, flinging her head up toward the open sky while she sang along to a senseless song with a funky groove about a black horse and a cherry tree.

Within ten minutes, she arrived at Ryan's building, drove around the back and into the underground garage. Damn it was dark in here. And quiet. She could see why Ryan hated it. She ran down the mental checklist. Kill the lights and radio. Close the roof. Turn off the heated seats. What else? Grab purse.

Check keys. Lock doors. She got out of the car, clicked the lock, and turned toward the elevator. She never saw the knife nor who was wielding it, just felt a burning sensation in the back of her throat when she opened her mouth to scream. But she couldn't. The knife severed her vocal chords and lodged in her larynx. She clutched the handle and tried to withdraw it but everything went black and she fell, first to her knees, and then face down, the handle of the knife hitting the concrete first, pushing the blade through her vertebrae and out the back of her neck.

Chapter 31

Ryan was getting a little worried. Karen wasn't returning any of her calls or text messages. For a moment, she wished she owned a landline instead of just a cell phone, but was that really necessary? To have a landline so she could call and check to see if Karen arrived at her apartment safely? How often did Karen do that? Once or twice a year? Why didn't Karen just answer her damn phone or shoot her a text?

"I hate those fuckin' things," Sheila said.

"Oh, I know. I do, too," Ryan said, though that wasn't entirely true.

She wasn't like some people who could text novels on their cell phones but she liked having all of her contacts at her fingertips. Life was fleeting and so were thoughts and at the weirdest moments she would receive a joke or a photograph in a text message from an old friend she hadn't heard from in years and there was no pressure to pretend to want to get together. *Linda O'Hanlon had a baby girl? Oh, that's great. What an adorable baby. But Linda married some stiff who's a big shot at Goldman Sachs and they live in Tom's River, New Jersey. I am never going to see her again nor do I feel the need to send the baby a present but thanks for the photo. It will serve as a conversation piece for some of the old friends I do see on occasion.*

"I can't stand when I'm out with a guy, or a girl, for that matter, and they spend more time friggin' around with their gadgets than they do with me," Sheila said, pulling out another cigarette. "Am I that bloody boring?"

"It's not you," Ryan said. "That pisses me off, too, and I swear, I do not usually do this, I'm just concerned that Karen hasn't gotten home yet and she won't return my calls or emails."

"Sounds like a job for the police."

"You think I'm being paranoid?"

Sheila shrugged. "She's your friend. Is this unusual for her?"

Ryan thought for a couple seconds. "Yeah, unless—"

"Unless she met a guy?"

"Yeah. That's what I'm thinking. Maybe she ran into someone. It happens in Woodlawn."

"Happens everywhere."

"I know, but in Woodlawn you can't walk down the street without running into someone you used to go to school with or who knows your family or whatever."

"Happens to me, too," Sheila said. "Everyone swears they know me from somewhere but it usually takes them a while to figure out it's from the diner. And then they're too ashamed to admit it, 'cause they remember they were loaded when they met me and they can't remember what they said. And I like to have a bit of fun with 'em, tell 'em they were in awful shape the last time we met and ask 'em if they really meant what they said."

Ryan laughed. "You do not."

"Sure, I do. I just chased off yer man there with that one." She pointed to the bartender with the snake tattoo and the ear-rings. "He admitted that he couldn't remember what he told me but he probably didn't mean it, whatever it was. So I told him to fuck off as well, then."

"He's kind of cute."

"Yeah, and likely to wind up like Declan, too. I wouldn't trust that one as far as I could throw him."

"I'm not into the tattoos or the piercings but if you could look beyond that…"

"How can you look beyond a snake tattoo on yer man's

neck? Wouldn't that be a constant reminder of his sinister past?"

"Ooh, a sinister past—some girls find that exciting. They want the challenge of taming the wild beast."

"Yeah? Well, I'm not one of them. Give me a quiet man who likes Van Morrison and flowers and can fix the toilet."

"You like sensitive, yet strong."

"That'll do. I'd take that in a heartbeat so I would."

Ryan chuckled. "You know, I've been living alone for a long time. And I've been known to do my own cooking and cleaning, a little bit of gardening and the occasional plumbing job."

"Is that right?"

"Yeah. And I *love* Van Morrison."

Sheila smiled at her. "Then the only thing you're missing is a penis."

"Would that be a deal-breaker?"

"It would, yeah."

"Ah, well. A girl can dream, can't she?"

"She has to. But she has to wake up at some point, too."

Right, Ryan thought. *We can't all play centerfield for the Yankees.*

Chapter 32

Barry Durkin went into the bedroom and kicked off his shoes, instinctively grabbing the remote control.

"Don't," his wife said.

"I just want to see if the Knicks won," Durkin said.

"Barry, this has been the nicest birthday I've had in years," Lisa said. "Don't fuck it up now."

She reached around and managed to unzip her black cocktail dress, a maneuver that would've been impossible until recently. Once she hit forty she became obsessed with making herself the most agile, well-conditioned specimen she could be. She joined the gym, jogged every day, became a certified yoga instructor, and drank a cocktail called Emerald Greens every morning, which supposedly had an abundance of every natural nutrient in each spoonful and kept her bowels moving like clockwork. He jokingly called the concoction *Soylent Green*, after the sci-fi movie he watched as a child when he was in the midst of his Charlton Heston fetish. Heston was *the man* for Durkin, the one who made it possible for the likes of Clint Eastwood, Charles Bronson, and Steve McQueen to carve out their snarling, sneering careers, firing handguns on film. From battling a planet full of apes to receiving the Ten Commandments, Heston was testosterone personified. Durkin lost interest around the time of Heston's "from my cold, dead hands" comment, when he was the face of the NRA. Having seen the effects of handguns on the job every day for nineteen years, his opinion differed on the matter. According to Durkin, guns and drugs did the most damage to society, at least in the blue-collar neighborhoods in which he worked. Some of his colleagues in tonier zip codes would argue that greed was public enemy number one but they had never responded to calls of children being shot in the head while watching television in their apartment buildings, victims of stray bullets fired by low-level drug dealers with unlicensed handguns they didn't know how to operate.

The sight of Lisa standing above him in a lacey black bra and thong underwear brought his mind back from Heston's cold, dead hands to his own warm, vibrant loins. His member instantly stiffened. He had seen the Victoria's Secret purchase when he checked the online bank account yesterday and was suspicious. Part of him was nervous. Lisa never bought fancy underwear, and she had been acting a little strange lately. While their daughter was away at college and had packed on fifteen pounds in two years, favoring sweatpants and oversized sweatshirts, Lisa had been working like a woman possessed to stave off Father Time, recreating her image and sculpting a new body. He liked the look of the new Lisa. Toned calves and biceps, almost a four-pack of abs—solid but not unattractively so, like those grotesque female bodybuilders who resembled an alien race—firm breasts begging to be fondled, pert nipples asking to be licked and nibbled. Women in short hair didn't usually appeal to him but this new cut suited her face, with spiky black wisps accentuating her high cheekbones and drawing attention to her fierce blue eyes. He just hoped that the new Lisa was still *his* Lisa. Was she doing this for him? Or for somebody else? He didn't have the energy to pursue his paranoia so he hoped for the best. The alternative was too much to consider.

As she slid off her panties and lowered herself onto him, he couldn't help but feel inadequate beneath her. His pale belly had spilled over his sides, forming two perfect love handles hanging over hips that had begun to creak and would one day need to be replaced. The hair on his head was rapidly disappearing, and his chest and pubic hair had turned gray. The bags under his eyes hung lower and darker, the result of drinking too many beers while staying up too late watching too many West Coast baseball games and too much Monday Night Football. But when you work nights, with Sundays and Mondays off, what else is a man to do? He generally made no effort whatsoever to make himself more attractive or appealing. *What did I do to deserve this goddess writhing on my lap? Most guys would have to pay for service like this, but that was meaningless, just a business transaction.* This beautiful, agile woman riding his rod was all his. *My God, I am the luckiest man alive,* he thought, flicking his tongue at her breasts as they brushed his face. All worries about his shortcomings disappeared. With one swift move, he wrapped his hands around her waist and rolled her over, straddling her. He'd start doing sit-ups tomorrow—tonight he'd be doing push-ups.

Chapter 33

I've never fired my weapon before," Alvarez said.

Keegan carefully placed a hand on his shoulder and patted. Alvarez shrugged it off and paced the room.

"It was an accident," Keegan said.

"No, it wasn't," Alvarez said. "I thought he was pulling a gun."

"So, it was self-defense."

"That doesn't make it okay. Hickey's dead."

When a colleague went down in the line of duty there was always a pang of regret and remorse, a smidgeon of survivor's guilt. The usual, *Why him and not me? What if that was me?* Oddly, Keegan didn't feel anything for Hickey. It was not like he was happy the guy was dead. He didn't wish that on anyone. But at least the guy didn't have any kids. He was married, all right, to some island girl he met on vacation or something, but the few times Keegan had seen her, she looked miserable and homesick. Maybe this would allow her the freedom she really longed for. Cops got killed. It was a hazard of the job. This was a tragic accident, no doubt. Never should've happened. But what the fuck was Hickey doing and why didn't he identify himself? Had it been his partner or his boss, Durkin, who was killed, then yeah, he would've felt sadness. But for Hickey? The asshole that took his starting position in high school, stole his girlfriend, dressed like a hipster grease ball, and was always carrying around containers of weird shit? Keegan just couldn't muster the crocodile tears for Hickey.

For all the talk about the police department being a fraternity or a brotherhood, Keegan didn't really see it or feel a part of it. Not the way he saw it among his friends in the fire department, anyway. Those guys were like family. They worked twenty-four-hour shifts, had mutual partners, cooked and ate meals together. They saw their co-workers more than they saw their wives and kids some months. Cops? Maybe they grabbed a hot dog or a sandwich, had some beers after work, but that was it. They didn't share sleeping quarters and work on each other's houses on their days off. They were more like office workers in that respect, only their offices were the streets and, instead of cubicles and emails, they sat in squad cars and traded text messages. They cared for their partners, of course, and had their backs, but it wasn't always easy. There was nothing in the manual that told you how to behave in situations like this. Some guys were huggers, some weren't. Keegan wasn't a hugger. And Alvarez didn't like being touched.

"You didn't do anything wrong," Keegan said.

"I killed Hickey."

"He could've killed *you*."

Alvarez sat back down and dropped his face in his hands.

"Just think about that for a second," Keegan said. "You're here for a reason."

"Yeah, 'cause I shot Hickey," Alvarez said, jumping out of the chair again.

This was going to be a long night, Keegan thought. "I meant that, you know, you got, like, your life's work to do here on earth first," Keegan said, "before God takes you, and you gotta be here—for your sister and shit."

Alvarez shook his head and paced then pointed his index finger at Keegan. "Just shut the fuck up for a minute, okay?"

That was fine with Keegan. This wasn't his strong suit and he couldn't fake it. He tried to talk down a jumper from a rooftop once to no avail. There was no way he could pull this off. What was there to say? The guy fucked up. Didn't identify himself as a police officer. Pulled the trigger too soon. It sucked, but it happened.

Nothing could be done about it now. *Life goes on for some*

of us. Just, you know, man up and cut the drama queen shit.

"It's gonna be okay," Keegan said. The minute it was out of his mouth he knew he shouldn't have said it. *Of course, it will be okay for me.* But for Alvarez, this was the kind of thing that kept you awake each night and haunted your thoughts for the rest of your life.

"I told you to shut the fuck up!" Alvarez screamed.

The heavy metal door opened and Dr. Dennis Cleary entered the room. Cleary had spent eighteen years on the force before going back to school and getting a PhD. in August of 2001. Never had a second career choice seemed more prescient. The ink on the diploma hadn't even dried before his services were pressed into duty. Since 9/11 he'd been counseling cops round the clock, some 100 hours of billable time a week. He'd packed on some pounds since Keegan last saw him. Understandable, Keegan surmised. Sitting on your ass all week listening to other people's problems, maybe taking them out for a burger and a beer wouldn't do much for your metabolism. He remembered Cleary from the basketball courts when they were little, and then again when they were teens hanging out on the courts at night. Quick guard, nice jumper, favored Michelob Light. If he had the size, he could've went somewhere with his basketball skills, maybe a Division III college upstate. But the PD pension was more secure and didn't require a college degree. Even better, the department paid for his education, provided he continued to work for them. Pressure was on to monitor and counsel police officers with itchy trigger fingers about racial profiling. There was one incident too many of white cops shooting unarmed minorities and the department had to do something to make it look like they were listening to the editorials in the daily rags and the Al Sharptons in the community. So Cleary was brought in to talk and listen to them, identify those who needed additional face time and guidance. He also helped when officers felt pangs of guilt whenever they used their weapons, justified or not. Some guys just didn't handle the rigors of the job well. Now, it seemed, more than ever. Maybe guys were getting soft, more sensitive. Watched too many movies on Lifetime, the television network for women. Whatever the reason, there always seemed to be an officer in distress and the force sent Dr. Cleary to make sure there were no suicidal tendencies present. He'd listen, hand the officer a prescription and a business card, tell him to call whenever he needed to talk. Nice work if you could get it, thought Keegan, though it did require time. He still preferred his idea of relocating to Florida and doing light security part-time while majoring in bikini watching on the beach full time.

"I've got bartender ears," Dr. Cleary always used to say to his prospective clients when trying to earn their trust.

He was starting to get a barfly's gut, Keegan noticed. The Cleary he remembered was skinny, wiry, with greasy, stringy black hair. This version was paunchy, with thinning, gray, dry hair.

Dr. Cleary fired questions at Alvarez, checking his memory of the events, recording his answers in shorthand on a yellow legal pad. It was standard operating procedure. Another officer had already gone through the same series of questions for the official police report. This was the monotony of the job Keegan couldn't stand. Sure, it was important to get all the facts correct, but while they were sitting in the interview room at the precinct, rehashing details of the shooting, cars were being broken into, drugs were being peddled, women and children were being assaulted and bar patrons along Katonah and McLean Avenues were getting behind the wheel under the influence of alcohol. No amount of police presence would ever put an end to criminal behavior, but they could curtail a portion of it. He was all for job security but he had a little bit of pride. Woodlawn was his neighborhood, too. He wanted its residents to feel safe.

"If you ever, and I mean ever, need to talk," Dr. Cleary said, "give me a call."

Keegan knew he shouldn't, but he kind of felt slighted. *I'm his partner* he wanted to say. *He can talk to me. Who knows him better than me?*

"How you doing, Keegan?" Dr. Cleary asked.

"Me?" he asked, startled. "I'm okay."

Cleary handed him a card, too. "If you need anything, this

is my cell. Don't hesitate to take advantage of the benefits the department provides."

Keegan took the flimsy card and looked down at it. Dr. Dennis Cleary. Psychiatrist. Member, NYPD. 917 555-1212. Could've been something done up on a home computer and an inkjet printer.

"Either of you have any questions?" Dr. Cleary asked.

"Where did you get your degree?" Keegan asked.

"I did my undergrad work at Lehman College and my masters at Mercy," Cleary said. "Doctorate from Capella."

"Not exactly Harvard, Yale, and Princeton," Keegan said with a smile.

"I wanted to stay close to home and continue working while I was going to school," Cleary replied, without a hint of being insulted.

Guys like Keegan couldn't insult Cleary.

Probably knocked off a lot of schoolwork while on the job, Keegan thought, picturing Cleary sitting in the squad car under a streetlamp scanning textbooks while he was supposed to be patrolling his detail in Washington Heights. To hell with the barrio, he was getting a doctorate.

"Are you thinking about pursuing an advanced degree?" Dr. Cleary asked, pushing the gunmetal frame of his glasses up the bridge of his nose.

"Me?" Keegan asked. "Oh, no. Nothing like that. My next degree would be my first. I'm not college material. Least that's what the old man told me. He gave me two pieces of advice when I turned sixteen: don't have any kids and don't waste money on college. Then he bought me a subscription to *The Chief* and a pack of rubbers."

Cleary wanted to laugh, but the timing didn't seem appropriate. Alvarez was in a fog.

"You'd be surprised," Cleary said. "If you find the subject matter that matches your interests, you'll be fascinated by what you can accomplish."

"Yeah? They offer any degrees in broads and booze?" Keegan said, laughing alone at his attempt at humor. "I think I did enough studying in high school."

"You should consider it," Cleary said. "Everyone should. You can't do this job forever, and now with the Internet, online classes, and email, it's so much easier to do research and get a degree. And if you can get the department to pay for it, even better. Let the job work for you."

"Yeah, maybe," Keegan said. "You can prescribe drugs, right?"

Cleary nodded.

"Can you write me a scrip for Vicodin? Or Oxycodone?"

"I could," Cleary said. "But there would have to be a reason for it."

"My back's fucked up," Keegan said.

"That stuff's dangerous," Cleary said. "Take some Advil. Or Tylenol. I can't write a scrip without seeing a patient first."

"You're seeing me right now."

"I'm here for Officer Alvarez," Cleary said.

Alvarez looked up at the mention of his name.

"Call me if you'd like to make an appointment, Officer Keegan," Cleary said.

Dr. Cleary turned toward the door, opened it, and stopped. He rubbed his belly, as if trying to decide whether that pang was hunger or gas, and then said, "Call me anytime if you need me, Officer Alvarez."

He shut the door behind him. Alvarez looked at Keegan, who shrugged, and looked back down at the card. "I know him from years ago," he said, feeling that he owed his partner an explanation for the lightness of his conversation given the circumstances. "Used to play hoops together at the courts near Kepler Field."

Right by where you just shot Hickey, he almost said. But he just looked down at the business card, as if studying the six words and ten digits on it in case there was a quiz later.

"Small world," he said. *And then you die*, he wanted to add, but again, he managed to hold his tongue.

Chapter 34

Ryan hadn't felt the time go by, but she always seemed to lose track of the time when she was drinking. She had been taking it easy, or so she thought. Sheila had lapped her several times with the drink orders, and was switching between healthy cocktails and beers, with the occasional shooter thrown in for good measure. Damn, these Irish broads could drink, she thought, looking around the crowded bar and seeing empty bottles and pint glasses covering every inch of each table. Four bartenders were on duty, each manning a side of the square bar and rotating every half an hour, all of them working non-stop, pulling pints, pouring shots, rinsing mugs, making change. All in a rush to get people drunk. When they were drunk, they left bigger tips. Or, they forgot to tip at all. But the generous drunks more than made up for the forgetful ones with the short arms and deep pockets.

"Should I take you home?" she finally said to Sheila, who was glassy-eyed and had begun cursing like a sailor.

"If I had a feckin' nickel for every feckin' time I heard that line tonight," Sheila said.

"I'm not hitting on you, Sheila," Ryan said. "I was just wondering if you'd had enough."

"Enough what, bitch?"

A part of Ryan wished she knew her better, so she could tell if she was serious or not, while an equal part wished that she had never started a conversation with the woman.

"Enough of this," Ryan said, waving her hand across the

scene, which was now populated with dozens of people in much the same shape as Sheila. "Do you want to go home?"

"Lemme get this straight, you cunt," Sheila said, pulling on an unlit cigarette. "You drag me out of my feckin' house, away from my *Law & Order* and Haagen-Dazs, and you want to know if I'm ready to go home?"

"That's right."

"Well, feck you, Detective. I'll tell you when it's feckin' time to go home."

Sheila took a fit of laughter, her skull bouncing like a bobble head doll, banging into anyone within three feet. None of them seemed to notice, or if they did, they quickly turned away and went back to their conversations. *Wow*, Ryan thought. *She is really shitfaced. How embarrassing. Is this what I look like when I'm bombed?* Normally, this question didn't faze her. She could care less what people thought of her. But when she went out drinking with Karen, they usually kept pace with one another. They either both got trashed or they both cut their losses and called it a night if there weren't good energy or vibes to the night. This was turning into a catastrophe. None of her goals were met. She was no closer to solving a murder, she was rapidly losing respect for who she thought was a new friend but was revealing herself to be a buzzkill of a belligerent drunk, and there wasn't a guy in the place that she would waste her time or energy on. Opening her purse, she flipped open her cell and called Karen.

"Oh, will you stop," Sheila said, lighting the cigarette in defiance of the smoking ban that went into effect six years earlier. "Shove that feckin' thing up your arse, why don't you, Detective?"

Her ranting drew a few quick looks from patrons and the attention of one of the bartenders, who made a slicing motion across his neck with an index finger, indicating that she was cut off.

"Is that some kind of threat? Because I don't find that too feckin' funny when a bartender just got his throat slashed with a feckin' beer bottle," she shouted.

"Go on, put the cigarette out, and go home," the bartender

said. "Don't you have coffee to serve in the morning?"

"If it's for you, I'll piss in it," she said, defiantly blowing smoke at him.

"Goodnight, Sheila," the bartender said, motioning toward one of the bouncers, a broad-chested guy with a crop of black curls, who up until this point had only been opening and closing the front door for patrons as they entered and exited the bar.

Sheila spied something or someone across the bar. She put down her healthy cocktail with a loud clank, spilling half of its contents and upending the straw. *Where is she going?* Ryan wondered. *After the guy with the snake tattoo?* No, she had already insulted him enough. Ryan lost sight of her in the crowd but saw heads and torsos turning in the direction she was headed. Then she spotted her, jostling her way through conversations, toward a petite but chunky blonde with high hair, circa 1985, a hairdo that required two cans of hairspray each weekend and was solely responsible for holes in the ozone layer.

Sheila tapped her on the shoulder and threw a cross right that caught her in the nose.

Chapter 35

I can't go in there," Sheila said, standing outside The Comfy Corner, holding some napkins to her eye.

"I'll go in and ask them for ice," Ryan said.

When the bouncers picked her up and threw her out, she'd caught a heel on a break in the sidewalk and landed on her face. There was a minor laceration and some immediate swelling just under the eye but nothing that needed medical attention, though Sheila had other plans.

"I'm going to sue that motherfucker Paddy Doyle for every last penny he's got."

"I'm not a lawyer, but I don't think you have much of a case," Ryan said.

Sheila straightened up and looked at her, aghast. Her mouth opened in shock, her eyes wide with surprise. "The feckin' nerve of you," she said. "Why, you lousy feckin' excuse for a human being."

"What?" Ryan said. "Sheila, you're piss drunk, fighting with everybody, cursing everyone out. You're lucky you escaped with just a scratch."

"That feckin' cunt deserved it. Walkin' off with me man last week."

"She didn't break any laws. You assaulted her. You should be in jail right now."

"Always the feckin' police officer, aren't you? Well, feck you and you're whole famn damily, Rileen Eyan."

Sheila took another fit of laughter, realizing that she had

slurred her speech. Ryan looked to flag down a gypsy cab so she could send her home.

"Sheila?" a voice called out.

They turned and saw Slats coming toward them, in his customary overcoat and huge headphones.

"What happened, Sheila?" he said.

"Oh, Tommy, it's all right. I had a bit of a fall, is all."

"Did somebody hit you?" he asked, glaring at Ryan with flared nostrils.

"No, no. I did this to myself," Sheila said.

He didn't quite believe her, looking back at Ryan.

"Don't be looking at her, Tommy. She didn't do anything. And if she tried, don't you think I could handle a skinny bitch like her?"

He didn't understand that Sheila would have a tough time standing up to a strong wind in her condition. He'd never seen her drunk before and still wasn't sure if she was, but he bought into her logic that she could handle anything Ryan could throw at her.

"Do you need any help?" he asked.

"Aren't you sweet? No, thanks, Tommy. Go on in and get yer breakfast. You've got a long day's work ahead of you."

Tommy stared at her through his bottle thick glasses. "You don't look okay. That needs ice. And some ointment."

He reached into the inside pocket of his overcoat and rummaged around, producing a wad of tin foil, coupons, string, a rubber band, some Band-Aids, and, finally, a dirty tube of triple antibiotic ointment.

"Jaysus, Tommy, for a second there I thought you were going to pull out a cat. You've enough toys there to keep one entertained for hours."

Either her remark didn't register with him due to the headphones or it went over his head. Whatever. She wasn't even sure if it made sense to her.

"I get a lot of cuts from the broken bottles," Tommy explained, handing her the tube. "This helps."

"You should wear gloves," Sheila said.

Though it didn't look like the most sanitary thing to be

handling, Sheila took the generic brand of antibiotic and squeezed out a translucent glob, smearing some of it under her eye.

"How's that?" she asked.

He didn't respond, just took his tube and put it back in his pocket.

"Thank you, Tommy. I think I'm all fixed up, now. Right as rain, so I am."

"Are you working?" he asked.

"Sure, what kind of work could I be doing standing out here on the sidewalk?"

He shrugged.

"I think Allison has the overnight shift. Go on in and get yer breakfast, Tommy. Most important meal of the day."

"I know," he said. "I hope you feel better."

"I do, Tommy. You fixed me up, so you did."

She gave him a playful pat on the head, and he walked into the diner, smiling from ear to ear.

Ryan shot her a look of disapproval.

"What?" Sheila demanded.

"Nothing."

"That's not nothing. That look says something. It says you don't approve of the way I talk to Tommy."

"That's not it."

"Then what is it? You think you're better than me?"

"No."

I think I'm a lot like you, Ryan wanted to say. *And I don't like myself very much right now. I actually make myself sick to my stomach.*

Ryan pointed to her mouth.

"What?"

She thought about making a run for The Comfy Corner's bathroom but was afraid she wouldn't make it and would let loose while people were chowing down either their very late dinners or very early breakfasts. Instead, she turned to the street, ducked between two parked cars, and heaved. Though she was thankful they were dry, they didn't seem as therapeutic as producing a stream of vomit that expunged toxins from her body. All they did was give her an instant, massive headache and serious nausea.

"Solpadeine?" Sheila asked.

Ryan shook her head. She just wanted her head to hit the pillow. Stepping out into the street, she nearly hurled herself in front of an oncoming taxi, which came to a screeching halt inches from her. She opened the back door and motioned for Sheila to get in.

"You're feckin' taking me home?" Sheila said, flicking a lit cigarette in her direction. "Some date. You didn't provide anything you promised. No men, no laughs, and no closer to solving a murder. And to think I missed *Law & feckin' Order* for this."

"I'm sure it'll be on some other channel when you get home," Ryan said.

They rode in silence to Sheila's apartment. Sheila got out, made no effort to pay, nor offered an excuse of any kind, and stumbled onto her porch. Ryan made the driver wait to see that she got in okay and then directed him to her apartment. The whole ride home her head was spinning. *What the hell was I thinking? I was actually attracted to her? Is that what I look like? This drinking thing just isn't working out for me anymore.*

Chapter 36

Ryan saw the police cruiser and the ambulance outside the entrance to the parking garage of her building and was glad she wasn't in her Jeep. There was never any street parking available around her building and it didn't look like they'd be letting anyone enter the garage any time soon. They'd probably check each driver, too, and she wouldn't pass a Breathalyzer. Exiting the cab, she hesitated, curious to see what the police activity was about, but more eager to get into her bed and make sure that Karen had made it home. She was officially off-duty for the night.

Rather than flicking on the lights and startling Karen, she opened the Flashlight app on her cell phone and followed the ray of light through the dark apartment. She was disappointed not to find Karen on the couch. That meant she was in her bed. *Oh, well. She deserves the bed.* Should she slide in next to her or take the couch?

She'd check the situation out. If Karen were curled in a ball on one side of the bed she'd slide in next to her but if she were sprawled out, spread-eagle, she'd grab a comforter and hit the couch. Kicking off her shoes, she tiptoed into the bedroom. The bed was in the same condition she had left it in, partially made and empty. Where the fuck was Karen?

Ryan called Karen's cell phone again. This time a gruff man's voice answered.

"Oh…I'm looking for Karen?" she said.

"Who's calling?" the man said.

"Eileen."

"Eileen who?"

Ryan didn't like the tone of the man's voice. Reminded her of some of her co-workers.

"Who are you?" Ryan asked. "Where's Karen?"

"Karen's dead."

Ryan screamed and dropped the phone. She ran to the bathroom and between sobs and screams managed to vomit up the last of the healthy cocktails.

Chapter 37

Durkin didn't want to answer the phone, and his wife certainly didn't want him to either but he simply couldn't ignore it. Ryan was his confidant on the job, the one person who he really felt understood the responsibility that came with it, and how and when to turn it off. If she were calling in the middle of the night on his wife's birthday, it meant one of two things: either she was piss drunk or she felt her life was in danger.

If she were drunk, it would be a quick, one-sided conversation and then he would pull the plug on the answering machine. If her life were in danger, then his wife's birthday celebration was officially over.

"This better be good," Durkin said.

"Karen's dead," Ryan said. "Knifed in the neck."

"What? Who's Karen?"

"My best friend."

"Oh, shit."

"Whoever did it thought she was me."

"What?"

"I'm scared, Durk. Someone's following me. They know exactly where I am at al—"

"Ryan, Slow down. Take a breath and tell me exactly what happened."

Ryan did as he said, sucking in a gulp of air and letting out a long sigh. "She was driving my car," she said. "To my apartment. Someone either followed her or was waiting for her and killed her. Stabbed through the mouth with a fuckin' butcher knife."

"Jesus."

Ryan's sobbing grew uncontrollable.

"Okay, take it easy. Try to breathe. Just relax."

"I can't fuckin' relax! My best friend is dead and it should've been me!"

"How do you know that? Maybe some nut just followed her. Did she piss somebody off? A jealous boyfriend? Or a case of road rage, maybe?"

"I seriously doubt it. She didn't have a boyfriend, and she drove like a grandma, which is why I let her drive my car."

Durkin rubbed his face, looked back at his beautiful wife, who kicked off the sheets and went into the bathroom, shooting him a glare that said happy friggin' birthday, indeed.

"Anything else out of the ordinary with it?" Durkin asked.

"There was a crucifix and a pair of rosary beads laid at her feet."

"Any prints?"

"I don't know. Forensics hasn't arrived yet."

"That's weird. Let me get on 'em and I'll get back to you."

"I'm scared, Durk."

"I know. But I promise, you'll be okay."

"Can you come over?"

Durk hesitated.

"Please, Durk?"

"Let me see what I can do."

"I'm scared, Durk."

"I know. Okay, I'll be over in a little bit."

Lisa opened the bathroom door and shot him *the look*. Then she slammed the door shut. She'd be doing some serious weightlifting and running in the morning to burn up the anger. Durkin grabbed a Post-it note from the pile on the nightstand and wrote *flowers* on it, to remind himself to bring home a bouquet before setting foot in the house again. He folded it neatly and stuck it in his wallet. Then he called forensics.

Chapter 38

There's nothing unusual about it, Lisa," Durkin said, fastening his belt. "The woman's life is in danger."

"I'll tell you what else is in danger, this marriage!" Lisa screamed at him.

"What the fuck do you want me to do? My best detective's life is in danger, and my top forensics guy was just killed by one of my guys. I have to go in."

"*Your* detective? *Your* forensics guy? Whaddya own these people? What about *your* wife? And *your* marriage? What's more important than that?"

"When are you going to grasp the nature of this job and what it entails? Before I retire would be nice."

"When are you going to grasp the responsibilities to your wife and family?"

"I know all about responsibility and wives and families. I also know a little something about working, too, which is what I have to do to support this family."

"Oh, fuck you. I sacrificed my career to raise a child."

"Yeah, by choice. And now that our daughter is eating her way through college, you can get back to work now, thank you very much."

"Don't you ever talk about my daughter like that."

"Our daughter, hon. *Our* daughter."

"Oh, fuck you, Lieutenant Dickbag!"

"Let's not forget who wanted me to take the lieutenant's test, and the sergeant's test, and the captain's test. I would've been perfectly happy to be a foot soldier or a transit cop for twenty years and collect a pension. *You* were the one that pushed me into this."

"Oh, so you're blaming me for giving you direction and motivation."

"I'm not blaming you for anything. But this is part of the job. You want the raise and the OT, you gotta put in the extra time and effort."

"I swear, if I find out you're lying about this—"

"Turn the TV on and see for yourself—"

"If you're going to a card game, or it's someone's bachelor party, or you've got a fuckin' girlfriend somewhere, some little Spanish girl—"

"What are you talking about?"

"I mean it. I'm onto you."

"You're onto me? You are so far away from me, it's not even funny."

"No, it's not funny, Barry. And it won't be funny if this marriage ends in divorce. 'Cause, believe me, it won't be pretty."

"You gotta stop watching those soap operas and cop shows. It's a lot less interesting in real life, believe me."

"Yeah, that's all I do, watch TV, right? Go to the gym and watch TV."

"And shop. Don't forget shopping. That goes right to the top of the list."

"I take care of everything for you. Your daughter, your food, your clothes. Your life only operates smoothly because I run it."

"Our daughter, Lisa. She's *our* daughter." Durkin slipped on his Merrells and flipped his hands at her in defeat. "Ah, what's the fuckin' point? Same shit, different day."

"Yeah, it *is* a different day. It's *my birthday*."

Durkin strapped on his holster and put on his jacket. "Well, I'm sorry death didn't take a holiday for your birthday, Lisa."

"I'm not getting any younger, you know."

"Couldn't tell by looking at you," Durkin said. "You look ten years younger."

Compliments usually got him out of a jam. Noticing a new haircut or that she had dropped a couple pounds was usually a game-changer.

"It's a little late for flattery," she snapped.

He'd have to go sugary. Pour it on a little thicker, like Bosco. "I'm serious. You look great. Better than the day I met you."

"Oh, please."

Durkin crossed the room and grabbed her in a bear hug. "I'm serious. I love you, Lisa. Why would I want anybody else? And who the fuck would want *me*, anyway?"

"I'm just warning you, Barry. If I ever find out that you were with another woman, it's over. You understand?"

"Yeah, I get it. And the same goes for you."

"Oh, right. Like that's what I'm about."

"I mean it. I catch you with another woman, and that's it...but I'm taking pictures first and posting them on the Internet."

"It's not a joke, Barry."

"Oh, I'm not joking."

She turned and went back into the bathroom.

"I gotta go," Durkin said. "Now can you please stop talkin' shit about our marriage? It doesn't help me do my job, and I've got a bitch of a day at work ahead of me."

"Just go. You'd rather be married to that job."

"Yeah, right. I'd rather leave my bed and a night of hot sex and a nice breakfast to go investigate a couple murders and drink shitty coffee. You know how many days until retirement, Lisa?" He checked his watch. "Two hundred seventy-eight and eleven hours."

"You better hope we make it."

"Two hundred seventy-eight days, ten hours and fifty-nine seconds, to be exact, and I'm all yours. Two hundred seventy-eight days, ten hours and fifty-five seconds...Two hundred seventy-eight days, ten hours—"

"Just go already. You sound like that stupid fuckin' song from *Rent*."

Chapter 39

Durkin parked in the precinct lot right next to Alvarez's vintage, fire-orange Camaro. Man, how he loved that car. Tricked it out with spinning rims, tinted glass, a fur-topped dashboard and a hi-def surround sound stereo system. It looked like something that belonged to a '70s-era pimp, or someone who spent his days evading police, not someone who shook down marginal criminals with zeal and gusto. He remembered the first day Alvarez was assigned to the precinct. The kid was wound so tight he took him out for a beer and a cheeseburger after his shift, told him to take his work seriously but don't take his co-workers too seriously. Respect them, give them some space, but don't be a hard-ass.

Nobody liked a hard-ass on the job. Alvarez was a good kid, meant well. A decent person who wanted to do the right thing. So how did he know the kid would fuck something up? It wasn't exactly a premonition but a strong feeling that somehow, this fresh-faced enthusiastic kid would find himself in trouble. Too gung-ho.

Being a cop in The Bronx meant letting a lot of the little stuff go. There were just too many people living in too small an area for there not to be minor discrepancies and differences. As long as they didn't escalate into full-blown warfare, you had to look the other way sometimes. They didn't teach that at the academy. That was what sergeants and lieutenants and captains and veterans taught the probees and the rookies, how to do their jobs in a particular precinct. Each one was different. A

Bronxville cop, for instance, might have to be learned in the ways of white-collar crime, mortgage scams, insider trading, pyramid schemes, and hedge fund cheats. Bronx cops had to be wise to the ways of the street. The kids snatching hubcaps and peddling grass might just need a stern talking to or someone to listen to them. Sometimes a kick in the ass was warranted, or the scare of spending a few hours in the lock-up. But drawing a gun on another officer without identifying yourself? That was PO 101. What the fuck was Alvarez thinking?

Granted, Hickey's story was odd, or at least the sketchy nuggets that had been relayed to Durkin were. Sure, guys became infatuated with girls and did weird things. Durkin himself had that Victoria Principal hang-up when she was on *Dallas* in the early '80s. Had it been the Internet age, Durkin certainly would've been browsing for images of Principal and visiting chat rooms dedicated to her whereabouts until the wee hours of the morning with a box of tissues and some lubricant within reach. But the Principal fetish was pure fantasy. Not like the crush he had on poor Jenna Cummings. Durk practically stalked her in eighth grade. All during homeroom, he'd drool over his marble notebook while he stared at her and pretended to read. She must've felt his eyes on her and ignored them but if she had known that he followed her home from five o'clock mass and nearly climbed in her bedroom window one evening, she would've been totally creeped out. Probably wouldn't have called the cops but she certainly would've told her father, the former high school linebacker turned ironworker with a drinking problem who took pleasure in beating the living shit out of adolescent boys. Well, at least his own sons, anyway.

Women in the precinct often brought out the weirdest in guys, who just didn't know how to act around a woman who carried a gun and a badge. They either shied away or tried to treat them like one of the guys, but of course they *weren't* one of the guys. There was professional protocol to follow and the department had ratcheted up the effort to be PC by mandating sensitivity training to stave off unprofessional conduct, but the fact remained that the academy and its $45,000 starting salary didn't always attract Rhodes Scholars with advanced degrees in etiquette. These were not always the sharpest knives in the drawer, as one captain in the academy used to say. Despite the training and the threats of termination for indecent conduct, female officers were still hit on by uncouth guys all the time. Some filed complaints, some sucked it up and kept it in, a few seemed to revel in the attention, and others hired lawyers. When Durk was at Midtown South, there was a beautiful brunette who wore her hair up in a bun under her cap on duty but whenever she'd bring in a perp and do paperwork, she'd shake it out and let it flow down beyond her shoulders, like she was doing a shampoo commercial. Every cop's head in the joint would turn and watch her. Officer Breck they used to call her. She became the object of many an officer's desires and the target of many sexist jokes and come-ons. One officer, having had a few too many at the Rangers game before starting his midnight shift, waved his dick at her in the lunchroom. She filed harassment charges, won a six-figure settlement. He went to jail, she did a spread in Playboy and turned in her badge before moving out east and landing a gig on the short-lived reality show, *The Housewives of The Hamptons.*

The Hickey thing was nothing like that case. Hickey's actions were calibrated, premeditated, well thought out, and let's face it, just plain weird any way you slice it. The guy had collections of hair and skin cells and fingernails and all kinds of wacky shit in his locker, along with soft core porn and spiked dog collars, powders, brushes, chemicals, pills, infrared lights, lasers, cameras, cassettes, CDs, Ziploc bags, cigar cases and tackle boxes. Was any of it evidence of a crime, or just proof that the guy was a little off? Was Hickey really into S and M? It was tough to find out because nobody on the force really liked the guy or took the time to find out who he was beneath the phony exterior. Whatever he was or wasn't, there was no point in leaking any of that information to the media or Hickey's wife. He was still one of them. Let everyone think he was a hero, maybe name a street after him, and let his secrets die with him. A box of Hickey's oddities was packed up and brought to Holly's Lane, a clearing in the woods beyond Van

Cortlandt Park East that was a popular keg party and bonfire site for teenagers, where an officer put a match to it. Officers told Durk that when they broke the news of Hickey's death to his wife, she almost seemed relieved that she could go back to the Sandals resort in Mexico—and not as a guest, but hoping to get her old job back.

It still didn't make any sense to Durkin. He needed to find out from Ryan what the extent of her relationship was with Hickey. But how did he tactfully approach that subject now that her best friend was dead? He was reminded of what a weary old sergeant had told him at Midtown South, "You aren't granted retirement from this job, you earn it." Time to start earning that pension, Durkin thought, as he grabbed the twenty-ounce coffee from the cup holder, exited his car, and made his way inside the crumbling brick facade of the precinct that violated a multitude of codes and wouldn't pass a routine building inspection.

Chapter 40

Ryan couldn't move. She sat at the breakfast nook, crying into her left hand and clutching a pistol in her right. Karen was the one person in the world she couldn't go on without. More than a family member, Karen was there for her, always. Since the third grade, when they sat next to each other in Ms. Chapman's class, holding hands and walking single file to the auditorium for an assembly and out the door to meet their waiting parents—or did their parents even meet them?—they were best friends. BFFs before the terminology existed. They walked to and from school together, played hopscotch and softball, and tried gymnastics and bowling, and quit after two weeks. They shared stories of boyfriends and a few actual boyfriends—not at the same time—and compared notes. Drinking partners and soul mates, they were an inseparable duo. They had even joked that if neither one was married by forty-five, they'd just move in together.

Both of Karen's parents had died and Ryan was actually grateful for that now. She couldn't bear the thought of breaking the news to them, two of the sweetest people she ever met. They had been small and frail, riddled with arthritis, and didn't age well. Her mother was an aide, taking care of older, frailer patients who opted to die at home under her watchful eye rather than alone in a nursing home or hospital. It almost seemed as if she had taken on the ailments of her patients, every day coming home with a new ache or pain and more gnarled hands. Her hips, knees, shoulders, all the bones and joints in her body, ached. She'd had trouble doing the eighteen stairs that led up to their front door, and couldn't carry groceries anymore. Her husband wasn't much help, either. A bricklayer by trade, his back had been arched from the day Ryan had met him, the result, she presumed, of stooping over for eight hours a day mixing mortar and stacking blocks.

Ryan remembered one evening back in high school in late December, smoking a joint with Karen in a bus shelter, while a light dusting of snow covered McLean Avenue, and then taking the number twenty-five bus up to the Cross County Shopping Center. Karen bought a pair of knee pads for both of her parents at Herman's Sporting Goods for a Christmas present, and they laughed all the way home, joking that the pads were for her parents to enjoy oral sex, because the sad reality was too much time on their knees scrubbing floors and building houses left neither of them able to walk without pain in their early fifties. Why didn't they just cut back on the work, Ryan wondered, sell the house, rent an apartment with an elevator, and send Karen to public school? Because they wanted better for their daughter, just like any parent. And now all the sacrifices they made, all the long hours of manual labor, what good did they do? Karen was as dead as they were, and it was all Ryan's fault.

She could philosophize away survivor's guilt when it didn't apply to her, but there was no mistaking that she was the intended target here, and no denying that she was responsible for getting Karen out of bed. *Karen should be the one crying*, Ryan thought. *I should be dead.*

She couldn't eat and tried to force herself to drink something but had trouble keeping anything down. Even the bottled water seemed to burn her esophagus. She made coffee she couldn't drink, tried chamomile tea again, and decided once and for all that she couldn't stomach it, sipped some Vitamin Water, but found it surprisingly sweeter than she remembered and a drop of orange juice that made the acid in her stomach boil. Should she try a beer? Or open a bottle of wine?

God, no. What a wicked disease. Taunting me in my weakest moments. What good could possibly come of that, and why would I want to turn this into a celebration of some sort or wallow in my pity? Isn't this enough torture?

The ringing of her cell phone startled her. Exhausted but unable to sleep, her nerves were now shot, too. She was relieved that it was Durkin.

"Ryan, how you doin'?" he asked.

"I've been better, but I honestly can't say if I've been worse."

"You can't blame yourself for this."

"Yeah, I can. And I will. So save your breath."

She walked over to her window, looked down at the George Washington Bridge, its arches lighting up the night, beckoning all comers to that fantasyland in the distance, a circus of a city where dreams are realized or meet a violent death.

"We don't know all the facts yet," Durkin said, trying to straddle the impossible line between detective, psychologist, and friend.

"We know enough of them."

"Don't jump to any conclusions."

Ryan looked down from her twelfth-floor window. "You should've stopped after 'jump.'"

"You're not suicidal, are you, Ryan?"

"I don't know what the fuck I am anymore. I'm just…sick."

"Okay. We'll get you some help."

"What kind of help? You gonna send Cleary over with a prescription? No, thanks. It won't bring Karen back."

"No. Nothing will bring Karen back," Durkin said. "Now we have to bring you back."

"I can't even think about work right now."

"I'm not talking about work. I mean your mental state."

"My mental state?"

"Yeah. Look, it's not easy to deal with the murder of a close friend so let's not sugarcoat this."

Ryan laughed. "What, are we baking cookies?"

"I'm serious. I've lost people before, Ryan. It's hard. And I'm not just talking about guys like Hickey."

"Hickey? Why'd you bring him up?"

Oh, shit, Durkin thought. *She doesn't even know about Hickey yet.*

"Durk? You there?"

"Yeah…it's just, ah, I don't know how to tell you this, Ryan, so I'm just going to tell you…"

"Durk? Maybe you shouldn't. I've had a bad day."

"Okay, try to get some sleep, then."

"Fat chance."

"Don't take any pills, all right?"

"Can you come over, Durk?"

"I don't know, Ryan. It's turned into a pretty shitty day for me, too."

"Well, if you need to talk about it, I'm sure I'll be awake all night."

"That won't help anything. Just go to sleep."

"You sound like my father now."

"Fathers are right sometimes."

She didn't remember saying goodbye, or hanging up the phone. Her thoughts turned to her father, unable to walk or get up without help or supervision. Now that the pervasive feeling of getting into a car and just driving far, far away from her job, the city, and her life overwhelmed her, she could imagine how frustrating it must be for him. Not being able to eat, drink, sleep, shit, move, even pick up a paper or a book and read or do a crossword puzzle without help must be hell. He was completely at the mercy of someone else, an overworked nurse or an underpaid aide. How could he stand it? In that respect, Karen was lucky to die all at once rather than a little bit each day. Hopefully, she didn't suffer too much. Ryan shook her head, trying to lose all the thoughts bouncing around in it. Now she was hoping Karen's killer was adept at stabbing her best friend in the neck so she didn't suffer too much. *What is wrong with me?*

Chapter 41

The persistent knocking on her door had been incorporated into her dream. She was on her knees in a confessional box, leaning into a tightly woven mesh screen, trying to speak words that wouldn't come out. On the other side of the screen she could make out thick glasses, a shock of white hair and a green stole draped over broad shoulders. The rest of the clothes were of an uncomfortable, starchy black material, maybe polyester. The priest's breath was hot and stale. Morning breath, with hints of coffee and Scotch, in need of a serious rinsing. She attempted to speak the words that began her confessions when she was a child, "Bless me, Father, for I have sinned, it has been…" How long since her last confession, thirty years? Did they even say that anymore? What was the protocol? What was it that she wanted to confess? What was she trying to say?

She opened her mouth, leaned closer to the screen to whisper, the priest's head resting on the other side in anticipation, when the knocking reached a crescendo and then there were fists pounding on the door. Ryan awoke with her cheek in a puddle of saliva on her pillow, her pistol still in her curled right hand, pointed ominously at her face. She slowly stood up, went to the front door, and spied Durkin through the peephole, pounding on her door.

"Ryan, wake up! It's me, Durk!"

Ryan unlocked the door and retreated into the kitchen. Durkin followed her with a brown paper bag.

"Holy shit, you okay?" he asked. "I was out there for fifteen minutes. I thought you were—" He caught himself before he said 'dead'.

"I was dreaming. I was in confession."

"Yeah, you were dreaming. What were you confessing?"

"I don't know. The words wouldn't come out."

Durkin removed two paper coffee cups from the bag and set them down on the counter.

"These are probably cold by now, but, what the hell? There's sugar in the bag, if you take it."

The sugar comment triggered her memory. "Sugarcoat."

"Hmm..." Durkin said, slurping his coffee.

"You said that last night...didn't you? You didn't want to sugarcoat something."

"Yeah. Sit down."

"I think I'll stand."

Durkin shrugged. "Suit yourself. This is going to sound weird, because it is—"

"Out with it."

"Hickey's dead. Shot once in the chest last night—by Alvarez."

"Alvarez? Keegan's partner?"

"Mmm-hmm."

Ryan sat down on the stool at the breakfast nook. "Were they on duty?"

"Alvarez and Keegan were."

"What happened?"

"I don't mean to pry, Ryan, but—"

"But you mean to pry."

"Exactly. How well did you know Hickey?"

"Not that well. I mean, he was from the neighborhood—"

"Yeah."

"I remember him a little bit."

"Did you two ever—"

"I never slept with him. Is that what he told you?"

"No. I was just wondering if you two ever went out."

"Once. But he creeped me out a bit—a lot, actually."

"Yeah. Had that effect on a lot of people, apparently."

"Why? What are people saying?"

"Well, he's not saying anything, obviously. But the officers who informed his wife thought she seemed relieved. Pretty strong word to use when a spouse dies tragically, don't you think?"

"Yeah."

"Had you had any contact with him recently?"

Ryan sighed.

"Ryan?"

"All right, Durk. Give me a fuckin' minute. This is a lot to digest."

She dumped some sugar into the coffee, took a swig, and ran to the sink to spit it out. "How can you drink this shit cold?"

"It's like iced coffee."

"But it's not. It's lukewarm coffee with curdled milk. It's horrible."

"Oh, right. I forgot you swallow it black."

She shot him a look. Was that a sexual reference? She was too tired to know if she was missing something.

Durkin shrugged and knocked back another arctic blast of coffee. She couldn't help but think that he would be the kind of guy to see shit stains in his underwear, shrug, and wear them anyway.

"When was the last time you saw Hickey?" he asked.

"This week. Just the other day." Ryan began making a fresh pot of coffee. "He called me, said he needed to talk to me about some fibers."

"And?"

"Durk, I'm telling you this as a friend, not as a cop."

"But you realize I'm a cop, right?"

"You're not interrogating me, you're asking me questions, because you're a concerned friend, aren't you?"

"Of course, Ryan, of course. You're not a suspect. We know who shot him. We have a confession and a witness. We're just wondering what the fuck he was doing dusting your car for prints."

"What?"

"Alvarez and Keegan swear they came across what they believed to be a robbery in progress on VCP East and 240, where there's been an uptick in car thefts and burglaries."

"Yeah, I know. I saw the CompStat numbers."

"Right. So they approached the suspect, Alvarez slipped on either a pile of shit or wet leaves, fell on his ass, his gun discharged, striking Hickey once in the chest. The end."

"Oh my God."

"Yeah. So, like I told you, my night sucked, too."

Ryan sighed. "How was Romero's?"

"Huh?"

It seemed so long ago. Was it only last night he had that terrific chicken scarpariello with hot and sweet sausage in brown sauce and a side of al dente ditalini in marinara sauce and sourdough bread to mop it up and a Brunello di Montalcino to wash it down? And for dessert, mascarpone and Lisa in frilly underwear? Jesus, that seemed like an eternity ago.

"Oh, nice. Real nice. You know, it's Romero's."

"Yeah." Ryan rubbed her face and checked the coffee. Still not ready. "Poor Alvarez. You believe him?"

"I don't have any reason not to—why? You know something I don't?"

"No. I bet that was the first time he fired his weapon."

"It was. Beginner's luck, huh?"

"What was Hickey doing to my car?"

"I don't know. I was hoping you could shed some light on that."

The coffee machine starting humming and Ryan couldn't wait for it to properly brew, shoving a Dunkin' Donuts ceramic mug under it to catch the first weak cup from the machine.

"I hadn't heard from Hickey in six years. This week, out of the blue, he calls me, tells me he found some hair at the crime scene of Declan McManus that match some hair that he collected from the headrest of his car six years ago."

"Yours?"

"Yeah."

"What did you say?"

"I said he was fuckin' weird and left him in the restaurant."

"Ohhh, so that's who you went to Romero's with?"

"Yeah."

Durkin shrugged. "At least he's got good taste in food."

"Yeah, it's not like he's Hannibal Lecter, but I was freaked out, Durk. The guy's a class-A fuckin' weirdo. Not to mention obsessed with '70s cop shows and '80s music and clothes."

"Can't kill a guy for that."

"Why did they kill him?"

"It was an accident."

"Did they identify themselves as cops?"

Durkin raised his eyebrows, sipped some coffee. "Does it matter now?"

"Yeah, it does. I mean, the guy's weird, but—it sounds like someone really fucked up."

"Everyone makes mistakes."

"But some are inexcusable. I'm even more freaked out that he was around my car, and then someone followed Karen in my car and killed her. Oh, shit. Do you think Hickey had anything to do with that?"

"Like I said, Ryan. He's not talking, and I've had a shitty night, too."

Durkin's cell phone buzzed and he checked the text message.

"And it looks like my day's not gonna be any better. Someone broke into Cleary's car and stole a bunch of prescription pads."

"Should be easy to track those."

"Not before a couple thousand tabs of OxyContin hit the street."

"Or Solpadeine."

"What's that again?"

"The Irish version."

"Right." Durkin's cell phone buzzed as he placed his coffee cup in the trash. "I gotta run. Call me if you need anything."

"I'll walk you down."

Chapter 42

Lisa Durkin was parked on Johnson Avenue in her friend Diana's car, a Volkswagen Golf with a sunroof. She didn't ask for the car but when she told her workout partner during their morning routine that she wanted to tail Barry because she thought he might be having an affair, Diana offered it to her. She declined Diana's offer to tag along, deciding to swap her Corolla for Diana's Golf so *she* could spy on her fuckball husband Ronnie, whom she *knew* was having an affair because she checked his email, bank account, and Facebook page regularly. What *he* didn't know was that she received text alerts about when and from which ATM cash was withdrawn, so she practically knew before he did where he was going for lunch and drinks and sex based on his whereabouts and the process of elimination. Armed with that information and her GPS, she could pretty much narrow down his choices of restaurants and hotels to two possibilities. Even if he knew or pretended to care, he wouldn't expect her to follow him. And certainly not in an eighteen year-old Toyota Corolla, anyway. If all went according to her plan, he wouldn't notice the tire iron she was wielding until it landed across his mouth or his balls, either.

Listening to Diana's rants had jacked up Lisa's own suspicions. Barry did spend a lot of time out of the house. There were plenty of nights when he had a few beers with the guys. He never came home smelling like perfume and she never found hotel or dinner receipts, but Diana had her convinced that he, too, was probably screwing around on her. She had given him the best years of her life and this was how he was going to repay her? The prick. On her birthday, of all nights.

Barry probably wouldn't have noticed anyone following him but seeing his own license plate in the rearview mirror all morning may make him a tad suspicious, so behind sunglasses, a painter's cap and the wheel of the VW, Lisa felt sufficiently disguised. She hadn't driven a stick shift in years and it took a bit of getting used to but it wasn't her clutch she was burning out and Diana's fuckball of a husband made a shitload of money trading something or other on Wall Street or Madison Avenue or somewhere. Enough so that he thought he was invincible, could have affairs and gamble on football and play cards with the guys on Friday nights. Asshole had another think coming once Diana got hold of him. And he could buy a new fuckin' clutch or even better, a new fuckin' car. An automatic this time, the cheap fuck. Thought he could fuck around on the wife he makes drive a stick shift to save a few dollars on gas? Bullshit on that.

Lisa settled into her People magazine, flipping pages while sipping a Grande Latte from Starbucks. If she were going to be on a stakeout, she'd allow herself a minor transgression from her strict dietary regimen. Okay, not exactly a minor transgression, a Grande transgression. She scanned pictures of Jennifer Aniston and Britney Spears in bikinis and thought her body looked as good if not better. Pictures of Kirstie Allie, Martha Stewart, and Oprah at the beach nearly made her gag but her nausea subsided when she spied Johnny Depp and Hugh Jackman shirtless on beaches somewhere far away. France or the Caribbean. Letting her mind wander, she imagined rolling in the sand with both of them, stroking her favorite pirate's soul patch, and melting in the biceps of the Australian Wolverine. She closed her eyes for a moment to savor it, felt herself getting moist and warm, and reopened them to see Barry standing at the doorway of 1886 Johnson Avenue in the arms of a woman who looked as if she had never set foot in a gym and hadn't slept in a week. Instinctively, she leaned on the horn. Both of them turned and looked in her direction but didn't seem to notice or care. He leaned in and quickly kissed the woman on the head, and she nodded and retreated into the apartment building. Barry slowly approached his unmarked Crown Vic, got in, and drove off, the same as if he had just picked up the morning paper and a roll at the newsstand. That fuck. That stupid fuck. She wished she had the tire iron. Who would get it first? The girl? Or Barry? It would be Barry, if only she could get the fuckin' car out of its parking space. She hadn't thought about the difficulties of starting the manual transmission while parked on such a steep hill. Was it gas, clutch, gas, or clutch, gas, clutch? Damn it, she couldn't remember. The Grande Latte wasn't helping. Her heart was racing as if she were finishing her crunch routine at the gym.

"Fuckin' bastard," she yelled. "Fuck, fuck, fuck!" as the VW coughed and whirred, coughed and whirred, coughed and whirred with each attempt she made to start it.

Chapter 43

Ryan couldn't sleep. She just wanted to get in her car and drive, with no direction in mind. Vermont, Florida, Chicago, San Francisco, Seattle, wherever. She just wanted to get lost in the wilderness or escape unnoticed in a foreign city. What was left for her here anyway? Her sister Maureen hadn't been home in decades, meeting up with some hippies at a Grateful Dead show senior year of high school and disappearing. Last postcard she got from her was from Portland in 1994, and she couldn't remember if it was from Maine or Oregon. One coast or the other, didn't matter. Maybe her father should've let her go to Vassar after all. Maybe she would've come back home once in a while to check on him.

Her brothers had moved to Connecticut to raise their kids, and she only saw them at Christmas, for a Hallmark celebration brought to you by LL Bean. They looked like Kennedy clan wannabes, their wives aging much better than was physically possible considering the amount of booze they gulped, the boys neatly jelled and coiffed and wearing matching red sweaters, khakis and deck shoes, the girls with their hair spun up in curls and decorated with red and green ribbons, just like the cascading branches of the eighteen-foot high and six-foot wide Douglas firs that didn't even dwarf the view of the yard from the bay windows on the far side of their cavernous living rooms. She would sit at the beverage station directly across from the tree and look down at the expansive yards below, always miraculously covered in a dusting of snow by that time of year, begging the question was it real or man-made, and imagine them playing touch football games by day, followed by nights nestled by the fire watching videos on the eighty-inch, flat-screen, LED HDTV and conversing about the bond market. Yeah, she was jealous of the wealth, the houses, the fireplaces, the well-stocked bars, the in-ground pools, the spas, the gyms and the game rooms in the basements. But part of that life seemed boring, too. Sheltered. If she really wanted solitude, she'd prefer a house in the mountains or the country, with no other houses in sight, rather than replica mansions dotting the hillsides surrounding each five-acre plot of land in Harmony Grove, where not one but both of her brothers had moved, put in pools, finished their basements, and built bonus rooms with the requisite man caves. Each 5,000-square foot home in the grove was visible when the leaves had fallen off the trees and each looked the same. Her brothers' kids seemed happy enough with all of the time-consuming distractions at their disposal, but they seemed most happy when they were huddled over their phones, texting the other children who lived similar or exact lives in the grove. She didn't even know exactly what her brothers did to make the kind of money to afford this lifestyle, and after the Madoff scandal was afraid to ask, but she knew they traded money or invested in "futures," whatever the hell that meant. She wondered if either of them would invest in her future and presumed that none of their children's futures would involve a career in law enforcement.

The older she got, the less people she liked but she still wanted to be around them. She wasn't a recluse and liked to know that other people around her were alive. Except now Karen wasn't. She cleared the mound of used tissues off her bureau and saw her date book. The word "Dad" was scribbled in for today. She had totally forgotten she had promised to have lunch with him. Pulling her hair up in a bun and coaxing it under a Yankees cap, she grabbed her car keys and then froze. Her Jeep had been impounded. Forensics wanted to give it a complete going-over to determine what exactly Hickey was doing to it and to make sure no foul play was involved. If only they had taken the Jeep when Hickey was shot, before Karen got in it, maybe she'd still be alive. *Idiots. Do they think the friggin' Jeep is responsible for everyone dying? Is the car possessed, like the one in that Stephen King book?* She almost called Karen to ask if she could borrow her car and began crying again. There was no one else she wanted to call. She'd have to take a taxi to visit her dad.

Chapter 44

Lisa was standing above the VW, trying to figure out how to start it. She had popped open the hood, as if that would do any good, and was poking around, not sure what she was supposed to be looking for. She grabbed a few wires to make sure they were securely fastened, then almost touched some caps and retracted her hand when she saw the words "Warning: HOT." What she really hoped was that some guy would come along and offer to help. Preferably, a young, good-looking guy, but anyone would do. She heard a car approaching and turned to see a black Lincoln slowing down. Was he stopping to help? Damn it, she should've brought her glasses.

She resisted the urge to wear them all the time but was ready to admit defeat. Her eyes were failing her. She needed glasses to see anything clearly beyond ten feet. How could she partake in a stakeout without glasses? The closer he got, the slower the car went. She threw up her hand and waved to it. The tinted passenger side window slowly descended and she peeked in to see an obese man cramped behind the wheel, with several layers of neck flab hanging over a starched collar. The smell of Indian food and BO smacked her in the face.

"Taxi?" the driver asked.

"Oh, no," Lisa said. "I was hoping you could help me start my car."

The driver laughed. "I can't do that. You want me to call you a tow truck?"

"No, I don't want a tow truck. It works. I just can't start it. I'm not used to driving a manual transmission."

"That's my cab!" a woman's voice shouted.

Lisa looked up to see a woman in a leather jacket and Yankees cap running for the taxi.

"I'm not looking for a cab," Lisa said. "I need help starting the car."

"You have triple A?" the woman asked, as she opened the back door of the taxi.

Lisa looked at her. Was that her? Was she really face to face with the woman who had ruined her fortieth birthday and destroyed her marriage? Her talks with Diana had pumped her up so much that she was convinced if she ever found out that Barry was cheating on her and she met the woman responsible, that she would gouge her eyes out. But all she could do was stare with her mouth agape. She wanted to hit her, punch her, kick her, and pull her hair but she couldn't move. She wanted to scream but she couldn't talk. She couldn't even blink.

"Call your insurance," Ryan finally said, getting into the taxi and shutting the door.

Normally she would've tried to help but if she let this cab go and had to wait for another she'd miss her lunch date with her father, which was sure to be the highlight of his day.

The taxi slowly rolled up to the crest of the hill, and Lisa stood in the street in a catatonic trance, watching its red brake lights fade as it began its decline.

Chapter 45

Her father was in a wheelchair facing the window at a corner table, sipping tea through a straw, a plate of mostly untouched food before him.

"Sorry I'm late, Dad," Ryan said.

His face instantly brightened. He didn't think she was coming. His sons would make plans to come visit but something always came up. The kids were sick or there was a business meeting or the car was in the shop. He understood. He couldn't stand these places, either. Who the hell wanted to visit with old, sick people? He appreciated Eileen's efforts. She always tried to make it for a meal. That was the hardest. Eating alone was depressing. Even when he was a kid back in the school cafeteria, he hated eating alone, thinking that other kids were talking about him or that he wasn't popular. Now eating was also a physical therapy session. Bringing a cup of hot tea to his lips and not spilling any was a challenge. Cutting a mouthful of meatloaf and steadying it on a fork was a major victory. Whatever caloric content a meal had, he expended the energy just getting some of it into his mouth. Today's selection of untouched lunch included a garden salad that he couldn't chew, piping hot vegetable soup, a hard roll with a frozen slab of butter in a packet he couldn't open with his hands, knife, or teeth, and a cup of Jell-O with a lid that must've been fastened with Gorilla Glue.

He had managed to puncture the cellophane top of the Jell-O with a fork and had sucked a few ounces down. The adage

was true—there was always room for Jell-O—even when you
didn't feel like eating.

"No wonder you're losing weight," Ryan said. "You can't
open any food."

Her father shrugged. "Don' wannit."

"You don't want it?" Ryan said, placing her bag down on
an empty seat and pulling up a chair across from him. "You
have to eat, Dad. They won't ever let you out of here if you
can't feed yourself."

He shrugged again.

"Don't you want to go home?"

Again, the shrug.

"Hey, that's good. You're moving both your shoulders really well now." She was trying anything to remain positive.

Another shrug.

"Show off," Ryan said, peeling apart the butter wrapper and
stuffing the pat into the roll.

She dipped a piece of it into the soup to soften it and handed it to him. He looked at it for a second, lost in thought. She
wondered if he knew what it was, or if his mind was else-
where. Then he shrugged and placed it into his mouth. Even
before the stroke he couldn't chew very well. He only had two
front teeth up top and four on the bottom, and a lone molar on
either side of his mouth. A bridge plate that cut into his gums
was before him in a plastic container.

"You want your teeth?" Ryan said, pointing to the container.

He shook his head then pointed to the roll. She dipped another piece in the soup and handed it to him. An aide in white
coveralls and a hairnet wheeled a cart through the aisles, collecting trays of uneaten food from other residents. What a
waste, Ryan thought. All this food going uneaten. Whole apples and oranges tossed. She looked around the room. Could
any of these people peel an orange or chew an apple anymore?
Sure, diets should be healthy and varied, and nobody ate
enough fruit, but this room consisted of strictly the soup and
oatmeal set. Any semblance of the act of chewing was difficult
to detect.

"Finished?" the aide asked.

"Does it look like he's finished?" Ryan asked.

The aide mumbled something unintelligible and continued down the aisle.

Her father's brow furrowed.

"Sorry," she said. Then she turned to the aide. "I'm sorry. I didn't mean to be rude—it's just, I had a hard day."

The aide nodded her head, offered a wave, and kept on clearing plates. She probably had days like this all the time, Ryan figured. People died in these places nearly every day, didn't they?

"What's 'smatter?" her father asked.

"Oh, everything, Dad—"

"Job?"

"Yeah, the job—and—"

Ryan dropped her head into her hands. She had told herself on the cab ride over not to cry in front of him. This wasn't supposed to be about her. She was going there for him. But there was no stopping the stream of tears that flowed down through her hands. She felt something brush against her hands and looked up to see her father holding out his Jell-O smeared napkin for her. Swallowing hard, she took it and dabbed at her eyes.

"Wha' happened?" he asked.

"Karen's dead—she was murdered last night—and it's all my fault!"

She bawled uncontrollably, unable to compose herself. All of the other patients and staff members were watching her. This was high drama, even for a rehabilitation center. Mealtime would bring the occasional dropped tray of food and maybe a few outbursts from frustrated diners who couldn't unwrap or cut their dinner but there was rarely someone cater-wauling at the tables and if there were, it was usually one of the patients, not one of their guests.

He pushed back from the table and managed to navigate the wheelchair around to her. He struggled to place his right arm around her shoulders but, at his first touch, she fell into his chest and wrapped her arms around him and the chair in an awkward, uncomfortable embrace. She felt his chest concave with a deep sigh and realized he had lost an awful lot of weight. God, he was slight. This was her father? The brick shithouse of a man who used to carry her on his shoulders through The Bronx Zoo so she could see the Kodiak bear over the crowds of people? She didn't want to let go. She was afraid of losing him, too. For what felt like hours she lay there, sobbing into his chest and clutching him. *And I thought I was coming here to comfort him*, she thought, finally rising and looking into his eyes. They were wet and red, too. He must've cried, too. *Great, I made my father cry. Oh, well.* The nurses warned her that they did get emotional at this age. And if ever he had a reason to cry, this was it. Widowed and lonely, in a rehabilitation center recuperating from a stroke, and his daughter comes to visit with a tale that reconfirms what little faith he had left in life and humanity. She wouldn't even tell him everything that happened. Not now. Someday, she would. When she got him back home to his house and had moved herself in and everything was in order. Maybe over a cup of tea and some soft cookies, those chocolate covered, orange marmalade filled Jaffa Cakes imported from Ireland, that he used to eat by the sleeve while engrossed in *The Daily News* or a Knicks game. She'd bring her HD, flat-screen TV and together they'd watch *Wheel of Fortune* and the Yankees and the Mets and she'd get her old room back, the one with the posters of Rick Springfield and Andy Gibb from *Tiger Beat Magazine* that still hung on the wall.

He had moved all of her brothers' stuff out—the baseball gloves and bats, the weight bench, the books and vinyl records—driving up to Harmony Grove one Sunday morning unannounced and dumping it all on their lawns. But he never bothered to touch anything in her room. Maybe somehow he knew that one day she'd be coming back to take care of him. He made it known he wanted to die in his house, that he would never live in Connecticut, no matter which of his children lived out there "in the sticks," and Maureen hadn't made an appearance since she hooked up with a band of hippies in the parking lot of the Nassau Coliseum at a Grateful Dead concert and toured the country in a Volkswagen bus. The last he heard from her she was working at a Napa Valley winery. So, Del Ryan would be coming home, and so would Eileen.

Chapter 46

When she saw Father McLanahan waltzing down the aisle to greet the casket, she wondered why she had bothered to have Karen buried. She would've preferred being cremated. Like any healthy thirty-seven-year-old, Karen didn't have a will. It would take a while for lawyers to figure out what to do with her assets but, in the meantime, Ryan had to decide the best way to honor her friend. She settled on two days of wakes at Dunphy's, a funeral mass at St. Sebastian's, and a burial plot at Gate of Heaven. Ryan realized that she did it for selfish reasons, so she would have somewhere to go and people to talk to. Karen's attitude would've been "fry me and scatter me at sea" but Ryan wanted a headstone to look at, with dates, a permanent reminder that this girl enjoyed life before it ended so senselessly and much too soon. The thought of sitting at home and saying goodnight to a copper urn or coffee can of ashes was too disturbing. She couldn't enjoy watching television while her father sat beside her in a wheelchair and Karen was in a container on her mantel.

The wake was surreal but ultimately necessary. Ryan needed to see old classmates and Karen's co-workers to cement the memories that she vowed to uphold. A collage of photographs adorned the open casket, in defiance of the semblance of the girl that lay in it.

The morticians had done a serviceable job but the girl lying on the silk pillow looked nothing like the girl in the pictures, nothing like the real Karen.

So many tears dropped into that casket over two days it was a wonder it didn't float down the aisle.

The sound of the church organ rattled in Ryan's chest. She could feel herself start to lose it as she followed the casket. At the wake she was engaged in conversation and telling stories and catching up with some people that, much to her surprise, she didn't mind seeing again. Girls she never thought would get married or have decent careers or both regaled her of stories of preschools and summer homes and vacations to Disney World that actually sounded like a nice life. And she was genuinely happy for them. Never could've seen a lot of it coming back in grammar and high school. Of course, she didn't see this coming, either. But now she could feel it. That empty hollow in her stomach. That awful nausea creeping in again. The sight of Father McLanahan marching toward the casket, his hand held high over his head, clutching a metal rod full of water. He doused the casket, and anyone in its proximity, with droplets of holy water. Ryan was actually relieved. The shock of it snapped her out of her thoughts and the beads mixed with her teardrops.

She dabbed at her eyes with a tissue and slowly walked up the aisle, sitting in the first pew, next to distant relatives of Karen she never knew existed. Second cousins from New Jersey, or so they said, though she still couldn't figure out how they were related. Probably unemployed former bankers who cased the obituaries and crashed funerals in the hopes that all the mourners would be invited back to a restaurant for a meal following the burial. She'd grill them back at Paddy Doyle's, where she had arranged for a buffet and open bar following Karen's burial at Gate of Heaven cemetery.

Ryan could barely hold her shit together during the readings. None of it registered. She just thought of not being able to call Karen when all of this was over to talk about how horrible these past couple of days were and kept scanning the pew for a place to vomit should the need arise. Had anyone ever thrown-up into the missalette holders? Or on the kneelers? Or the multi-colored carpet with the crucifix and fleur de lis patterns? Where did they find that? Navy blue carpet with red crucifixes and gold fleur de lis? Looked like a remnant from a wild Mardi-Gras party.

With her head down, she fixated on the carpet and tried to stave off vomiting. *Concentrate,* she said to herself, over and over. It became her mantra. *Con-cen-trate. Con-cen-trate. Con-cen-trate. Breathe. Con-cen-trate. Con-cen-trate. Con-cen-trate. Breathe. Con-cen-trate. Con-cen-trate. Con-cen-trate. Breathe. Con-cen-trate. Con-cen-trate. Con-cen-trate. Breathe.*

She looked at the red crucifixes, imagined them covered in blood, and thought of the crucifix and rosary beads left at Karen's feet at the crime scene. Was it a message? A clue? The mark of a serial killer, like the Zodiac killer? The Crucifix Killer? She couldn't think of any crazy church lady who lived in her building and may have stumbled across a dead body and arranged rosary beads on it. Who would do that?

Father McLanahan's voice boomed over the microphone and she picked her head up, trying to make eye contact with him. *Con-cen-trate. Con-cen-trate. Con-cen-trate. Breathe.* His shock of white hair came into view. *Oh my God.* She felt a pang in her gut. It was *him.*

Chapter 47

She didn't remember fainting, or being taken in the ambulance to Our Lady of Angels Medical Center. As her eyes adjusted to the bright lights she heard faint voices.

Is that my mother's voice? Am I dead?

She heard a low beeping noise and the humming of a machine. Then she saw a familiar shock of white hair. Father McLanahan.

No, I'm not dead. Karen's dead. And Father McLanahan killed her.

His face was within reach. She wanted to remove his glasses and scratch his eyes out. He leaned in closer to her. She tried to lift her hand to stop him but there was something holding it down, a vice grip of sorts on her left arm, a rope of some kind on her right.

"Congratulations," Father McLanahan said.

She wanted to reply, *"You bastard!"* but she couldn't speak due to the oxygen mask covering her mouth. She realized that she was in a hospital bed, with an IV bag on a drip administering fluids through a tube in her arm. The firm yet soothing voice she thought was her mother's belonged to a nurse who was reading her blood pressure.

"Almost back to normal," the nurse said.

Everyone has an opinion, Ryan thought.

The nurse removed the Velcro strap from her arm and Ryan felt life come back to her extremities.

"I think we can remove this now," the nurse said, delicately removing the oxygen mask from her face. "Okay?" she asked.

Ryan didn't respond. She was still groggy, confused.

"I'll get you some water and lunch," the nurse said, leaving the room before Ryan had the chance to respond.

"I'm not dead," Ryan finally said, defiantly.

"No," Father McLanahan said. "You're pregnant."

Chapter 48

Cleary was in his office at One Police Plaza, sending faxes to all the pharmacies in the city. This was the drudgery of office work that he hated but there wasn't enough money in the budget for him to have a permanent assistant so it all fell on him. The NYPD was still behind the curve with technology and hadn't yet been able to amass an email list of all the city's pharmacies so the archaic, time consuming fax machine was engaged nearly all week. But there was an upside to the menial tasks, however, at least for Cleary. The paperwork, the phone calls, the research, the faxing—all of it—was billable time. Faxing 1,100 pharmacies added up to a lot of overtime, as did crafting the letter in which he advised them not to fill any prescriptions that had his name on them before contacting the police to make sure they were legit. The knock on the door caught him off guard. Officers usually called or emailed when they sought his services. He opened the door and saw a sheepish Officer Alvarez, his head down, gazing at the floor.

"Officer Alvarez," Cleary said.

Alvarez didn't look up.

"Come on in," Cleary said. "Have a seat."

Alvarez walked in, looked at the chair, but remained standing. The bleating of the fax machine caught his attention. Cleary had managed to figure out a way to program all the pharmacy phone numbers into the machine and feed a stack of letters into it so that each time a line opened up, the fax would go through. He hadn't yet figured out how to silence the machine, so those annoying blips would provide the soundtrack for the evening.

"Does that bother you?" Cleary asked.

Alvarez shook his head and looked around the room at the framed degrees from Lehman and Mercy College hanging on the wall, and another one from a school in Arizona that he thought he recognized from a banner ad on his Yahoo email account, an online degree of some sort. Maybe he could do something like that. Get a technical degree and make a living fixing fax machines, if email didn't make them obsolete in the near future. He'd have to find something, because this cop thing wasn't working out.

"What's going on?" Cleary asked.

"I think I need help," Alvarez said.

I hope he doesn't want a prescription, Cleary thought. He'd already sent 560 faxes to area pharmacists telling them to contact the police if anyone sought to fill one with his name on it. There were probably some sample packs of antidepressants, sleeping pills, and antipsychotics laying around the drawers that could get him through the week.

"What kind of help?" Cleary asked.

Alvarez shrugged.

"Sit down," Cleary said. "Let's talk."

Alvarez refused to sit, fidgeting with the plastic clasp of a baseball cap that he held in his hands.

"I think I need to leave," Alvarez said.

"Leave?" Cleary asked. "Leave what? The state? The country?"

"The job."

"Oh," Cleary said, pushing back on his chair.

He'd heard this before. Cops who used their weapons in the line of duty often had trouble reconciling the need to use force. In this case, the feelings were certainly justified, from what Cleary knew about it. Couple guys had come in before, attempting to get out on three-quarters pay for some bullshit mental disability. They found a badly beaten dog and their love of animals was too great to have to witness such a sight, blah, blah, blah. Everyone wanted a scam. But Alvarez looked genuinely troubled.

"I don't think I can do this," Alvarez said.

"Well, let's not rush to any conclusions," Cleary said.

"I didn't rush. I've been thinking about it for a while now. This incident just kind of cemented the idea for me."

"You're not the only officer to have an accident on the job," Cleary said.

Alvarez sighed and fidgeted some more with the cap.

"I looked over your files," Cleary said, rocking back in his chair. "You have several commendations from Durkin. He thinks you're a good cop. And a good man."

Alvarez's eyebrows arched. He didn't agree. Truth of the matter was, he'd rather be fishing than working as a police officer. He only took the test as a fallback. A history teacher of his in high school, Italian guy with a name he couldn't pronounce, sounded something like Paparazzi, told them to apply for all the civil service jobs they could, as soon as they were eligible. When the time came, if they weren't interested, they could refuse. But if things didn't work out for those with dreams of playing in the NFL or the NBA, they may want to put in twenty years as a fireman or a cop or a court officer or a sanitation worker, retire with benefits and a pension, and then go coach the sports they loved. Not a bad plan, Alvarez thought, though most of his classmates treated the advice as if it were coming from their fathers. They didn't listen. Alvarez knew he wasn't NFL material and didn't know what to study if he went to college. Police officer was a job that would keep him close to home, where he could keep an eye on his sister and family, and retire in twenty years to a house on City Island, where his boat was docked. But now, one stupid mistake, and it was all out the fuckin' window.

"I'm not a good man," Alvarez said. "And I'm not a good *police*man. I don't want to do this anymore. I just...can't."

Alvarez reached into his waistband, pulled out his revolver, and placed it on the desk. Then he took his badge out of his back pocket and gently placed it down next to it.

Nobody had ever done that before. Cleary wondered what

the protocol was. *Do I turn it in? Should I send him to Durkin? There must be some phone calls and paperwork involved.*

"Have you spoken to Ramon?" Cleary asked.

"Who's Ramon?"

"Garcia. Head of the Latin Policemen's Association?"

"Why the fuck would I talk to Ramon?" Alvarez asked.

Cleary was certain he had seen the well-coiffed and polished Garcia on television in the hours following the incident, defending Alvarez's actions and promising that he'd be cleared of any wrongdoing, pending a thorough investigation. He'd just assumed that Garcia had already reached out to Alvarez.

"He gave the impression that he had spoken to you when I saw him interviewed," Cleary said.

"Nah, he hasn't spoken to me, only to the reporters," Alvarez said. "He's only interested in hearing himself talk."

His loss, my gain, Cleary thought, as the fax machine bleated away like a cash register at Christmas time, music to his ears. *There's going to be a nice little OT check this week.*

Chapter 49

Ryan felt like puncturing holes in McLanahan's chest and twisting his heart out with her bare hands. He had a look of glee on his face, as if he were the proud father to be.

Pregnant? What the fuck was he talking about? This must be a dream.

"I know I'm not dead so I must be dreaming," Ryan said.

"It's no dream," Father McLanahan said.

"My ass it ain't. This is a fuckin' nightmare."

McLanahan rubbed his chin, looked down at her in the bed, as if contemplating his next move.

"What?" Ryan said. "What? Don't fuckin' sit there with that condescending look on your face. Don't you fuckin' judge me!"

McLanahan just smiled at her.

God, she wanted to smack that smirk off his face.

"What the fuck are you doing here, anyway? What happened?"

"You fainted during the service," McLanahan said. "Someone called nine-one-one. You were malnourished. Dehydrated. Not to mention stressed out, overwhelmed, and in shock."

Ryan wanted to cry, but the tears weren't coming. Still dehydrated, she guessed.

"I missed Karen's funeral?" she asked.

"The show must go on," McLanahan said.

"Is that what it is to you, a show? Is that why you're here?

For show? To make it look like you're a good guy, and not some murdering, lying, gambling, homosexual?"

"Anything else you'd like to add to that?"

"Sleazeball."

"Who's the one judging?" McLanahan said, an arrogant smile spreading across his face.

"Get out of here. I don't want you here."

McLanahan took a small, blue plastic bottle of out of his windbreaker pocket. He twisted off the cap, sprinkled some holy water on his fingers and made the sign of the cross over her.

"God bless you—" McLanahan said.

"Fuck you," Ryan said.

"—and the baby," McLanahan added, as he placed a Yankees cap upon his shock of white hair and zipped up his Members Only windbreaker before exiting the room.

Baby? Ryan thought. *Bullshit. There ain't no baby.*

The nurse entered with the lunch she had promised, a small salad, vegetable soup, a breast of chicken smothered in cream sauce surrounded by baby carrots and green beans, with a small bottle of water, a Styrofoam cup of hot water with a tea bag, and a small container of skim milk. It looked like way too much food for one person, especially one who was in a hospital bed. How could she work that off?

She wouldn't touch half of it. The amount of food being wasted in these institutions was appalling. Not to mention the impact on the environment.

Why are we still using Styrofoam? Doesn't everyone know it doesn't break down? The Styrofoam industry must have some dynamite lawyers lobbying for their interests. It's not like we don't have alternatives. There's cardboard, paper, plastic. What the hell am I thinking about? Am I that dehydrated? I must be drunk. Or high. I'm delusional. What's in that IV drip? Heroin? Solpadeine? Vodka? Did McLanahan spike the holy water?

"We're recommending a low fat, low salt diet," the nurse said, "no coffee for now but we gave you some tea to stave off the caffeine headache, if that's an issue for you, and I'll swipe some fruit from somewhere, too. None of it looked ripe so I threw it out. Any questions?"

The nurse put the tray of food down before Ryan. She drank the entire water bottle in one gulp.

"Is it true?" Ryan asked.

"Is what true?" the nurse asked.

"Am I pregnant?"

"Oh, yeah," the nurse said. "Either that, or you swallowed a grapefruit with a heartbeat."

Ryan looked down at her stomach. It didn't seem like anything was in there. It seemed empty. Tears welled up in her eyes. And they weren't tears of joy.

Chapter 50

Keegan had only been to City Island a handful of times in his life. The first time was on a Mother's Day, around 1980, when his father yelled at them to get in the effing car after church, they were going to eat. It was a hot day and the window crank didn't work. His face was pressed up against the back window of the Chevy Impala, his father chain smoking behind the wheel, his mother fighting back tears in the passenger seat, and his three older brothers cupping farts and pressing their hands over his nose while they sat in bumper to bumper traffic on the two-lane bridge, a single lane for getting onto the island and one for getting off.

Once on the island, his father pulled into the parking lot of another church, St. Savior's by the Sea, made a U-turn, and headed back off the island. Despite the reservations his mother had made at the Lobster Loft for her special day, his father decided the traffic wasn't worth it and steered the car in the direction of the McDonald's drive-through on Pelham Parkway instead. The second time was in high school, when he piled into a car with a bunch of guys from Woodlawn and drove over to kick some guy's ass for grabbing someone's girlfriend's ass at the movies. Couldn't remember the kid's name or where he lived, only that the cops showed up shortly after they arrived outside a small A-frame with water views, a dozen of them banging baseball bats and bits of pipe on the cars and mailboxes that lined the quiet street. Nobody was arrested. They drove back to Kepler Field and finished a quarter keg of

Bud and the story had been evolving ever since. Different versions of it were still repeated in bars along Katonah Avenue whenever members of the crew met up. The third time he was on City Island he was supposed to be going to Alvarez's annual party on Memorial Day weekend. But, like his father, he ran into traffic and pulled a U-turn. If he were going to sit in traffic on a bridge on a holiday weekend, he'd rather be sitting on the Whitestone on the way to a bar in Long Beach, which is exactly what he did.

There was no traffic this time. And now he had a GPS with Alvarez's address punched into it, with a gravel-throated Australian voice directing him to the driveway. "Arriving at destination on right," it told him. He wished it offered him a "G'day, mate," but that would have to suffice.

Keegan cut the engine and slowly walked up the narrow pathway to the modest two-family house. There was a street level apartment in the basement and eight steps up to the front door. Both doors had steel bars protecting them, as did the windows.

A bit overdone for City Island, thought Keegan. *What the fuck is he protecting in there, gold? Drugs?* He heard the low, deep bark of a dog from the ground floor apartment. He decided to take the stairs to the top apartment, unsure which one was Alvarez's. When he rang the bell, another dog started barking.

Maybe there were drugs in there. Instinctively or reflexively, he reached for his holster, just in case. If a pit bull came charging through the door, he'd use his revolver, the way he did back in '99, when he chased some perp down an alleyway in Mott Haven, only to come across a dogfight in progress. Despite the fact that almost everyone in attendance was carrying a piece, he brandished his and shot the pit bull charging at him. He was cleared when one of the hoodlums he recognized from walking the beat testified that the dog's owner gave the command to attack.

When a woman in about her mid-fifties, in a bathrobe and curlers, opened the door with one hand and restrained a Boxer with the other, he felt at ease. He recognized both of them from photos he had seen on Alvarez's iPhone: his mother and his dog.

She must've recognized him, too, because she waved him in.

"Hi, nice to see you. I'm Brian, Eduardo's partner?"

"Si, si, come in."

She yelled for Eduardo as Keegan petted the dog and walked into the house. He looked around the walls at the framed pictures of Jesus, Eduardo making his first Communion and graduating from high school and the academy, and of a little girl in a wheelchair, smiling in every photo, despite her handicap.

Eduardo walked into the room, in a wife beater and board shorts, holding a bottle of Corona. "Whatchoo want?" he asked.

"I just wanted to talk to you for a minute. Is this a bad time?"

Eduardo shrugged. His mother said something in Spanish and Alvarez shushed her. She retreated into the kitchen, where he heard the refrigerator open, some glass rattling, and the unmistakable sound of a bottle cap being popped. He could picture the little puff of frosty air and the carbonation sending bubbles to the rim of the bottle. His mother returned, holding out a longneck bottle of Budweiser to Keegan.

"Oh, thank you," Keegan said. "Muchas gracious...*para la cerveza*. Did I say that right? That's about the extent of my Spanish. That's all I learned from the barrio."

"What do you want, Keegan?" Alvarez repeated.

"I'd prefer a Corona, to be honest."

Neither Alvarez nor his mother made any indication that they understood what he said.

"Nah, just kidding. This'll do. I just wanted to see how you were doing. I heard you were thinking about packing it in."

Alvarez said something to his mother and motioned for her to leave the room. She obeyed, but not before admonishing him with a ferocious, staccato tongue-lashing. Keegan found her kind of sexy, imagined she was quite a looker back in her day. A hot Latin lover, something out of *West Side Story*. Not that he had ever seen the play or the movie, but he heard people talk about it. He wouldn't put it past himself on a hot summer night with a couple cold ones in him to imagine she was Salma Hayek or Maria Conchita Alonso and not Alvarez's mom.

"Yeah, I'm done," Alvarez said.

"I think you're making a mistake," Keegan said.

"I made the mistake already. Now I have to pay for it."

"That's not true. Look, mistakes are made all the time. On every job. You can't just pack it in. You're a good cop. You gotta get back on the horse."

That last line didn't sound right to either of them. They weren't mounted police. What the fuck did horses have to do with it?

"I know I'm not saying it right, but you know what I'm saying, right?" Keegan asked, peeling at the label of the Budweiser.

"Let's take a walk," Alvarez said.

He led him out of the house and down Fordham Street to where several small boats were docked. Stepping onto a Boston Whaler with the name Bonito Suena stamped on the side, Alvarez motioned for Keegan to get on board.

"I hate the water, man," Keegan said. "I get sea sick watching *The Love Boat*."

"Maybe it's the love that gets you sick," Alvarez said. "Just get on, pussy."

Keegan chugged the last of his Bud and stepped onto the boat.

"There's more in the cooler," Alvarez said, pointing to a large Rubbermaid with six-inch wheels and a towing handle.

Keegan unlatched the clip and saw at least two mixed cases of Corona, Heineken, and Dos Equis on ice. Maybe he could learn to like boating.

Alvarez turned the engine and put down the throttle, moving the Whaler out into the sound. Keegan sipped a Heineken and watched as Alvarez, in his wraparound shades, navigated the gentle waters. This wasn't really boating, Keegan thought, this was like one of those rides at an amusement park, where plastic puppets in pirate regalia popped out and said "Arg" every couple minutes. The Olde Maid, or something like that, at Rye Playland, where the St. Sebastian's altar boys used to go for their class trip every year. Only there were no pirates, and he was now drinking beer and wouldn't need a Gatorade until morning to replenish electrolytes.

Two beers into the ride, Alvarez cut the engine and they drifted. He cut up some squid and rigged up two fishing poles, handing one to Keegan.

"I don't fish," Keegan said.

"Just take it. Otherwise, you're just drinking."

"What's wrong with just drinking?"

"This is more productive. Like playing darts in a bar. Or shooting pool. At least you're active, forcing your mind and your body to do a little work. Otherwise, your brain and your body just atrophy, like that fat fuck over there."

Keegan looked up to see a tanned man sans T-shirt sitting on the bow of boat, a smile etched across his face and a gut hanging down to his knees. A living Buddha. Looked like he hadn't shaved or bathed in a month and the only exercise he got was pulling his pants down to shit. Probably couldn't even reach around to wipe. Keegan picked up a pole and tried to imitate how Alvarez cast out his line. Alvarez laughed and switched poles.

"You fish like a girl," Alvarez said. "Actually, you're worse. Even my sister can cast better than that, and she's—"

Keegan sensed his uneasiness. He caught himself before he actually said it, but he had never come that close before. Maybe it was the beer.

"What's wrong with your sister, anyway?" Keegan asked. "I saw the pictures of her in a wheelchair. She looks really happy, kinda like those kids with Down Syndrome."

"It's not Down Syndrome."

"No, I know it's not, I was just saying she seemed happy like that…you know how those kids are always smiling?"

"She don't always smile." Alvarez cast out again. "And when she does, it's because she doesn't know any better."

"Compared to a lot of people, she's got it pretty good.

She's got a loving mother and a brother looking out for her."

"Yeah, lot of fuckin' good that does her."

"C'mon, man. You're really fuckin' hard on yourself. Life ain't perfect, you know? And neither are people. We're all fuck ups. I fuck up every day. I don't bury my head in the sand and give in."

"Look, Keegan. You're happy about being a fuck up, that's your business. But you don't know shit about me or my life, and that's the way I like it."

"I'm just saying, you don't have to do this."

"I don't want to be a fuckin' cop anymore. I only did it so I could retire in twenty years. So, this just sped up the process. If I don't go to jail, I'm retired."

"You're not going to jail."

"We'll see. It's already like being in prison."

"This—" Keegan said, gesturing with his hand over the expanse of the sound, "—is nothing like prison. This is fuckin' beautiful. Prison is hell."

"You have no idea how it feels," Alvarez said. "It's like *I* died when I shot Hickey."

"Yeah, I do," Keegan said. "I know exactly how you feel."

"You ain't never killed no one."

"Yeah, I have."

Alvarez looked up at him, tried to detect if he was squinting from the sun or afraid to look him in the eye.

Keegan reached into his back pocket and pulled out a yellowed page of *The Daily News*. The dateline was highlighted in orange. March 18, 1995. The headline read: *Officer Killed By Friendly Fire.*

Alvarez looked up at him.

"Read it," Keegan said.

During a drug bust gone bad on the West Side of Manhattan last night, rookie police officer Kenneth McIheny was stuck by friendly fire and killed. Police were carrying out a raid at 355 West 38th Street, a suspected crack cocaine den, when shots were fired on the roof of 354 West 37th Street. Officer McIheny climbed the fire escape in pursuit of a fleeing suspect and was struck by a single bullet wound in the neck. Paramedics pronounced him dead on arrival at St. Vincent's Hospital.

Sergeant Barry Durkin from the Midtown South precinct said, "It was just a case of being in the wrong place at the wrong time. A freak accident."

The officer who shot McIheny has been identified as Brian Keegan, also a rookie, who was in pursuit of a suspect accused of armed robbery on the corner of West 36th Street and 10th Avenue. Keegan, who was in a patrol car when the call came in, took off on foot after the suspect, following him up to the roof of West 37th Street, where the suspect opened fire. When Keegan returned fire, he allegedly struck Officer McIlheny, who was responding to the shots from the fire escape of the building on West 38th Street. The suspect that Officer Keegan was pursuing was not apprehended.

"This is just a sad, sad day for the police department," Commissioner Raymond Kerry said. "We lost a very brave and dedicated officer due to the actions of another fellow brave and dedicated officer. Accidents happen in this line of work, too. Unfortunately, this one turned out to be fatal. Our thoughts and prayers go out to the McIheny and Keegan families."

Two suspects were apprehended from the apartment on West 38th Street, at the intended address of the drug raid. A cache of weapons, $200,000 in cash, three kilos of cocaine, and crack vials worth an estimated $80,000 on the street were also taken into police custody.

Alvarez held out the article to Keegan, who refused it.

"I don't need that anymore," Keegan said.

Alvarez crumpled it up into a ball and threw it overboard. They watched it rise on the crest of the tiny waves and then slowly descend out of view.

"I think I felt something," Keegan said, looking down at the tension on his fishing line.

"Reel it in!" Alvarez said, coming to his aid.

Keegan made a few spastic attempts to turn the reel.

"No, like this."

Alvarez jerked the line up and vigorously circled his right hand. He let out a little tension on the line and then reeled in again. "Grab the net," he instructed.

Keegan reached under the seat and grabbed the handle of a long fishing net. Seconds later he was looking at a ten-inch bluefish through the mesh.

"You caught a fish, man," Alvarez said.

"*You* caught it."

"I just reeled it in. You hooked it. Keep it."

Alvarez expertly removed the hook form the fish's mouth and wiped some blood on his shorts.

"Nah, you keep it," Keegan said. "I don't eat fish. What is it, anyway?"

"Bluefish."

"Yeah? Are they good?"

"Nah. All fatty and shit. Unless you make fish cakes out of 'em. Should we throw it back?"

"No, way, man. That's my fish. Here, hold it."

Alvarez took the net while Keegan pulled out his cell phone and took a picture of the fish, still wriggling. Admiring the photo, he opened his contacts list and emailed it as an attachment to Alvarez.

"We make a pretty good team," he said.

Chapter 51

Durkin shuffled through the hospital corridors with two large containers of coffee, as if he were browsing for furniture. Should've put the glasses on before he bought the coffee he noted to himself. There was no way he could hold both cups and manage to put glasses on now. He walked up to several doors to read the patients' names before finding Ryan's room.

"Ryan," he said, as if it were routine to see her in a hospital bed.

"Hey, Durk," Ryan said, still bleary-eyed.

"Got you some coffee," Durk said. "Real coffee. Not the crap they serve here or at the precinct."

"I'm not supposed to have any."

"Says who?"

"The doctors and the nurses. They got me on a low fat, low salt, low caffeine diet."

"What for? You pregnant?" Durk said, slurping his coffee.

"Bingo."

"You're too young to be shoutin' 'bingo.'"

"I am—pregnant."

God it was hard to say that when it applied to oneself, Ryan thought. Under the right circumstances—married to a bread winner, nice house in the suburbs or high-rise in the city, didn't have to work, could stay home, watch daytime TV and raise the kids, just like her sisters-in-law—it may even sound joyful, hopeful. But now, in her circumstances, it was nothing of the sort. Being pregnant sounded like a death sentence.

"Never a dull moment with you, huh?"

Durk slugged more coffee. If she drank coffee the way he did, she'd have to attach a bedpan to her backside. It went right through her. How could anyone drink that much coffee?

"You don't sound very shocked."

"Ryan, I'm one of ten kids. I got one of my own. I know how science and the law of averages work."

"What do you mean?"

"You know what I mean."

"No, I don't think I do."

"C'mon, iRye, it's me. Don't get defensive."

"I'm not getting defensive. I'd like to hear you're reasoning."

"Would I lose you with a baseball analogy?" he asked, sipping more coffee. He didn't wait for a response. "A good hitter hits three hundred. Seven out of ten times he makes an out, but regardless of how they pitch to him, he still manages to make contact. Could have a broken bat base hit. Or you catch the defense off guard, back on their heels, and drop down a bunt. You butcher boy one, a Baltimore chop. Point is, eventually, a bloop drops in or a ten hopper finds a hole and squirts through the infield. You know what I'm saying?"

Ryan felt her heart sink then that ubiquitous lump in her throat. Fuck, she thought. Not now. Not here. She didn't want to throw up again. On herself, in a hospital gown.

Durk noticed her complexion had turned ashen.

"Ryan, you okay?"

She didn't answer.

"You need something?"

Yes, she needed a bucket in case she let fly with the vomit, but then decided that his face would do in the event she couldn't hold it down.

"You want me to get a nurse?"

She wanted him to get a clue and realize that he sounded like an insensitive jerk, like one of the other assholes on the force, not the one guy she considered a friend and confidant on the job. Maybe she was wrong about him. Maybe he was just like the others. Maybe he was one of the mean kids. She'd never let her baby grow up to be one of the mean kids.

Chapter 52

Keegan was on his fifth beer when Alvarez sparked up another doobie and offered it him. He hadn't smoked pot in years but what the fuck, anything to help a partner in need. Inhaling deeply, he immediately coughed out a stream of smoke and Alvarez laughed.

"Rookie?"

Keegan shook his head but couldn't talk yet. His whole face was flushed red as he hacked some sputum over the side of the boat.

"Haven't smoked in years," Keegan said. "Makes me stupid."

"It ain't the smoke."

"Fuck you."

Keegan took another toke, letting the smoke settle into his lungs and blowing out a steady plume. His eyelids instantly grew heavy.

"Wow," he said.

"Yeah," Alvarez said, taking it back and sucking in a hit. "That ain't your father's smoke. That's Uganda blue."

The sun was setting and the sky resembled rainbow sherbet to Keegan, with slivers of raspberry, orange and lemon.

"You got any food on this boat?" he asked.

Alvarez shrugged, tossing him a knapsack. Keegan opened it and found a bag of Cheetos, alongside a Ziploc bag full of buds and a .22 caliber pistol.

"You carry this shit around with you?"

"In case I get the munchies," Alvarez said.

"I meant the other stuff."

"Keeps me calm on the open waters."

"And the gun?"

"For protection," Alvarez said, casting out his fishing line. "From pirates."

Keegan found that so funny that his laugh morphed into another coughing fit, and he launched more phlegm into the sound. Then he sat back down and popped another Heineken. He liked fishing.

⌘⌘⌘

It was dark by the time they headed back in, and Keegan joked that they needed a nautical GPS to find their way back. Low fog had rolled in, making visibility more difficult. The pot didn't help, either. Keegan was ready to take a nap. Or eat a pizza pie by himself. The kind with cheese in the crust. And a side of sauce. He always wondered who those commercials were aimed at, where a large, cheese pizza sits on a table, someone rips off a piece of cheese-filled crust and dips it into a side of sauce, essentially eating a pizza stick as an appetizer for the pizza. Now it dawned on him. What was better than pizza? Why wouldn't you want pizza for an appetizer and pizza for an entrée? And what was better with pizza than beer? He opened another Heineken, in anticipation of washing down a pizza with another Heineken, because, what was better than Heineken for an appetizer than Heineken with the main course?

He never noticed the blue and white boat approaching them at a deliberate pace, and neither, apparently, did Alvarez, whom he presumed was still awake. With those wraparound black shades he couldn't be sure, but he heard him on his cell phone minutes earlier, while he was dreaming of pizza. Now it dawned on him that they were about to collide with this boat. Didn't Alvarez see it? He looked back at Alvarez, whose head was down, still talking lowly on a cell phone.

"Hey!" Keegan shouted, getting to his feet. "Look out!"

Keegan suddenly found himself bathed in the brightness of a searchlight coming from the approaching boat. Another light was thrown on Alvarez, who still had a joint dangling from his lips and a cell phone to his ear. The blue and white boat pulled up beside the Bonito Suena and two men in blue jumpsuits and boots stepped onto it. Both of them had rifles.

Holy Shit, Keegan thought. Alvarez wasn't kidding. There *are* pirates on the Long Island Sound. The City Island pirates? His heart was racing. What did they want? Nothing on his person. Sixty bucks, driver's license, Foodtown bonus card, losing Lotto ticket, a grocery receipt, Lieutenant's Benevolent Association card. *I'm a dead man.* His first instinct was to reach for the piece in his waistband but he resisted. The last time he and Alvarez pulled guns too quick, things got really fucked up.

Keegan noticed the white NYPD emblazoned across their navy jumpsuits. Fuckin' harbor patrol. The guys that usually checked under bridges for explosives. What did they want on Alvarez's boat?

"Relax," the first officer said. "You look like you've seen a ghost."

As he brushed past Keegan and started toward Alvarez, Keegan caught a glimpse of the name sewn onto the suit: Ripken.

He tried to think of any Ripkens he might know. A family of cops from The Bronx, perhaps? Nope. Nothing other than the family of baseball players who were deified in Baltimore came to mind. Despite Ripken's order, Keegan couldn't relax. He was too stoned. This was why he had stopped smoking pot years ago. Couldn't handle the immediacy and potency of the high. Made him paranoid. Why the fuck did he smoke that joint with Alvarez? This was what friends are for? To get stoned and possibly arrested together?

The second officer approached and asked Keegan for identification.

"I'm on the job," Keegan said.

"Really? What job is that?" the officer said.

Great. What kind of an asshole is this, Keegan thought. "I'm an officer," Keegan said. "In the four-seven."

"Then you should know it's illegal to be boating under the influence of alcohol and that possession of large quantities of marijuana is a felony and conviction of a felony is grounds for dismissal from the police force, right?"

If they were attempting to be a buzzkill, mission accomplished. Keegan wasn't sure how to reply so he didn't. He just handed over his wallet with his identification in it and watched as Ripken walked toward Alvarez, who looked completely lost in the haze, as if he were imagining the whole scene, or trying to convince himself it was only a dream.

"Hanson" read the nametag of the officer looking over his identification. That name rang a bell.

"Hanson?" Keegan said, reaching for straws. "Didn't you used to work out of the five-two? With Devaney and Flynn?"

"No," Hanson said. "Used to be in forensics. After 9/11 I transferred to harbor patrol."

Oh, right. There was a Hanson who worked with Hickey in forensics years ago. Douchebag, just like Hickey.

Ripken asked Alvarez for identification but Alvarez just looked at him, as if he didn't comprehend.

"What are you, a wise guy?" Ripken continued. "Show me some ID."

"Show him your ID!" Keegan yelled at him.

Alvarez snapped to, reaching into his back pocket, but then rethought his decision. "I don't have any," he said.

"Oh no?" Ripken asked. "This your boat?"

Alvarez shook his head, no.

What the fuck is he doing? Keegan wondered. *He's making this worse.* He tried to think of someone he knew who worked on harbor patrol but drew a blank. Never thought he'd need to know anyone on harbor patrol because he never boated. Why didn't Alvarez know these guys?

"This isn't your boat?" Ripken asked incredulously. Then he turned to Keegan. "This your boat?"

"No," Keegan said.

"Well, who's boat is it?" Ripken asked.

Neither of them answered.

"You don't know?"

The officer looking through Keegan's wallet spoke up. "This one's a cop."

"We both are," Keegan said. "He's my partner."

Ripken had a moment of recognition. "Wait a minute. I know you—I saw you on the news."

Then he turned to his partner. "Mikey, this is the guy who shot Hickey."

Hanson looked him over, as if determining if that were the case, and then looked back at Keegan.

"Is he the guy?" Hanson asked, his face turning sour.

Sonofabitch, Mikey Hanson, Keegan thought. *Of all the scumbag cops to come across on the open water. He's the perfect cop for this job. Harassing Hispanic fishermen who don't have proper licenses or speak proper English and treating them as potential terrorists.* He'd heard stories about these guys. Hadn't found a bomb yet but managed to make dozens of arrests each week, from Boating While Intoxicated to possession to trafficking.

"It was an accident," Keegan said.

"Yeah?" the officer standing above Alvarez said. "And would it be an accident if I shot you guys, and dumped yous in the sound?"

Keegan saw Alvarez glance at the knapsack by his feet and knew what he was thinking: *Do I have time to reach in and pull the trigger twice?*

"Whaddya think, Mikey? Would it be an accident if we shot these guys and dumped them in the sound?" Ripken asked.

"That depends. It might be and it might not be. 'Course, we could always make it look like an accident—or we could say we were acting in self-defense—"

"And if this guy doesn't have any ID on him, who's gonna know who the fuck he is when his body washes up in a couple weeks?"

"Hold on," Alvarez said. "I think I do have my ID."

He gave a quick peek over at Keegan, then crouched down, and grabbed his knapsack. His fingers trembled as he slowly pulled back the zipper. Keegan shook his head, hoping he wouldn't follow through with it, then reached into his waist-band in case he did.

"Open the bag!" Ripken yelled at him.

Alvarez obeyed and stuck in his hand. In one swift motion, he pulled out the .22 and fired a shot into Ripken's neck. Ripken fell backward, firing shots into the air as he tumbled overboard and splashed into the sound. Hanson stood catatonic for what was probably only a few seconds but felt like hours, before screaming in anger as he ran at Alvarez with the butt of his rifle turned like a bayonet aimed at his face. Alvarez calmly fired twice more, with both shots ripping through Hanson's chest.

Chapter 53

The shock of being pregnant had subsided and she had settled into her situation, not so gracefully but not so reluctantly, either. It was kind of a pleasant surprise. She had all but given up the idea of ever having kids and had convinced herself that she didn't want them. Now she was realizing that wasn't entirely true. How many times had she caught herself at TJ Maxx and Marshall's wandering over to the infant sections and seeing those adorable pink feety pajamas and blue onesies? She wished they sold them in her size, for those days when she didn't want to get out of bed and would just lay around and watch television and sleep and eat cereal without milk by the handful. The Slanket and the Snuggie had come close, but they weren't quite the same. She'd bought baby outfits on occasion because they were so damn cute and cheap and she'd always know someone who was having a baby, right? The bottom drawer of her dresser contained no fewer than ten such items, "just in case" purchases in blue and pink, for babies ranging anywhere from 0-3 months to 6-9 years. Now that she was actually casing the clearance racks for her own baby, she could feel the adrenaline rush surging through her body. My God, something she actually needed that was on sale! The baby must've felt it, too, because it was kicking like crazy. Probably a girl. A champion of the clearance racks, just like her mom. Maybe she'd name her Mandee. Or Marshall. Or TJ Maxx.

The only down side to the pregnancy so far—well, other

than the morning, noon, and night sickness—was not being able to share these moments with Karen. She had made amends with passing out at her funeral, understanding now that it was because of malnourishment and being pregnant. Durk had assured her that McLanahan had been investigated and had an alibi for his whereabouts the evening of her murder: he was sequestered in an Atlanta hotel room, during three days of testimony before a grand jury investigation into a sex abuse scandal at a school for deaf children where he had worked prior to coming to St. Sebastian's. He was not named in the inquiry and, in fact, had played the role of whistle blower when one of the boy's parents contacted him. While she didn't fully believe it, Durk assured her it was rock solid. Whatever. She had to move on, for her baby's sake.

She made frequent trips to Gate of Heaven cemetery to talk to Karen and brought her photos of the sonogram. "Wouldn't it be cool if we were both pregnant? If we raised our kids together? If they were best friends like we were best friends and we went on vacations together to those places with wave pools and super slides? All those places our parents never brought us and we pretended we didn't want to go to anyway but secretly we did and were really jealous of all the kids who did go?"

Then she'd laugh at herself, standing in the rain talking to a headstone with dates that didn't make sense, and then she'd cry about something from her childhood, telling Karen all she wanted to do was go apple picking just once, like the little girls in some book that she read, even if they did get sick from the cider that wasn't pasteurized and one of them bit into a Macintosh and found half a worm. Just once, she wanted her mother and father to wake her up early on a Sunday morning and drive her up to one of those orchards in Fishkill or Scratch Your Ass, NY to go apple picking. She didn't even like apples but wasn't a little girl supposed to climb on her father's shoulders, pluck apples from trees, bite into them on the car ride home, and then peel them and cut them with her mother and bake them in a pie in the oven so the house was filled with that wonderful smell, just like Arturi's bakery? Well, that's what she was going to do with her daughter, or son—she didn't want to know—even if she didn't know how to bake a pie. She would Google a pie recipe.

And then she'd thank Karen for listening and get back in the car and go home, or maybe stop by the Goodwill store first, to see if anyone had dropped off a car seat or a high chair. She hadn't even changed a diaper yet but already felt guilty about the amount of them she'd be contributing to landfills. There was no way she was going cloth. She'd find some other way to reduce the carbon footprint of her infant. Buying used plastic chairs was a start.

She had filled her father's basement with the baby stuff she was accumulating. "Nesting" as all the expectant parents' books called it. She had also taken to sleeping in her old bedroom in her parent's house. There was no name for that in any of the books, but she wasn't going back to the apartment building where someone had killed her best friend who was driving her car. Still no leads, and the sketchy video from the cameras trained on the garage doors only showed cars coming in and out, no pedestrians. The elevator cameras weren't in working order and the ones mounted to the ceiling were dummies. So much for the high security promises from co-op management. Granted, Karen's murder was the only crime she could recall happening since she moved into the building, other than the guy she had dubbed The Stealth Bomber, who on occasion would drop a deuce in the elevator. At least she assumed it was a guy and by the looks of things he was eating healthy. Both suspects remained at large and it crossed her mind a time or two that they may be one and the same. At least he didn't leave a turd near Karen. Maybe he had since found some twisted religion, converting from The Stealth Bomber to The Crucifix or Rosary Bead Killer. Who knew? The whole thing was maddening and didn't make any sense. It was hard to remove herself from the case, being that it was her best friend, it happened in her apartment complex, and she was a cop, but she was under strict orders from both the department and her OBGYN not to meddle with it. Her OGBYN, whom she referred to as OBI-WAN, was adamant that she stay away from any scenarios that may upset the baby she was nourishing.

She still hadn't been back to the garage and she never entered the building at night. Lately, she'd been phoning in favors to colleagues to help her move stuff from the apartment to her father's house in Woodlawn, with the intention of clearing out the place entirely by spring and putting it on the market. With a fresh coat of paint and some luck, she'd clear enough to open a college fund for the little one that was kicking the shit out of her stomach. Maybe the kid wouldn't need the college fund after all. It felt like a budding soccer scholarship was in her womb. How about the name Pelé for a boy? Or Mia Hamm for a girl?

She had forgotten what a nightmare the parking situation was on those cramped Woodlawn streets. Thankfully, her parents' house was one of the few that had a built-in garage at street level. The few snowstorms of the past season reminded her of those years when her neighbors were at the ready with shovels anticipating the first flurries to fall. There was simply nowhere to put the snow. Secondary and tertiary streets like theirs didn't see snowplows for a few days or even a week after a significant accumulation. Residents couldn't wait on plows. Instead, they designated one or two flagstone or slate slabs of the sidewalk to building up mountains of snow. The tolerance of neighbors was tested by tumbling blocks of snow and ice and the fighting over air space above their sidewalks and parking spots. If a car were parked in a legal spot and covered under a blanket of snow, it didn't move until the snow cleared, out of fear of never getting the spot back. If a legal parking spot were vacant, residents resorted to filling it with snow so nobody could park there for days. Some would walk the snow down by the shovelful, others would pile it into wheelbarrows and transform it into a mountain that kids and dogs would eventually turn into their playground. Ah, well. Winter was a long ways away. Maybe she'd even look forward to a snowfall someday, when she could bundle up her baby and pull it on a sled.

Ryan had gotten over her fear of parking garages by returning home. In the initial weeks after Karen's death, she had sworn off of them. No more indoor mall shopping for her.

Goodbye Westchester and Galleria, hello Central Avenue strip malls, Cross County Shopping Center, and if she were up for the hour ride, Woodbury Commons Outlet Center. She could make a vacation out of that place, with hundreds of name brand outlets nestled in the foothills of the mountains, dotted with fast food kiosks along the walkways. She preferred shopping outdoors anyway. But there was also something to be said for returning home and opening a garage door with the push of a button and entering her father's house through the stairs that was very convenient and comforting. She was happy to return to her childhood bedroom, and even happier that there was a teenager living across the street who volunteered to rake her leaves or clear her sidewalk for twenty dollars each time it snowed. From the smell of his camouflage army jacket, she imagined he used the money to buy weed, but who was she to judge? As long as he worked for it, he was free to do what he liked with it. Sometimes being neighborly superseded being a cop.

With snow removal and leaf raking taken care of, there really wasn't as much maintenance involved with the house as she thought there would be. Much of it was in decent condition. At her father's insistence a few years earlier her brothers had promised to paint the interior but they reneged and hired some Mexicans to do the job instead. It was just as well. They didn't know how to paint and the day laborers did a fine job. They took a little longer than expected, because they kept pointing out other jobs around the house that needed fixing, from patching the roof to hanging new gutters and installing a temperature gauge on the hot water heater. This last item was the one that sent her brothers reeling. They thought these guys were just charging for whatever would yield some extra dough. Her father was happy to have them around, though, and he did see a drop in his electricity and water bills, so he was a fan. He didn't shower much anymore anyway and as he always used to say, every nickel helps. Now that a baby would be in the house again, Ryan was relieved that it wouldn't be scalded when she bathed it in the tub or the sink. She remembered seeing a picture of her with a mop top of suds sitting naked in the kitchen sink sucking on a bottle while her mother gave her a bath. Oddly enough, Karen took a similar picture of her about twenty years later, while she was on spring break in Ft. Lauderdale. Only she was in a hot tub and it wasn't milk in the bottle.

She had taken bereavement leave from the job and then medical leave, trying to put it out of her mind, but that wasn't entirely possible. Everywhere she went she was confronted with reminders. The television news was full of crime stories and all other programming was full of commercials for the upcoming news. When she'd click on the Yahoo home page to check her email, the day's top crime stories called out to her. How did any cop really retire? *After spending your life solving or thwarting crimes, how do you just turn that off?* She couldn't pick up a newspaper without getting agitated and had to resist the urge to speed off after some suspect or follow up some lead. If it weren't for the persistent kicking of the growing basketball in her gut, she'd be out pursuing miscreants though the bowels of The Bronx. But her priorities had changed. The baby kept her grounded, and for the most part, homebound, other than her daily trips to see her father, who was steadily improving.

The news of the baby and her frequent visits were largely responsible for his rebound, or so the therapists told her. If patients improved and went home, they looked better in the eyes of their superiors and the rehabilitation center retained its lofty reputation. There was never a shortage of patients, only a shortage of beds. The more they turned over and sent home, the more money they could charge and collect. Even the health care business was all about numbers and volume. For most of the patients, this was a win-win situation for all involved. Rehab, get better, go home. But now it was starting to dawn on Ryan. *How the hell do I care for a baby and my father?*

While it was great to see him wheeling his chair down the hallway and raising his right hand to wave at some of the other patients, the reality was, he was getting closer to coming home. Not just *his* home anymore. To *my* home, Ryan thought. *Our home.* This wasn't the way she imagined it would be. *But God, look at him*, she thought. He was actually smiling. When was the last time she had seen her father flash a complete smile? Like her, he had spent the last few months of his life crying. But when he saw her coming down the hall toward his room, carrying some flowers she had picked up in the lobby store to brighten his room and battle those industrial strength hospital smells, he was ecstatic to see her and hell bent on impressing her. The power in his left hand wasn't there yet, but he was fastidiously pumping his right, which was enough to propel the wheelchair at breakneck speed down the hallway. Other patients looked at him, some impressed, some in shock, some so jealous they couldn't mask it. Nobody liked a show off. There was a reason The Rockettes weren't performing at Walter Reade Hospital for the troops who had lost their limbs.

"Go home, Del," one man yelled at him from a doorway.

"Slow down," another yelled at him, as if he were driving a car too fast down a suburban street where children were playing.

And one woman smiled and batted her lashes at him, as if he were showing off his new convertible outside of the high school a week before prom, looking for a date, and she was making it known she was impressed and available.

Ryan felt the baby kick and wondered if it knew that grandpa was racing toward them. It was at that moment she understood that this was what she was supposed to do with her life. She had to stay home and raise her child and nurse her father back to health. In some twisted way, this must be what it was like to have twins, she thought. They weren't identical or fraternal, nor Irish twins like her brothers, born eleven months apart in the same calendar year, but they were both going to be relying on her to wipe their asses and change their diapers for a few years, weren't they? Was there a name for these kinds of twins? One at the beginning of life, progressively getting larger and more capable, and another toward the end, shrinking and regressing? "Bookend twins" seemed like an apt moniker. She'd have to Google it when she got home, maybe trademark it.

Chapter 54

Ryan clicked on *The New York Post* web site, her daily
morning guilty pleasure now that she had stopped
drinking coffee, and saw Alvarez's face staring back at
her. The headline screamed: *COP KILLER*. Durk was right.
The kid did make the papers. A lot. Or at least the online versions of them. Who read an actual paper anymore? The online
version of *The Post* made Alvarez out to be some sort of serial
cop killer and readers were posting comments questioning his
motives and associations and linking him to every crime imag-
inable. Were cops his only target? Was he involved with terrorists? They were pinning every unsolved murder in the city
on him, it seemed, except for Karen's.

She felt for both Alvarez and Keegan, though neither one
came off as a very sympathetic character in the tabloids. It was
tough to know the whole story, since Alvarez wasn't talking,
and nobody could believe anything Keegan said. All the other
witnesses at the scenes were dead. As much as she wanted to
reach out and offer support, she was afraid to go near them.
She didn't know the officers on harbor patrol, but she'd heard
stories.

They weren't well liked by foot patrol. Then again, foot patrol didn't much care for anyone but themselves. They des-
pised bike patrol, made fun of transit cops, and looked down
upon housing, the lowest possible rung. Who wanted to grow
up in a busted or dysfunctional home and spend the bulk of

their adult lives breaking up other people's domestic quarrels? Trawling the projects and deciding which fights and drug deals to interfere with or ignore was a thankless job. No one was jealous of a housing cop. Harbor patrol, though, was a different story. They may as well have been firemen. Harbor patrol logged lots of overtime despite not having much to do, other than run drills and pluck washed up corpses out of the water. It was a great job until there was an actual emergency. Didn't happen often, but should a plane land in the Hudson River, you were forced into duty.

If there were a jumper on a bridge, you were expected to respond. And if the day ever came when terrorists blew up some bridges, well, that would totally suck, even with the ridiculous overtime. But on most days, harbor patrol was the safest place for a NYC police officer to be. Unless, of course, you happened to come across a depressed and stoned Eduardo Alvarez, who was battling substance abuse and rapidly sinking under the weight of the pressure to do good by his mother, his sister and his job.

Alvarez had already been suspended pending the Hickey investigation and now Keegan would be too, awaiting the result of the fallout from what News 12 would refer to as *The Harbor Patrol Murders*. They had thought about dumping Hanson overboard, turning the Bonito Suena loose and heading out of the sound, maybe for Bridgeport, Connecticut where Alvarez had some friends that he could swap boats with and pick up enough supplies to make it down to North Carolina and get lost in some college town, pick up some coeds and reinvent themselves. But when the effects of the pot wore off, and Alvarez remembered his sister, he decided against it. Keegan called in the incident, they returned the boat to City Island, and awaited their fate.

Ryan just shook her head. None of it made any sense. She felt her womb, nervous that there wasn't any kicking while she read the disturbing news. Whenever she found something upsetting, it was like a hockey game broke out in her belly, complete with fistfights and hard checking into the boards. She looked down to see what looked like a hand make its way completely across her midsection from left to right, as if the baby had let out a big yawn and rolled over and waved at her and now was completely at rest again. That was a relief. At least the baby was alive.

The doorbell startled her. She hadn't ordered Chinese food. Who else would be ringing her bell? She reached into her shoulder bag, grabbed her LadySmith, and attempted to put it in her waistband but duh, there was a baby blocking it. She couldn't use the ankle holster anymore because she could barely bend down to tie her shoes, not that her fat feet could fit into anything these days other than slippers and Crocs, those plastic eyesores for gardeners with square shaped feet. She decided to leave the gun where it was, in her shoulder bag, and wore it to the door.

Durkin's face filled the window, the ubiquitous coffee cup to his mouth. She unbolted the two new locks she had installed and opened the door.

"Going somewhere?" Durkin said, motioning to the handbag.

"Oh, I was just on my way out to do some shopping."

"Where you going?"

"Just to get a few items from the store."

"What store?"

"Geez, Durk, you always such a detective?"

"No, I was just wondering, 'cause I could ride along and carry some packages for you or something. You shouldn't be lifting shit in your condition."

"Oh, thank you," Ryan said. "That's very nice of you."

Durkin shrugged, slugged some coffee.

He was probably looking for a place to hide, now that two of his officers were involved in a second shooting of fellow policemen. There were probably reporters trailing him, too. She didn't want to be seen with him in public.

"Do you want to come in?"

"Aren't you going shopping?"

"It can wait."

"You sure? I thought you needed some things."

"No, I only need toilet paper. Come on in."

"All right, in that case," Durkin said as he stepped in, "but stop me before I use your bathroom."

"Deal."

Durkin glanced over the newly painted walls and tastefully, yet sparsely, decorated living room.

"Your father keeps a neat place," he said.

"Yeah, he kept it in decent shape," Ryan said, admiring her recent handiwork with the curtains and drapes. "'Course, a woman's touch helps."

"So you're serious about this?" Durk said with a wave of the hand, motioning to a wide-open living room that led into the dining room, with lots of space for a wheelchair and a toddler to navigate.

"Yeah, this is it. This is my life now." She found herself unconsciously rubbing her belly. "*Our* life."

"Well, best of luck to you," Durk said, hoisting his coffee in a toast.

"Thanks, Durk." She felt a bit uncomfortable, not having a drink to toast back with, but that was something she'd have to get used to. Her drinking days, at least for the time being, were over. "Any news with you?"

"Hmm?" he said, distractedly, lost in a photo collage hanging over the recliner, pictures of her and her sister and brothers swimming in a pool in the Catskills, the one summer vacation any of them could remember, probably because the pictures served as proof. It was either the only vacation her family ever took or the only one in which they brought along a camera.

She didn't want to broach the subject of Keegan and Alvarez. Let him bring it up if he wanted to talk about it. She was more interested in finding out who killed Karen and Declan.

"Any news on Karen's case, Durk? Any leads?"

"Oh, ah, no—sorry to say, that case is colder than my wife."

"Don't say that."

"She left."

"What?"

"Lisa left me. Ran off with a fire hydrant. Some squatty guinea with a washboard stomach. Drives a convertible. House on the Jersey Shore, condo in Bronxville. Owns a couple gyms, including the one she's been working out at for the past couple years."

"You're lying."

"You're right. I'm not telling the entire truth. She actually asked me to leave. She's having the fuckin' affair and wants me to leave? Can you believe the balls of this bitch?"

"Oh, my God, are you serious?"

"You've known me a long time, iRye. Granted, I've been known to have a wild sense of humor and tell a yarn or two, but I shit you not."

"Durk, I'm so sorry—"

"I'm not."

"I know you don't mean that."

"Well, I am and I ain't, you know? I'll be okay. It just sucks for my daughter. Studying for exams in college and her mother's fuckin' around. I'm sure she'll pull a 4.0 GPA this semester."

"Well, she doesn't have to know, right? Not *now*, anyway."

"Lisa thought she did. Texted her this morning. Considerate of her, wasn't it? One year left in college, she'll probably fuckin' drop out now and become a cop, hundred and eighty grand down the fuckin' tubes. At least I only dropped out of community college."

"I don't know what to say, Durk."

"Don't say anything."

He perused more pictures on the wall. Perhaps they brought back memories of a happier time but she got the feeling he wasn't even registering what he was seeing. Was he really interested in her sister's communion party or her brothers' Little League baseball teams? He didn't look well. Pale, gaunt. Hadn't been sleeping, obviously. Bags and dark circles under his eyes. Sickly, like he had meningitis or the flu or something. At least he was drinking coffee and not whiskey.

She worried about him. So close to retirement, with a lifetime of solid police work and a decent marriage unraveling at warp speed. She could picture him filling his days sitting in some dungeon of a bar drinking what was left of his life and wife away, angry at her and worried about their daughter, though he wouldn't tell anyone, not even the bartender. He'd just sit and sip his drinks, watch the ballgames, go back to some dingy apartment, and die a lonely man. Half the bars right up the street were full of those guys. In a way, while she watched him and rubbed her belly, she was glad she didn't know who the father of her baby was and had no intention of finding out.

"You know what the worst part is?" Durk asked. "She'd been accusing me of fuckin' around on her for years. Makes me wonder how long it's been going on. Was I that much of an idiot? Was I totally in the dark all these years? How fuckin' stupid am I?"

"You're not stupid, Durk," she said. "You're not stupid at all. You can't blame yourself. It's not your fault."

She didn't remember how it happened, but she found herself stroking the back of his head while he held her tightly around the waist and cried into her shoulder. She caught a reflection of herself in the mirror above the couch. All of a sudden, she was the mother hen, and everyone was coming home to roost.

Chapter 55

She had been dyeing her hair blonde for so long that she had forgotten its real color. Now that there was no need to pretend to be someone else, to put on the war paint and body armor, and slay the dating scene, she was going back to basics. Gone were the push-up bras that gave her the appearance of a C-cup, the press-on nails she used for digging into backs, even the Spanx to hide the paunch. A bag of hair care products went into the trash. Spritzers for height, sprays for volume, bleach for the blonde, all of it, gone. Her baby would not be ingesting those toxins.

Her hair was thinning and the bags under her eyes were darkening, but overall she thought she looked okay. She looked her age, maybe a bit older. Funny how in her teenage years she wanted to look those few years older, so she could get into bars and get more mature guys into her. Now she wouldn't mind looking a few years closer to thirty rather than forty. But she knew the rules and the consequences and she was willing to face them. Of course, she had regrets, everyone did. Not everyone could or would admit to them but she definitely had more than a few, though, surprisingly enough, being pregnant wasn't one of them. It actually brought her more joy than she could ever imagine, and not just because she had no guilt for craving and eating Oreos and milk at midnight, but she was excited about her future for the first time since she was a teenager looking forward to adulthood. Now she felt that she had finally arrived. *This is what a grown up looks like*, she thought, staring into the mirror above the vanity. Though she could only see half of it, she thought her ass was holding up pretty well for a woman her age in her condition. She probably only had a few more weeks before she had to relinquish normal jeans for the dreaded panel pants, that abominable creation with the elastic waistband and eight inches of stretchy material atop the denim. Wasn't there a better, more fashionable option for wearing jeans without suffocating your unborn child?

There were more gray hairs than she would've liked, but she knew she'd earned them all. Father Time was actually being pretty kind, she thought. She had more red highlights than she had remembered, which was a welcome surprise. She rubbed at the shadows under her tired eyes with a wet cotton ball, but it wasn't mascara and it wasn't coming off. Her fingers were dry and her hands callused from too many days at the firing range. Her joints ached from arthritis. The extra weight was causing her spine to bunch up, sending sporadic shooting pain down her legs and to the balls of her feet. Sciatica, Obi-Wan told her. Her knees creaked each time she bent. Would she ever jog again? Probably not. But maybe, if she found one of those baby-jogging strollers at Goodwill, she'd consider it, as long as it wasn't covered in vomit. More so from the mother than the baby, probably.

She presumed the baby joggers were like home gym or NordicTrack purchases, with over eighty percent of them ending up being nothing more than expensive and elaborate space-eating coat racks. The only workout many ever got from those was the four hours spent assembling them and the subsequent five minutes moving them to the curb for bulk garbage collection years later, to make room for more stuff. She was no exercise freak but even she knew that was just too long an interval and not enough exertion to develop any muscle tone.

Maybe she'd pick up some weights instead, because how many pictures of dusty old weight sets had she seen accompanying the pronouncement Curb Alert! on Craigslist? Too many to count. Who was she kidding? She wasn't the workout kind. She liked to walk. But not too far. Six blocks to McLean Avenue was enough. She'd stop at Arturi's for a homemade Italian ice and share it with the baby and then watch its face bunch up at the sour apple flavor or its eyes light up at the taste of a watermelon. That's what she wanted. Now. Homemade Italian ice from Arturi's. Pina colada flavored. Or maybe cream. No, a scoop of both. But first she'd put on some lipstick because, well, you just never knew whom you might meet. The shade of maroon made her checks look paler than they actually were. She pursed her lips together to smear it on evenly and sucked her cheekbones in.

Oh my God, she thought. *I look just like my mother.*

Chapter 56

The walk up Martha Avenue to Arturi's took her past St. Sebastian's, something she wasn't thinking about as she set out. The rumbling in her stomach wasn't coming from the baby. It was from thoughts of Father McLanahan. Memories of Karen's funeral. The image of him in the throes of ecstasy. She felt her pace quickening. Just two blocks to go. She'd walk a different route home.

She couldn't even be fully sure what it was about him that conjured up such violent feelings. It was like she projected all of her negative feelings about the Catholic Church and its sordid scandals onto this one individual, whether he was responsible for any of them or not. Kind of like the way some residents of The South Bronx used to treat police officers. If they were harassed or arrested by one—even for a good reason—they hated cops. *All* cops. One of her first nights on patrol around Yankee Stadium, on 165th and the Grand Concourse, a television fell from a roof, missing her and another cop by a couple feet.

A group of kids on the sidewalk that they didn't bother, even though they were selling knockoff hats and jerseys, broke into a spontaneous chorus of "Fuck The Police."

Thanks, rap music. She still hated it for that reason. She hadn't even made an arrest in her career yet, but she had made enemies, simply by wearing the uniform. Somehow the memory of those kids laughing that she was nearly killed and screaming "Fuck The Police" made her feel a bit of sympathy for McLanahan. Maybe he wasn't such a bad guy. What did she really know about him? Had he molested any children or covered up any wrongdoings by clergymen? Not that she knew of. She was pretty sure—no, she was positive—that she saw him getting a blowjob in the basement of a bar after hours, but she couldn't hold that against him, as she on occasion found herself in similar situations.

And did she really believe that he had plunged a knife into Karen's throat, thinking it was her? He might be a horndog, but was he really a killer? Why would he stay at her bedside in the hospital after she fainted? Was he trying to kill her? Or was he trying to save her? The things she thought about him would make a helluva movie of the week, but only if HBO did it and a slightly younger Michael Caine or Gene Hackman played McLanahan.

She looked up as she turned the corner of McLean, about to dart into Arturi's, and found herself face to face with McLanahan. The weather-beaten face that she wanted to sink her nails into and tear to pieces, now perpetually shielded from the sun by the ubiquitous Yankees cap, suddenly seemed wise and forgiving, kind and open. He was just an old man, trying to survive, like her father minus the anger. Her legs turned to jelly and she began quaking at the knees. Tears streamed down her face as she fell into him. He caught her, but not before dropping his waxed paper bag containing hot coffee and a jelly donut.

"I'm sorry," she sobbed into him.

"It's okay."

"I'm so sorry—for—everything."

God, what is happening to me?

She was an emotional wreck. Was it the hormones? Was this what being pregnant was? Falling to fuckin' pieces in public? Her thoughts fired like random neurons, not fully connecting. Such anxiety. What would happen to her baby? Her father? Herself?

"I'm a mess," she cried. "I'm so sorry."

"Don't be," Father McLanahan said. "I didn't need the donut anyhow, but we all give in to temptation."

"Oh, please, don't fuckin' lecture me now."

"No, no, not at all. This isn't a lecture."

She pulled away from him and wiped her tears.

"Did you want to go somewhere to talk?" he asked.

"I don't know...I..."

"Not that I mind, but, you know, people may get the wrong idea if they see us hugging and crying on the avenue here, given your condition."

"Oh, please. I think everyone knows I'm not your type. You're not fooling anyone with the Yankees cap, either."

"I am a fan, but I use it mainly for protection—something, apparently, you don't know much about."

"Thank you for reminding me why I hate you, you arrogant prick."

"Anything else you'd like to get off your chest?"

"I just—wanted—an ice—that's all. I just want to enjoy a fuckin' ice without getting emotional or being lectured or feeling inferior. Is that too much to ask?"

She brushed past him and entered the bakery, unsure if the confrontation had even taken place, or if she were in some delusional dream state. Could it be lingering effects of the Solpadeine? Was that stuff like LSD, capable of producing flashbacks? Would it affect the baby? She looked beyond the attendant, at the giant coffee urn and stacks of chocolate cigars. Maybe she needed to drink coffee again. Caffeine wasn't so bad for a baby, was it? Better than Solpadeine, which had not only caffeine, but codeine and acetaminophen. And chocolate had some healthy properties. Antioxidants. She should step up the caffeine and antioxidants, for her sake and her baby's.

Then she looked down and saw what she had really come for, the tubs of multicolored, flavored ice. They all looked so enticing. Cherry, lemon, watermelon, peach, sour apple, chocolate, coffee, cream, pina colada, rainbow, orange, and blue raspberry.

"May I help you?" the cheery, round faced teen behind the counter asked her.

She wondered why she didn't work here when she was a

teenager then remembered that she had a sweet tooth and a tendency to swallow baked goods whole. Pies, cakes, donuts, and cookies made up a large part of her diet as a child. It wasn't until a nasty bout of constipation left her straining, pushing, and bloated, resulting in recurring hemorrhoids, that she turned into a fruit and salad eater.

Obi-Wan had warned her that giving birth would be like taking the biggest dump of her life. She had already stocked up on Tucks medicated pads in anticipation of *The Return of the Hemorrhoids*. Sounded like a movie starring Obi-Wan.

"I really would like one of each," Ryan said, "but I do have a conscience. Even though I'm very spontaneous, I'm afraid I'll have to stick to the plan somewhat."

Chapter 57

Moments later, she turned the corner with a pint of ice and a plastic spoon.

McLanahan was waiting for her on a park bench, sipping what was left of his coffee.

"Are you waiting for me?" she asked.

"I'm just having some coffee," he said.

Ryan thought about her options. Walk home and let some of the ice melt, eat while walking home—running the risk of tripping over a raised portion of sidewalk she wouldn't see beneath her tub of ice and protruding belly and fall to the ground, injuring her baby—or sitting on the bench next to him and enjoying her ice. She sat down and popped the top. She had settled on mixing four different flavors: pina colada, cream, coffee, and chocolate. The blue raspberry beckoned too, as did the rainbow, but there'd be other days. God, this was good. The way the chocolate and the cream mixed together in that icy cool sweetness…*this* was heaven.

"You have to try this," she said.

"No, thank you. Gives me brain freeze."

He said that like it was a bad thing. That was part of the enjoyment. It was like catching a buzz without the hangover. She dug into the ice, each mouthful a celebration of the simple pleasures in life. Sure, they were empty calories. But they weren't heavy and filling like ice cream and no bits of caramel stuck in your teeth like a candy bar. In lieu of everything else she had given up, she could allow herself to indulge in the occasional Italian ice without guilt. It was a better choice than a cannoli.

She got halfway through before being sated. Now the decision: would she take it home and try to re-freeze it or just throw it out? She wrestled with the choice as if she were choosing a name for the baby. Aidan for a boy? Phoebe for a girl?

A woman walked by, looked at the two of them, and smiled. Not an innocent smile. A smirk. As if she were making some sort of inference from the two of them sitting there, her pregnant with a pint of ice and him incognito under a hat sipping coffee. Did she know he was a priest or did she think he was her father, or some dirty old man? *Will people actually think we were a couple? I don't look that old, do I?*

She used to sit on the same bench with her father some thirty odd years ago and think about sitting here with her own kids someday, sampling their ices. Though the baby was kicking away, probably hopped up from the chocolate, it still didn't seem real to her. Was she really going to be a mother?

"Do you plan on having the baby baptized?" McLanahan asked.

"I haven't thought about that."

"'Cause if you are, you'd have to be in good standing with the church and all."

"Oh, really? And am I in good standing with the church?"

"I'd have to look into it. Have you made all your sacraments? Are you a member of the parish? Do you put your envelopes in for the collections at mass?"

"Is that all you give a shit about? Life and death are all just business transactions to you?"

"Of course not. The sacred gift of life is much more than that."

"So why would you ask?"

"I'm only trying to make conversation, Eileen."

"Did you kill Karen McGuire?"

"What?"

"You heard me."

"Are you only trying to make conversation?"

"Answer the question."

"Absolutely not."

"Do you know who killed Declan McManus?"

"I don't have a clue."

"Were you getting a blowjob in the basement of MacGuffin's?"

"Miss Ryan, with all due respect—"

"Just answer the question."

"I don't care for your line of questioning.'

"And I don't care for your line of shit. Why would I bring my baby to be blessed by a liar? I saw you in the basement of MacGuffin's. I've asked you twice now and you've denied it both times."

"You must have me confused with somebody else."

"Your evil twin, I suppose."

"I don't have a twin."

"Let me guess, then. You were sleepwalking."

"I've never walked in my sleep to the best of my knowledge."

"Do you guys practice denying all charges made against you?"

"No charges have ever been brought against me."

"Let me ask you one more time, and I want you to answer me with a straight face. Did you get a blowjob in the basement of MacGuffin's?"

McLanahan stared into Ryan's blue eyes and answered, "No."

Ryan dropped her hands in exasperation, causing a chunk of her ice to fall to the ground. She attempted to bend over and scoop it up with her napkin but her belly made it difficult. McLanahan took the napkins from her, picked it up, and tossed them in the trashcan on the corner.

"Either I need glasses, or you're full of shit. Either way, I'll see you in hell, then."

"Don't be so sure of that."

"Why? You don't believe in hell? Or you think you're better than me?"

"I'm not better than anyone. We're not here to judge. Only

the Lord knows where we'll end up, but it's up to us to make the decision easy for him."

"So, it's all about forgiveness then? Confess your sins, say a few Hail Marys, and party on?"

"There would have to be contrition, of course."

"Of course. I'm sure Peter showed contrition after denying he knew Christ three times. He was the rock of the church, after all, wasn't he?"

"Would you like to discuss scripture, Miss Ryan?"

"No, thanks. I prefer contemporary fiction."

Ryan began to waddle back down Martha Avenue before turning back to him.

"So you deny your sins in public but then confess them in private to another priest, say an act of contrition, and you get to go to heaven? Is that the way it works for you guys? Is that the fraternity of the priesthood? That gives you carte blanche to do whatever you want? Does that make any sense?"

McLanahan flashed her a smirk. She'd seen that kind of look on the job before, from wiseguys who knew that charges wouldn't stick to them and from co-workers who knew there were certain laws they could break and get away with, like the ones who reserved some parking spaces at Yankee Stadium or drank a few beers in public, knowing if they were ever confronted they could flash a badge and keep drinking.

"You must have us confused with the police department," McLanahan said with a toothy grin. "Whaddya call it? The Wall of Silence? Or The Blue Shield, is it?"

Touché, Ryan thought, holding her tongue.

"I'll keep you and the baby in my prayers," McLanahan said.

"Go pray yourself," Ryan said.

She had another verb in mind still couldn't bring herself to say it to the priest's face, at least not in public. She turned her back on him and headed home.

Though the ice was satisfying for a few minutes, she already felt the after effects. She needed another nap. Those were totally empty calories. She passed the sidewall of a building with an Irish flag painted on the bricks and as much as she

felt at home in Woodlawn, she felt the weight of the Irish enclave around her. She needed to blame someone so she blamed
everyone. It wasn't easy growing up anywhere, but this neighborhood presented some unique hurdles. The prevalence and
destruction of alcoholism were on display on every block, as
was the lapsed Catholic thing. The guilt. The shame. She could
put on a tough facade like the best of them but she couldn't lie
to herself. This wasn't easy.

At least she could take solace in the fact that she wasn't a
man and didn't suffer from the other Irish curse of the small
penis. But all the other ones, she had them. And as much as
she wouldn't wish them on anyone, she didn't want anyone
else's problems, either.

The devil you know, she thought, looking back once more
over her shoulder at the smirking priest on the bench, who held
his coffee cup up to her in salute.

Chapter 58

Ryan flipped through the pages of a *Modern Business Magazine* that alternatively preached future doom and gloom and a hearty rebound from the recession, smiling meekly at the other women coming in and taking seats around Obi-Wan's waiting room. All of them had to pee. Another joy of pregnancy nobody had mentioned to her, the unbearable pressure to pee. The little buggers must be stomping on our bladders, she thought, as one after another the expectant mothers made their way to the cramped bathroom off the waiting room. Why would Obi-Wan schedule so many appointments at the same time? Did that many pregnant women cancel? Possibly. Come to think of it, she herself had almost bailed, tempted by the aromas of the roadside gyro stand. Thankfully, her real feelings about the dangers of eating street meat won out.

Okay, that wasn't entirely true. The lack of a parking space kept her moving. But really now, eight women in the office at once? Maybe some of them had second thoughts between appointments and historically, those eight would dwindle to say, five or six. It had crossed her mind on occasion. Being pregnant was not always fun. The ability of the skin to stretch would never cease to amaze her but it wasn't easy walking around with all that extra girth. The thoughts of raising a child alone would creep in, the amount of time, care, and money it required, and she'd have moments of doubts in her ability to do it. Maybe she wasn't prepared to be a good mother. Maybe she should give it up to some family in Connecticut who couldn't conceive or find time to make love or just terminate it and move on.

But then she'd hear her mother's voice saying, "Two wrongs don't make a right," something she'd always say to her children when they had inevitable spats and retaliated against a sibling who had started it. Ultimately, she decided this was what she wanted and what was wanted of her. In keeping with the consistencies of the contradictions that seemed to govern her life, she wasn't crazy about the Catholic Church or a lot of priests but she still believed in some higher power and divine intervention.

At times, she even entertained the bizarre notion that she was the recipient of another immaculate conception because she couldn't for the life of her figure out who produced the miraculous sperm that slipped past her IUD. The ParaGard was supposed to last ten years with a less than one percent chance of failure so it'd have to be one lucky Leprechaun who beat those odds. But then again, there was supposed to be a pot o'gold at the end of a rainbow and not a dead body outside The Pot O'Gold, so luck might have nothing to do with it.

Most of the women in the office were further along than she was and some looked ready to go at any minute. They could hardly fit into the chairs anymore and required the help of others to get out. Watching them made her glad that she wasn't obese. She couldn't imagine having such difficulty getting into and out of a chair if she were just fat and not pregnant. Her belly was a fairly neat protrusion compared to the rest of the patients. In typical fashion, all of the women stared at each other's bumps and, whether they realized it or not, made instant judgments about the mothers and the babies. Ryan had the expectant baby population in the room pegged at six girls and two boys, based on the simple criteria that her mother had employed to successfully predict the sex of babies with a staggeringly high rate of accuracy: girls take the beauty away from their mothers and boys don't.

She didn't know any of the other eight women in the room but, to put it mildly, six of them weren't exactly lookers. There were a lot of ugly people out there having sex, Ryan thought, and apparently the recession had cut into the condom budget. Like the elderly population on a budget who chose food over medicine, their younger counterparts were choosing food over condoms and sex over vacations. The popularity of the stay-cation not only crippled the economy of tourist destinations, it was also putting a strain on Medicare and the insurance indus-try. Cutbacks and furloughs tended to place people in cramped quarters in the vicinity of cheap booze and this packed waiting room was the result. *Do we really need more ugly people in the world?* Maybe she'd write a letter into *Modern Business Magazine* from her perspective in Obi-Wan's office in the north Bronx.

"Eileen Ryan?" the receptionist called.

"Here!" she yelled.

"You're next."

She wanted to feel relieved that it was her turn for five minutes alone with Obi-Wan but whenever she was called she felt nervous. It meant she was one step closer to having to care for another life while her own was rapidly crumbling. In the past six months, she had lost her best friend and there were no leads. In the last detail she'd been assigned, the investigation of the death of a guy she happened to have slept with, she also couldn't find any solid leads.

A forensics officer that she happened to have dated once al-so turned up dead, shot by an officer who subsequently shot two more officers. Her best comrade and confidant on the job was going through a messy divorce and had literally fallen into her arms, seeking support.

She was pregnant but didn't know who the father was and had taken an extended leave of absence from her job, officially out on bereavement. And she would have to care for her father, who had suffered a stroke and was confined to a wheelchair. Not exactly how she had drawn up her career or life path. She needed more than Obi-Wan—for starters, a life coach and a nanny.

Chapter 59

O h, looks like big baby," Dr. Oh told her.

A small man with an unusually large head, Dr. Oh seemed genuinely interested in delivering babies. She had researched him online, found out that he was born in Japan, did his undergrad work at Cornell, and had his doctorate from Columbia, but what impressed her even more was that his C-Section rate was the second lowest in the state of New York. Since the only OB-GYN with a lower rate practiced in Buffalo and didn't take her insurance, Dr. Oh became the de facto choice. That he happened to deliver in Montefiore, a simple taxi or bus ride away should she be unable to drive herself to the hospital, cemented the deal. She would let Dr. Oh deliver her baby. Hell, she'd even let him nurse it and rock it to sleep every night if he was willing but she'd settle for a safe and traditional vaginal delivery.

"You're gaining weight," Dr. Oh said.

He finished each sentence with a smile, as if everything he said was the greatest news in the world. She wasn't sure how other women felt, but she didn't like hearing about gaining weight and having to deliver a big baby.

"It's not too big, right? You're not going to cut me open, are you?"

"No-o-o-o-o," he said with a big smile. "You big girl, you push."

Okay, she could push, but she didn't want scars. Or tears. No episiotomies, please.

"Let me listen," he said, smiling as he reached for his stethoscope, "and make sure you don't have two babies."

Twins? Oh, God, no.

"Well, if I do, you have my permission to get rid of one right now. I don't want to be faced with *Sophie's Choice* down the line," Ryan said, proud of her ability to reference one of the few books she had read as an adult into a conversation. But wait—had she read the book? Or had she seen the movie on television when she was too hungover to get up and find the remote? Yes, that was it. In fact, that was the day she stumbled across her hangover remedy, when she couldn't decide whether to drink Vitamin Water or take Alka-Seltzer. *Ryan's Choice* was to combine them and voila, goodbye hangover, hello Vitamin Seltzer...Or Alka-Water?

"No, no," Dr. Oh said. "Just one baby. One big baby."

He squirted some cold petroleum jelly-like substance onto her belly and turned on the machine that looked like the television set on the swinging arm that her father had in his room at the rehabilitation center. Then he strapped some Velcro paddles on her gut and stuck a dildo-like wand inside her.

And to think, I pay him for this.

"Sorry about the chill," Dr. Oh said.

"Easy, doc," she said, but he was all business.

She wasn't expecting any foreplay, not with a room full of patients awaiting the same treatment, but a gentler touch would've been appreciated. This bordered on illegal. But then the television revealed a show she had never seen before: a fetus, moving and twisting and turning. Not just any fetus, *her* fetus. She could see a head and little arms that looked as if they were shielding eyes from a bright light and a foot and then another foot and was that a penis? *Oh my God*, she thought. *There's a little man inside of me. And by the looks of things he doesn't have the Irish curse.*

A rush of emotions overcame her. Tears rolled down her face but she was smiling, as was Dr. Oh. There was such a sweetness about him, as if he were seeing this show for the first time, too, but wasn't this what he did all day? Why was this still so amazing to him?

"Is everything okay?" she asked him.

"Listen," he said with a smile.

He turned a dial on the machine and the rapid thumping of a heartbeat drowned out the sound of the swishing fluids.

"That's your baby's heartbeat," he said with a laugh. "It sounds beautiful."

"It does," Ryan said. "It really does."

He hit a few more buttons on the machine and the whir of a printer kicked on. Then he turned the screen off.

"Don't turn it off," Ryan said.

He laughed. "I make you a picture."

He withdrew the wand, cleaned off the jelly, unstrapped the paddles from her belly and handed her some tissues to wipe herself. The whole ritual was a lot like the act of sex itself. She wished Dr. Oh were the father, or at least someone as enthusiastic about seeing the baby.

"If I had one of these machines, I'd never leave the house," she said. "I'd just watch baby movies all day in real time."

Dr. Oh laughed and repeated, "I make you a picture." He handed her a five-by-seven-inch black and white picture of the image on the screen. Somehow seeing a still shot of it wasn't as spectacular. Watching it move and hearing its heartbeat was awesome but this could be anybody's baby. Except for that large penis that looked like a third leg. Okay, so the father probably wasn't Irish, which would help her narrow down her suspects, but if he were, she would be putting a popular myth to rest and giving birth to the future porn star McTripod or, perhaps, Ryepod.

Chapter 60

As she signaled to turn into her garage, she was surprised and annoyed to see a car parked in front of it. Then she saw who was sitting in it and kept driving.

"What the fuck does Keegan want?" she found herself saying aloud as she circled the block.

This couldn't be good news. Whatever it was, she wasn't going to let it affect her day. This was the most excited she had felt about being a mother since she found that collapsible playpen in mint condition at the Goodwill store for ten bucks. Not that she would be going anywhere anytime soon, but she just liked knowing that she could be ready in a moment's notice to take her little tripod with her wherever and whenever she wanted to go. No, she wasn't going to let Keegan ruin her day.

She pulled the Jeep up alongside Keegan's Camry and zapped her window down.

"Keegan, get out of my driveway," she said.

Keegan looked up from his iPhone and waved. He removed earbuds and attempted to answer her before realizing his window was closed. Then he opened the door.

"Ryan, I gotta talk to you."

"You gotta move your car."

"Okay, I will. But I gotta talk to you."

"I'm really not in the mood for conversation."

"Please, it's important…it's about the job."

"I'm not on the job anymore. Doctor's orders."

"Okay, but, there's some things you need to know."

He reached into his breast pocket and pulled out a cassette tape. Had it been John Cusack behind the wheel the gesture might've been cute but in Keegan's hand it just looked pathetic. She had an inkling that he liked her, but she could never reciprocate those feelings. Not that she was major league anymore, but Keegan couldn't make the minors. There were the complete players, the "five tool guys" who had it all, then there were those who were competent in one or more areas and had potential in others, and then there was just the tool. Keegan wasn't a complete tool but he wouldn't be getting any playing time with her.

"You made me a mixtape? That's so…retro."

She had flashbacks to high school, when Eliot Ingalls made her a mixtape of crappy love songs by REO Speedwagon, Journey, Def Leppard, bad Rod Stewart, and Survivor's "Eye of the Tiger." That last one was only on there because it was on the soundtrack of *Rocky III*, and Eliot was so obsessed with Sylvester Stallone movies that he regularly quoted monosyllabic scenes from all the *Rocky* films, as well as *First Blood*, *Nighthawks*, *F.I.S.T.* and *The Lords of Flatbush*. The last time she had thought about Ingalls was when she saw his name on a police report, listed as a possible suspect in a steroids peddling scheme at a Bronx gym. Did not surprise her one bit.

"It's not a mixtape," Keegan said. "Please, Ryan, give me a little credit. I do own a computer and know how to burn a playlist to a CD."

"What is it?"

"I don't know. Hickey's widow brought it into the station, said to give it to you."

"Oh, God. I don't want it."

"Neither do I," Keegan said. "Do what you want with it."

"You mean to tell me a dead officer's widow brings a tape into the precinct and nobody listened to it?"

"Me and Durk were outside bullshitting when she walked up to us and handed it over. Durk asked me to bring it to you, said he had to meet with his lawyer…he's getting divorced."

"Yeah, I know."

"He's…ah…not taking it too well."

"Who does?"

"I took mine pretty well."

She had totally forgotten that Keegan was once married. Didn't last more than a few months. Guys in the precinct even had a pool going on how long it would last.

"Some things just aren't meant to be, you know?" Keegan said. "We all make mistakes when we're young."

"Yeah," she agreed. "And some when we're not so young."

He looked down at her belly. "That's not a mistake," he said. "You'll make a great mother."

She didn't exactly need Keegan's vote of confidence or his opinions on any matters but he seemed genuine, and from what she read in the papers, he was going through a pretty big ordeal, the poor bastard. Maybe she was wrong about him. Maybe he had potential.

"Thanks, Keegs," she said. "How's everything going with you?"

"Oh, great, in case you haven't heard," he said with exaggerated sarcasm. He didn't do subtlety. "Things are really looking up. I'm being investigated by Internal Affairs, got shuffled to desk duty, and word on the street is that I'm going to be forced to turn in my badge."

"Really?"

"There's been a lot of white shirts doing inspections down at the stationhouse, complaining about the lack of activity in general and my numbers specifically."

"The quarter's not up, though. You still have time to pay the rent before evaluations. Get yourself a couple 250s, step up your C Summons count, and these things have way of straightening themselves out. Durk will vouch for you."

"The hounds are putting a lot of heat on Durk, too. Blaming him for the low activity for such a heavy precinct."

"But the four-seven's not that heavy."

"The XO and the Borough Patrol Commander seem to think so. They did an inspection during roll call and started tossing CDs around like crazy. No whistle, CD. No flashlight, CD. Shirt untucked, CD."

"Any time a cop's in the news, they start in with that bullshit," she said. "As if that had anything to do with it."

This was part of the job she didn't miss hearing about. In-ter-office politics and pressure to fill quotas—not that anyone would ever admit to quotas on the force. But when patrol officers were pressured to bring up their numbers or face disciplinary action or a transfer, what else could you possibly call them?

"If it's three strikes and you're out, I guess I'm out of a job," Keegan said. "Just got hit with my third CD."

"For what?"

"Reading the paper on duty."

"Are you serious?"

"Yeah, I'm guilty, too. I was also eating a sandwich. Two-thirty in the morning, parked near the Thruway where all them cars were getting broken into? What the fuck am I supposed to do? Drive back to the stationhouse and eat from the vending machine?"

"What bullshit. What were the other two?"

"The night Hickey was killed. Cited me for failure to iden-tify myself as a police officer."

"Is that true?"

"Technically, yes, but Alvarez shot off his weapon, not me. I don't deserve a Command Discipline for that...And then I had a little incident some years back on a rooftop in Hell's Kitchen."

"Oh, right...I remember that."

"And now this fuckin' disaster on the boat with Alvarez—" He looked away, squinting into the sun. "He's probably al-ready left for Cuba, or someplace—won't return my calls, no-body answers the door. Fuckin' guy just left me twisting in the wind. He's got Ramon Garcia and the Latin Policemen's As-sociation doing all his talking for him, what do I got? I can't leave my house without some asshole shoving a camera in my face."

Ryan didn't know what to say, other than "Sorry."

"It's cool, you know, I don't mean to vent to you," Keegan said. "My conscience is clear. I sleep at night. I'm confident no charges will be brought against me. I'm going to move to Florida, start all over. Gonna sell all my shit on eBay and hit the fuckin' road. Got an in with the Tampa Bay Devil Rays, working security. If you ever come down to check out a Yankees game, give me a holler."

Ryan smiled, just to be polite. "Okay," she said, as she held up the tape. "Thanks."

"You bet."

"Good luck."

"Yeah, you too."

He stood awkwardly outside of his car for a few seconds. Was he expecting a kiss or a hug?

"Ah, Keegs?"

"Yeah?"

"I still need you to move your car."

Chapter 61

She fixed a cup of tea, grabbed a box of Social Tea biscuits, and sat in the recliner before the Lloyds stereo. The machine was a dinosaur, a floor model her father bought from Alexander's on Fordham Road back in the 1970s because he didn't trust the new model in the box.

"How do I know that one works?" he asked the salesman.

The Hispanic kid with a pencil thin mustache, couldn't have been more than sixteen, just shrugged his shoulders and pointed at the floor model. "You want that one?" he asked.

Her father had brought along a cassette tape of traditional Irish songs, a blast of reels featuring flutes, fiddles, and accordions, and placed it in the floor model. Then he cocked an ear to each speaker to make sure they both worked and walked back a bit to hear it from a distance. When he was satisfied, he said, "Yeah, I'll take this one."

Ryan was by his side, along with her older brother Patrick, who hid behind a mop of black curly hair, too embarrassed to even look at the salesman as he carted away the unopened box with the new stereo and returned to tape up the plastic cover of the turntable on the floor model instead.

"Why would he buy the floor model?" Patrick asked her once they got home and were out of earshot. "Doesn't he know kids are always messing around with the floor model? That thing is probably already broken."

"It sounded fine in the store," she said.

"A new one would sound better," Patrick said.

But the floor model must've sounded just fine, because that's where she would often find Patrick after school, reclining before the Lloyds stereo with her Princess Leia earphones perched on his head. His eyes would be closed, the faint odor of marijuana wafting from his jean jacket while he sang off-key to Pink Floyd's "Shine On, You Crazy Diamond." The floor model had held up. It was still the house stereo. The eight-track tape machine had stopped working years ago but the only eight-track in the house was Don McLean's "American Pie" and nobody had expressed interest in hearing that in more than thirty years, so it wasn't an issue. There were still crates of vinyl LPs scattered about in closets, and in the basement, despite her father's efforts to rid the house of them after the boys moved away, and the turntable and the receiver still worked.

Her father was perfectly happy with the purchase, for he only listened to the radio and an occasional record, but mostly because he got the floor model at a twenty-percent discount, something he only divulged years later. Ryan was a quick study, having outfitted her apartment with a floor model bed frame, dresser, flat-screen television, and microwave, all at deep discounts.

As Ryan settled into the recliner, she reached back to hit the power button and open the cassette desk but couldn't quite manage. She stretched, but her belly simply wouldn't budge. Playing the cassette Keegan gave her would require a dismount from the recliner and a walk—more of a waddle—around it. She decided the cassette could wait. She would enjoy her tea and biscuits instead. Then she made the effort to get up, walk around the chair, press play, and sit back down, reclining with her eyes closed. Several seconds of hissing were interrupted by Hickey's voice, in a roadie baritone, "Check, check...check one."

What an asshole, she thought. Then he cleared his throat and began speaking.

"Ryan, if you're listening to this tape it means that something has happened—something bad. I don't know where to begin so I'll just say it. I've always admired your skills as a patrol officer and a detective, and it's no secret I guess, that I've always found you attractive. That being said, I don't want you to think I'm some nut, 'cause I'm not. I'm a happily married man, and whatever our relationship was is in the past—"

Ryan rolled her eyes. What relationship? A pizza dinner six years ago?

"—the reason I'm recording this is simple. I think your life may be in danger. I've been trying to document my findings because some of them may be disturbing, some evidence may be purely circumstantial, and I don't ever want to see an innocent person accused of anything they didn't do. If all of this sounds like some sort of riddle, I'm sorry, but the nature of my work precludes me from divulging sensitive information—"

"Just get on with it," Ryan said. "The guy thinks he's Captain Kirk or in the fuckin' *The Twilight Zone.*"

"—I found some things at the scene of Declan McManus's murder that may be of interest to many people, especially you. Of the hair samples I've collected, the only match in the database was yours. Your fingerprints were also at the scene, on a beer bottle and on the wall. There was another set of fingerprints that matched samples collected in our database that belong to an unknown male. These prints were also found at two other locations within the last sixteen months where crimes were committed, one in the men's bathroom of an after-hours joint on the Lower East Side of Manhattan, where a woman was raped and assaulted at approximately five-fifteen in the morning, and the other took place in Prospect Park in Brooklyn—"

Ryan kicked the footrest of the recliner down and pressed the stop button on the cassette player of the stereo. She ejected the cassette, grabbed her cell phone and car keys and quick waddled to the door.

Chapter 62

Y eah," Durkin answered.

"Durk, where are you?"

"Somewhere no one will find me."

"Durk, we gotta talk."

She had intended on listening to the cassette as she drove but had forgotten there was no tape deck in her Jeep, only a CD player and a jack to plug in an iPod or an MP3 player.

"Do you have a cassette player?" she asked.

"What?"

"Do you have a cassette player in your car?"

"Yeah."

"Meet me outside the stationhouse in ten minutes."

"Can't do that."

"Why not?"

"I don't want to be seen anywhere near there."

"Aren't you working today?"

"I'm never working again."

"What?"

"I quit. Bunch of white shirts were up my ass about getting the activity up, 'specting us to do more with less, bringing in bags of shit, and making up charges. Told 'em to go fuck 'emselves."

She nearly crashed into the back of a tow truck that was stopped at a red light on the corner of Katonah and East 233rd St. "Durk! You're wasted."

"You bet yer ass I am. I'm cooked. Stick a fork in me—lemme get 'nother, Jimmy."

"Where are you?"

"None of yer business."

"You're not in that dive on Webster Avenue, are you?"

There was a pub on the corner of Webster and Bainbridge Avenues, a retired old man's shot and a beer joint by day and a home to off-duty cops in the mornings, when they had finished their overnight shifts. From eight in the morning until one or two in the afternoon, it was either the safest place to drink or the most dangerous, depending on your perspective, since all the patrons were packing heat. Usually the sergeants and lieutenants would avoid these joints, but it was a magnet for the rookies, trying to fit the mold, and for the lifers on patrol with no ambition to climb the ladder—the guys who just wanted to punch in, punch out, belly up, and collect a pension after twenty years.

"Whaddya want from me, Ryan?"

"I want you to help me catch a killer."

"Ah, fuck it."

Either the call or the phone was dropped because Durk was no longer on the other end of the line. She made an illegal U-turn in the Hess station, nearly taking out a gas pump in the process. With her cell phone on speaker, she redialed Durk's number as she drove down Katonah Avenue.

"Leave me alone," he shouted.

"Listen, asshole, I will check every single bar in The Bronx until I find you, so you may as well tell me. I already know the bartender's name is Jimmy, so really, how hard will it be?"

Durk considered her logic. There were probably lots of Jimmys tending bar in The Bronx, not that he could think of any at the moment, except for the one before him pouring a double.

Ryan figured she would stop into the first bar on the avenue, Gilligan's Aisle, and simply ask the bartender which member of the fraternity named Jimmy was working days today, but then she spotted Slats in his ubiquitous overcoat, headphones, and untied New Balance sneakers, lollygagging down the avenue, oblivious to all. She rolled to a stop, put on her hazards, and zipped down the window.

"Tommy!" she called, but he didn't answer. "Tommy!"

She didn't realize she was blocking a bus stop until the bus driver behind her leaned on his horn.

"Fuckin' Slats," she muttered to herself as she drove down the block and into a handicapped parking space to let the bus pull over. Reaching into her wallet, she pulled out a Lieutenants Benevolent Association card that Durk had given her and placed it on the dashboard. She never used it to score parking spaces but, if ever she were going to, now was the time. If this wasn't handicapped, what was? All women who were six months pregnant should have one of these. There ought to be a Pregnant Woman's Benevolent Association card, or a sticker with the logo of a big belly that they could place on their windshields so they could park in the best spots.

She attempted to march across the street in an authoritative manner but any chance of that happening was negated by her protrusion. She was all belly. This thing must be squatting ass first because that was all she could picture—a big ass resting on her bladder and the occasional punch or a succession of swift kicks. If she weren't carrying the personification of the Notre Dame Fighting Irish Leprechaun, then she would be giving birth to a mixed martial arts champion or Michael Flatley's child, because The Lord of The Dance was about to make her wet her pants. Her march quickly morphed into an unsteady, unintimidating waddle. Ah, well. She didn't need to intimidate Slats. It was not like he'd responded well to the tough-talking cop routine in the past. She just needed an honest answer, and the only way to get it was to talk straight to him.

His gaze froze her. She had never noticed it before, but he sort of resembled a white Stevie Wonder. He wasn't totally blind but his eyesight was awful, he was overweight, had big teeth and thick lips, and smiled a lot as his head lolled from side to side in synch to whatever music was playing on his headphones, completely lost in the symphony of his own world. Must be nice to be oblivious to the odor of the fish shop, the exhaust of the number thirty-four bus, and the hot stream of chemicals escaping from the dry cleaners' vents. This was no place for a pregnant woman to stand. As she approached him, his initial reaction was to avoid any confrontation, and he instinctively moved toward the street. She moved directly into his path and he finally looked up to see who was accosting him.

She smiled and waved at him. It took him a few seconds of concentrating through his Coke bottle glasses to recognize her face. Then he smiled in return.

"Hiya, Tommy," she said, realizing that she sounded like an old housewife greeting a young paperboy, circa 1957.

He gave her a hug that she wasn't expecting, as evidenced by the reaction on her face, which garnered the attention of passersby who wondered if this was something she was okay with. Everyone in the neighborhood knew Tommy by face, if not by name, but he didn't bear hug people with any regularity. Some of the old timers just assumed he could be dangerous, because he was a little off, had a penchant for looking through garbage cans and Dumpsters, and smelled of BO and beer, but not as if he had been drinking, just as if he had been sleeping in a bar or on a subway.

"Wow," Ryan said. "Thank you. Good to see you, too."

"What?"

Ryan removed his headphones. She could hear the sound of water splashing over stones. Tommy was listening to relaxation tapes?

"I said it's good to see you, too."

"Thank you. It's good to see you, too."

Okay, that had been established, but she didn't really have time for small talk. "Tommy, do you know a bartender named Jimmy who works days around here?"

"Did you ever find out who killed Declan?"

"Ah, no, police are still working on it."

"Will they ever find out?"

"I certainly hope so. Tommy, do you know of any bartenders named Jimmy?"

"Jimmy?"

"Yeah. Works the day shift."

"Why? Did he have anything to do with Declan's murder?"

"No, it's nothing like that."

"What is it, then?"

"I'm afraid I can't discuss it. You know, police stuff."

"Yeah?" He laughed, then smiled and sang, "'Fuck the po-lice. Fuck the police.'"

Great. Thanks again, rap music. "Tommy, it's really important that I find him…can you help me out?"

Tommy put his head down and swayed from side to side, shuffling his weight from one untied New Balance to the other.

"There's a Jimmy that works at The Celtic Cross up the street. Jimmy Coughlin."

"Is he working today?"

"Should be. He usually works Mondays."

"Thank you, Tommy. You're an angel. Take care of yourself, and say 'hi' to Sheila for me."

His face suddenly turned ashen. "Tommy? Are you okay?"

He shook his head.

"What is it? Is it Sheila?"

He nodded.

"Is she okay?"

"She got a boyfriend. They moved back to Ireland."

"Oh, I'm sorry to hear that—I mean, I'm happy for her, but I'm sad for you. You must miss her."

He nodded.

"Is there someone else at The Comfy who takes care of you now?"

"It's not the same without Sheila."

"Well, if she's happy, I guess we should be happy for her, too, right?"

He didn't agree. He put his headphones back on and started ambling down the avenue, singing "Fuck The Police," and gathering stares from old ladies while Ryan headed back to her Jeep.

Chapter 63

The Celtic Cross was only two blocks away but Ryan wasn't walking in her condition. Obi-Wan had warned her that if she remained uncomfortable on her feet for long periods of time, she would have to be put on strict bed rest. She told him that wasn't an option, as she lived alone and would soon be taking in her father as well. He advised her to keep the long distance walking to a minimum, in case her sciatica acted up. The back pain wasn't so bad when she drove, as she could adjust the steering column into a position that would allow her gut to slide safely under the wheel, and the seat reclined enough for her back to receive proper lumbar support.

Faced with the choice of parking at a fire hydrant or another handicapped space, she opted for the handicapped space. This shouldn't take long, anyway, she thought, picturing herself grabbing Durk by the elbow and leading him out of the bar, the way she had witnessed so many mothers and wives over the years pulling their husbands and children out of the pubs by the elbow, the ear, or the hair on their head.

Her own father once came to drag her out of McSwillagins on McLean Avenue back when she was a freshman in high school. She and Karen had gone down to a shop in Times Square and purchased fake college student IDs that said they went to Fordham University and that they were nineteen years old, the legal drinking age at the time.

On the way home, they stopped off at a few pubs to see if the IDs worked and were surprised to find that they did, despite the fact they were each wearing the same shirts they had on in their new photo ID. The following night they put on a little too much make-up and perfume, walked into McSwillagins, and drank vodka and orange juice until her father waltzed in the door and took her out. One of the other patrons, she still hadn't found out whom, had recognized her and made an anonymous call to the house.

Her father calmly walked in the door, told the bartender, "If you ever serve these two girls again, your ass is grass," and silently followed the girls out, scowling back at the bartender over his shoulder. It was the only time she remembered being grounded by her parents, and the only time she ever set foot in McSwilligans.

She shook off the trip down memory lane as she swung open the heavy wooden door and let in an obtrusive burst of daylight. A shadowy figure at the bar moaned displeasure. As the door slowly shut her vision adjusted and she could make out three men drinking alone. There wasn't a bartender in sight but there was a Shane McGowan look-alike circa 1989 with greasy hair and a ratty goatee defiantly smoking a cigarette wedged between browned picket-fence teeth, despite the ban, in the near corner of the bar. Beside him was a man in adidas sweatpants, Timberland boots and a baseball cap feeding bills into the flashing CD jukebox that was blasting Van Morrison's "Moondance." The McGowan doppelganger turned and glanced at her belly with a look of disgust. "Jaysus, will you ever stop?" he said in a thick, Northern Irish brogue.

She ignored him, walking passed a second, older man, whose head was down on the bar, before a full stein of draft beer and an empty shot glass. A third man in an Irish cap and white tee shirt had his back to the door in the far corner of the bar, looking up at a television that was tuned to the game show *Who Wants To Be A Millionaire?* Seemed like something Durk would do. He certainly wouldn't converse with the others. It wasn't like him to mingle or make small talk, especially when most of it would be indecipherable.

"Let's go," she said.

He kept his back to her, engrossed in the $64,000 question.

She found herself looking up at the screen, thinking that Meredith Vieira wasn't bad looking for a mother her age. Maybe she could age as gracefully. Legs were never her strong point, but Meredith's were pretty nice. Then she noticed the question.

Who was the lead guitarist for The Rolling Stones after the death of Brian Jones and before Ron Wood joined the band:
A. Mick Ronson
B. Jeff Beck
C. Lyndsey Buckingham
D. Mick Taylor

Surprisingly, Ryan knew the answer, remembering her older brothers arguing with friends that Mick Taylor was the best guitarist the Stones ever had.

"It's not Lyndsey Buckingham," the contestant said, a nerdy man about her age in dark glasses and a crisp blazer over a black satin shirt. "He was in Fleetwood Mac. I know that. I think it's one of the Micks but I'm not sure. They both sound familiar, but…could be Jeff Beck, too. I know he was in The Yardbirds but he also played with some other groups. He played with Rod Stewart, but so did Ron Wood…am I mixing them up?"

"It's D, Mick Taylor," Ryan said.

"I'm going to use my fifty/fifty," the contestant said.

Dumb ass, Ryan thought, hanging her head. She wasn't a frequent watcher, but whenever she did tune in, it seemed that if a contestant talked out the possible answers using the process of elimination that the "computerized" response was always to give them the fifty/fifty choice that didn't help them one iota. She looked back up at the screen to see:

Who among the following was the lead guitarist for The Rolling Stones after the death of Brian Jones and before Ron Wood joined the band:
A. Mick Ronson
D. Mick Taylor

"It's Mick Taylor," Ryan repeated.

"Mick Ronson played with Bowie," Shane McGowan shouted from the corner.

"Right," Ryan said, leaning down. "Now, let's get the hell out of here." She tapped the shoulder before her. "Let's go!" she screamed.

The man turned to see who had tapped him. Ryan's mouth dropped open. Those green eyes and that intriguing smile.

"Eileen, what a surprise," he said. "What brings you *here*? At this hour of the day?"

Conor turned around fully in his seat and noticed that she was pregnant. She was too shocked to speak.

"Oh…ah, congratulations," Conor said, nervously rubbing his two-day stubble. "That's, ah, not mine, is it?"

She nearly grabbed the Amstel Light bottle from off the bar and smashed it over his head but thought better of it. She couldn't risk cutting open a vein in her wrist or slicing a finger. Instead, she just balled up her fist the way her brothers had taught her and punched him right in the nose. He barely flinched. Then she hit him with a left upper cut and a cross right to the side of the jaw that sent him off of his chair. That hurt—both of them. She felt the sting in her right index finger, thought it might be broken. *Great. There goes the trigger finger.*

Conor rubbed the side of his jaw.

"Ryan?" she heard Durk call out.

She whirled to see a disheveled figure exiting the men's room.

"What are you doing?"

"Yeah, what the fuck are you doing?" Conor asked.

She heard the quickened steps of someone coming up the stairs behind the bar and looked to see the bartender, carrying a bucket of ice, emerging from the trap door.

"What the fuck is goin' on here?" he asked, his skinny black punk rock tie askew and his white dress shirt stained with tomato sauce. She wondered why the bartender at The Celtic Cross had to dress up in vintage attire but figured that, if he didn't, he'd be confused for one of the clientele.

"Ah, you missed it, Jimmy," Shane McGowan said. "The lass with the bump here is after punching Conor's lights out."

"Put that fuckin' cigarette out, you," Jimmy said. "Take it outside, all of you. This is all I fuckin' need on a Monday morning. C'mon, get out. The whole lot of you cunts, out, now!"

"Relax, Jimmy," Durk said.

"You relax. Get out! Now! And don't you fuckin' wake Liam, for Chrissakes, whatever you do."

Ryan looked at the man face down asleep on the bar, his curly black hair resting on sunburned arms. She'd been there before, when she was young and stupid and drinking kamikaze shots with varsity football players after winning a big game against a high school rival. What seemed like fun then just struck her as really sad now. That was someone's son, maybe a husband and a father. And it was twelve-thirty on a Monday afternoon.

"C'mon, Durk," she said.

Shane McGowan opened the door but the sunlight didn't bother Liam, who remained sleeping. The Cranberries' "Linger" faded out and the eerie opening strains of The Moody Blues' "Tuesday Afternoon" drifted out of the jukebox's speakers. *Should've called that one "Monday Afternoon,"* Ryan thought.

"See you tomorrow, Jimmy," McGowan shouted back as he held the door open for them.

"Fuck off," Jimmy shouted back.

Then again, maybe "Tuesday Afternoon" is scarier.

McGowan tossed his cigarette butt out into the gutter and made a U-turn into Gilligan's Aisle. Conor looked at Ryan and Durk, who was swaying from the booze, and decided they must be a couple, so he followed McGowan's lead, while the guy in the adidas sweats and Timberlands pulled the baseball cap tight over his eyes and shuffled slowly behind, a cell phone to his face.

Durk had a pained expression on his face. "What did you ask me?"

"Do you have a cassette player in your car?" Ryan said,

getting back to the heart of the matter, as if nothing else had transpired since their last conversation.

"Yeah," Durk said, taking what appeared to be a sip from an invisible or imaginary glass.

Retirement just wasn't the right option for some people. Unfortunately, Durk was one of them.

Chapter 64

Durk, I don't care what you do with your life but you can't do that," she said to him as they walked toward the Jeep.

"Call me crazy, but I don't think that's true."

He had a drunken smile on his face, which was reddened by either the sun, the wind, high blood pressure, or some combination. Another of the Irish curses, the pale skin that blistered at the mere hint of sunshine. Durk couldn't occupy the window seat of a pub or a car without getting third degree burns.

"No, Durk, you can't. You've got a daughter to take care of."

"I meant the part that you don't care."

"Well, you're right. I do care. You can't be a lush or a deadbeat dad."

"How'd you find me?"

"I'm a detective, remember?"

"Yeah. Damn good one, too."

"Ran into Slats."

"Ah. Woodlawn's Deep Throat."

"Poor guy's crushed over his favorite waitress leaving him."

"I can sympathize with that."

"If your wife ever heard you refer to her as a waitress—"

"Ex-wife," Durk corrected her, as he tried to light half a cigar with a Zippo. "And she was a waitress when I met her."

"Throw that disgusting thing out," she said, snatching the cigar from his mouth.

"Hey! That's a Cuban."

"Looks like something you plop in a toilet, not your mouth."

She tossed it into the gutter.

"Littering is illegal, Ryan."

"So are Cuban cigars. Where's your car?"

"I don't know."

"What do you mean 'you don't know'?"

"I ditched it last night."

"You've been out since last night?"

Durk raised his eyebrows at her and hiccupped. "As if you've never pulled an all-nighter."

"Ah, Durk, come on. You're too old for this. Acting like you're eighteen isn't going to bring Lisa back."

"I don't want Lisa back."

"No? You'd rather trawl the bowels of The Bronx after hours?"

"I gotta say, you meet some interesting people in Woodlawn between closing time and the opening bell."

"Yeah? Like who? Slats? Father McLanahan? Bartenders?"

"You're batting a thousand."

"The Five O'Clock Club?"

"I don't know what that means."

"A bunch of guys drinking, drugging, playing cards, screwing around on their wives with some underage coke sluts."

"Yeah, that's what happens between four a.m. and noon, unless you're in Vegas, where it happens 'round the cock."

She knew he meant clock and that he was just drunken slurring but she wasn't going to call his attention to it. He was remarkably coherent for someone who was out drinking all night. She just shook her head in disgust and got into her Jeep. Durk walked around to the passenger side and climbed in.

"You've been on the job, Ryan. Whaddya expect at that hour? Hopscotch and lemonade?"

"I just expect more from you, Durk."

"Spare me the guilt trip."

"What about your daughter?"

"My daughter's twenty. She's an adult. No longer my responsibility."

"Oh, bullshit, Durk. She may be more mature than you but she's still your responsibility. Some example you set. Living out of your car and you can't even find it."

"Ignorance is bliss."

"Yeah? And where's the ignoramus sleeping tonight?"

Durk shrugged. The weight of his shoulders crashing down nearly knocked him out cold.

"Durk! Stay awake!" She pressed on the gas and merged into traffic without signaling.

"You know you were parked in a handicapped spot, right?" Durk asked.

"I'm pregnant and you're drunk. We *are* handicapped."

"I noticed you didn't signal, either."

"I noticed you're not wearing your wedding ring."

"I'm not married anymore."

"Until that divorce if finalized, technically, you are."

"Whatever."

"That's exactly how I feel about my illegal lane change. Whatever."

She got on the northbound Major Deegan.

"Where the fuck are we going? Can we at least pick up something to drink for the ride?"

"You're done drinking."

"I'm not the pregnant one, I can drink whatever I want."

"Not around me and my baby you can't."

"Fine, then drop me off at the deli."

"We need to find your car."

"Why? I can't drive it anyway."

"'Cause you need someplace to sleep it off. And you need to hear this tape."

"What tape?"

"This cassette that Hickey's wife gave you."

"Oh."

"You didn't listen to it?"

"No."

"Come on. Really?"

"I swear."

"Durk, a dead cop's widow hands over a cassette, and you don't listen to it?"

"Ryan, she said to give it to you. I had a bunch of white shirts up my ass, drawing up citations for everyone in the house, and Keegan shows up wanting to talk shop. I figure nothing good is gonna come out of this thing, let me just blow the fuckin' joint up right now. I told Keegan to give the tape to you, told the white shirts to stick it up their ass, and walked out. I'm officially off the fuckin' job."

"So, this is nothing more than work to you?" she said, flailing the cassette in his face with her right hand while she steered with her left.

"Two hands on the wheel, please."

Ryan slammed on the brakes and brought the Jeep to a dead stop in the right lane. Durk nervously looked over his shoulder at the honking traffic that swerved to avoid them.

"Ryan, what the fuck are you doing?"

"Goddamn it, Durk! Don't you fuckin' get it?" Ryan started crying. "Someone tried to kill me! My best friend is dead! I broke my finger punching that leprechaun in the face, and I think I'm in love with you, you fuckin' idiot!"

She's drunk, Durk thought. *No, wait, I'm drunk. Even so, if we don't get moving out of this lane, we're going to die.* "Okay, Ryan, I get it!" he yelled. "Now can you please step on the gas and get off the fuckin' highway before you get us all killed!"

Chapter 65

She'd given up trying to find Durk's car, in part because he couldn't remember where he started drinking and when he started taking cabs. Could've been at the east end of McLean Avenue at Fibber McGlone's, Ronnie Dingle's, or The Water's Edge, or maybe it was on the west end at Paddy Doyle's, McQuade's, or Minion's. It was somewhere along McLean Avenue, and he was definitely walking—or at least doing some semblance of walking—by the time he embarked on the Katonah Avenue pub crawl. The cabs were getting expensive and he reasoned he needed the exercise if he were going to be putting himself back out there in that pathetic over-forty dating scene.

Before bringing him back to her house—which she really didn't want to do because she didn't want her neighbors to see her in her condition bringing home Durk in his condition on a Monday afternoon; gossip was still the number one recreational sport in Woodlawn and this would be fodder for the Hall of Fame—she tried finding a cassette player at the Goodwill store in Yonkers but was shit out of luck. *You know something is a dinosaur when the Goodwill store no longer carries it.* There wasn't even a broken one. There were broken MP3 players and a portable Coby CD player, even a stereo unit with a turntable but no cassette players. People were still nostalgic for vinyl, cassettes not so much. Fast-forwarding and rewinding and flipping over a cassette to find the beginning of the one song you liked buried on side B amounted to a level of aggravation for which no one yearned, except apparently for this douche-bag Hickey, God rest his soul.

Of course, she didn't really mean what she said to Durk, not that he believed her anyway. What she meant was that he was her best friend now, and without Karen to confide in, Durk was going to be the one she went to with all her fears and secrets and feelings. She needed a peer, someone close in age who understood her, the neighborhood, her profession, and parenting. It wasn't like she ever found him attractive. He had tired, sunken eyes with dark, sleep deprived bags under them, and high cheekbones with sallow cheeks and fading freck-les...or was it melanoma?...dotting the pasty white skin of his forearms.

From the neck up, he resembled an Irish cadaver, or one of those grainy black and white still photographs from those PBS specials on *The Famine*. His skin was weathered from too many hours spent at outdoor ballgames and keg parties without a hat in his youth and too many hours in the window seat of the pub as an adult. He wasn't fat, but the eight-pack abs that had graduated in recent years to twelve-pack status now hung over the belt. So, he wouldn't be gracing the cover of *Playgirl* anytime soon. But he was smart. And she knew that he was kind. The fact that he had a penis and nowhere to put it any-more—and she could accommodate that need and wanted the occasional penis to fill her needs—just complicated the matter. Did she really want to wake up to that? she wondered, as she saw him poking through her refrigerator.

"What the hell do you eat?" he called out. "Don't you have any frozen pizzas or burritos?"

"No."

"It's all yogurt and wheat germ and shit."

"Yeah, I eat a lot of shit. I think there's some pretzels on the counter."

"No booze?"

"No. Doesn't agree with the baby."

"That kid ain't Irish. Or German, Russian, or Lithuanian."

"Can you just grab some water and listen to the tape, please?"

Durk poured a glass of water from the sink, stuffed a few pretzels in his mouth and sat on the recliner. She pressed play on the cassette and left to pee. On her way back from the bathroom she stopped in the hallway to listen to Hickey's voice.

"...I found some things at the scene of Declan McManus's murder that may be of interest to many people, especially you. Of the hair samples I've collected, the only match in the database was yours. Your fingerprints were also at the scene, on a beer bottle and on the wall. There was another set of fingerprints that matched samples collected in our database that belong to an unknown male. These prints were also found at two other locations within the last sixteen months where crimes were committed, one in the men's bathroom of a bar on the Lower East Side of Manhattan, where a woman was raped and assaulted at approximately five-fifteen in the morning, and the other took place in Prospect Park in Brooklyn—"

"That's the key, Durk!" she said excitedly, hurrying into the living room to hit pause on the cassette player. She looked down at Durk, who was asleep in the recliner.

Bag of shit. That was what cops called the guys who hung around the streets of The Bronx doing just enough to get by. "Getting by" meant having enough money to buy booze and drugs and take a lady out dancing and get her pregnant. Most of them hadn't finished school, collected unemployment, worked off the books if they worked at all, came from broken homes, and liked to get high and play Lotto in the hopes of forgetting about all those things, or at least to afford better booze and drugs. For the most part, they were harmless. Part of the scenery. They may have been hit with a couple C summonses here and there, for an open container, littering, graffiti, or loitering, or a B summons for using a cell phone while driving or running a red light. Maybe even possession of a small amount of weed. But they weren't shooting one another and they weren't in gangs. In order words, they were just like the guys hanging in the bars along Katonah and McLean Avenue, getting high and getting by. The only difference was booze was the drug of choice in Woodlawn, whereas marijuana was in the other neighborhoods, in part because it was a cheaper and more immediate high with little or no hangover. For a couple dollars a couple puffs in a couple seconds changed your worldview. It was a little more expensive and time consuming with alcohol and the hangovers were severe. Ironically, one of the alleged cures for a hangover was a couple puffs of marijuana and the vicious cycle was set in motion again. Of course, Ryan didn't think they were bags of shit any more than she thought Durk was, but it had become somewhat of a habit amongst her peers to call one another a bag of shit at these moments, when in need of a friend. To the patrol officers whom the white shirts harped on to boost their numbers, it meant bringing in a bag of shit and then finding a crime to pin on them. Everyone was guilty of something. Ryan was pretty confident she could bring any random person in off a Bronx street and find a crime to charge them with: tax evasion, jaywalking, littering, loitering, gambling, expired license, possession of weed or weapon, failure to recycle, whatever. Who amongst us wasn't a bag of shit?

She thought about kicking Durk to wake him when her cell phone rang, a call from a name and number she didn't recognize. Which bag of shit could this be?

"Yeah?" she answered.

"I-neen?"

It took her a few seconds to realize whose garbled speech it was. "Dad?"

"I'm coming home," he said through his tears.

She felt her own tears coming on, choking her. A few drops squeezed out and rolled down her cheeks before she could find her voice. "That's great, Dad! When?"

"Now."

She knew this day was imminent but not *this* imminent. Now? As in, *today* now? "Are you sure?"

"Nyes."

She liked the way he pronounced yes. It sounded Russian, or some combination of both yes and no, kind of like how she would answer guys in bars who asked her if she'd like to go home with them when she had too much to drink. Part of her always did; another part of her knew she'd regret it. "No" meant "no," but "nyes" was a gray area. When she said *nyes*, the yes part usually won out.

"That's great. Can you put one of the administrators on, please?"

She was waiting for what seemed like an hour while she heard nurses and therapists yelling and patients calling out. *I don't ever want to be in one of those places. God, if ever I do have a stroke, please, make it a massive one. Just take me. I can't live at that speed. I have absolutely zero tolerance and patience for institutions.* She kicked Durk's feet, which were dangling off the recliner, but he didn't move.

"Bag of shit," she said.

"Hello?" a familiar voice finally said.

"Hi, this is Eileen Ryan. My dad thinks he's coming home today?"

"Yes, he's met all his goals," Katherine with a K said.

That's how Ryan remembered the administrator at Browne Rehabilitation. She introduced herself that way to everyone. "Hi, I'm Katherine, with a K."

Wasn't that weird? *Who does that?*

"Oh."

"You don't sound impressed," Katherine with a K said.

"Oh, I am. Believe me, I am. There was a point when I didn't think this day would ever come. It's just that, I didn't think it would be today. Nobody called me."

"We thought you'd like to hear it directly from your dad."

"Normally, I love surprises," Ryan said, trying not to sound too sarcastic, as she caught a glimpse of her protruding belly in the living room mirror, and Durk passed out in the recliner while the voice of a dead forensics inspector warning that her life was in danger was paused on her vintage Lloyds stereo. "But I don't know if I'm prepared for this. I almost didn't answer this call. I didn't recognize the number."

"It's my cell. Call anytime. But, I'm sure you'll do fine," Katherine with a K said. "He's really eager to come home."

"I bet he is," Ryan said.

"When can we expect you?"

"Oh…ah, would it be possible for you to send him home?"

That must've sounded harsh, because Katherine with a K didn't reply. An awkward moment of silence hung in the air for what seemed like enough time to fill a cavity in a molar.

"In an ambulette, or something," Ryan clarified. "I'm six months pregnant, so I really can't be pushing a wheelchair around."

"Oh. Is there anyone who could help you?" Katherine with a K said. "Because I don't think his insurance will pay for an ambulette."

Usually, she'd appreciate Katherine with a K taking into consideration an unnecessary expense, but this was one instance where she felt the old man could spend a couple dollars on himself. After all, he'd gotten off pretty easy with his wife's death. She went suddenly, on the sidewalk. No doctors' or hospital fees, no copayments, nothing; just the funeral and burial expenses, which they had the foresight to prepay in a trust that actually accrued interest. Even the flowers were covered.

"A sibling, or a friend..." Katherine with a K said.

This one's a tightwad, Ryan thought. "...or a bag of shit?" she imagined Katherine with a K saying.

"I got nothing," Ryan said. "Put him in an ambulette. I'll pay for it."

"I'll see what we can arrange."

Katherine with a K put her on hold, and Ryan tried to rouse Durk from his stupor. Kicks and smacks did nothing but send gobs of saliva spewing from his mouth. She put a vase of fresh cut flowers under his nose to no effect. Then she dumped some water from the vase onto his face. Still no response. Bag of shit was out cold.

"We can get a driver at four-thirty," Katherine with a K said.

"That's great," Ryan said. "Thank you."

"You're welcome. That'll be two hundred and thirty-five dollars."

"That's fine," Ryan said.

"And your address is still 1155 Johnson Avenue?"

"No, it's not," Ryan said. *Thank you, Katherine with a K.*

"I've moved into my father's house, so I could take care of him."

"That's sweet," Katherine with a K said.

But not entirely true. Big part of the reason was because, "My best friend was murdered at 1155 Johnson Avenue!" she wanted to yell at Katherine with a K but she managed to restrain herself.

"Is he still at 1212 East 238th Street?" Katherine with a K asked.

"Yes."

"Great, thank you. And good luck."

Ryan hung up and looked at Durk.

"You got three hours to wake up, listen to this tape, and get the fuck out of here, got it?"

This is what marriage must be like, she thought, as she climbed into the recliner opposite him and kicked her feet back. The house was relatively clean and clutter free since she had been nesting for her baby's arrival. She wasn't expecting her father to be delivered before her baby but she was learning to expect the unexpected while she was expecting. A dog-eared copy of *What To Expect When You're Expecting*, another Goodwill find, lay on the coffee table. The book, like life itself, could be summed up in three words: *expect the unexpected*. A big sigh escaped as she leaned back in the chair. She was going to need a power nap if she were going to be taking care of all these handicapped men for the foreseeable future.

Chapter 66

The buzzing of the doorbell woke her but not Durk.
"Shit!" she yelled, slamming down the footrest. "Durk!
Get up!"

He didn't budge. She walked over to his recliner, thought of dumping him out of it before realizing a) she wasn't capable of lifting the chair with him in it, and b) she was six months pregnant and incapable of hoisting much more than a spoonful of Haagen-Dazs to her mouth. Then she noticed the depressed pause button on the cassette player. She pressed stop and eject, removed the cassette, and stuck it in Durk's shirt pocket, then grabbed him by his ears and yanked him forward. He awoke with a start.

"What the fuck?" he said, rubbing his head. "What happened?"

"You're shitfaced. You gotta get out of here. Listen to the tape in your pocket when you get a chance."

Durk was groggy, hungover. It felt like a jackhammer was digging into the base of his skull and blood was gushing from his brain like a BP oil rig. He clutched the tape in his shirt pocket and looked up at her, trying to piece together the events that led to this moment. *Was I dreaming or did she say that she loved me?*

"You made me a mixtape?" he asked.

The doorbell buzzed again.

"No, asshole, Hickey made me that tape. You need to listen to it so we can find a killer."

His mouth was so chalky it hurt to form words. "Water?" he managed to say.

"Hold on. You need to help me get my father settled in."

"What?"

"That's my father at the door."

"Didn't he have a stroke?"

"He's back."

"Well, then…" Durk said. *I guess there goes the idea of me crashing here.* "You better let him in."

Ryan checked herself in the mirror, not so much as to impress her father, who could care less what she looked like, but to make sure that he didn't think she and Durk were fooling around. *Of course, he must know by now that I'm sexually active, right? I mean, I am six months pregnant. And he never was much of a believer in the Immaculate Conception.*

When she opened the door, two burly black guys in blue jumpsuits stood before her. The name Browne was embroidered in white script letters across their hearts. People could easily mistake them for having the last name Browne, not being employed by Browne Rehabilitation Center. She'd be skeptical, if not for the fact that she could see the wheelchair behind them.

"Eileen Ryan?" the one wearing the red do-rag said.

"That's me," she answered.

"Sign here," the one in the sideways Yankees cap said, handing her a clipboard.

This was business as usual to these guys, she thought, like delivering a mattress or a sofa.

"Not until I inspect the merchandise," she said.

They stepped aside, revealing a pale, gaunt version of her father. *Who shrank Del Ryan?* He must've lost twenty pounds. Oh, well. She had gained twenty-four so it almost equaled out.

"Daddy!" she called, throwing her arms around his neck. The tears immediately began flowing—his and hers. She noticed the Browne brothers impatiently fidgeting. "Let's get you inside," she said.

She tried to lift the chair over the one big step into the house but deferred to the Browne brothers. Each one grabbed a handle and lifted him into the hallway, the same as if they were hoisting a keg of beer.

"You shouldn't be doing any heavy lifting," the Browne in the do-rag said. "Not in your condition."

"I know…it's, just…I thought I'd make an exception for this occasion," Ryan said.

Since she hadn't married and no one carried her over the threshold on her wedding night, then the least she could do was carry her father into the house on his return from purgatory.

"No exceptions, or you'll wind up in a chair, just like him," the do-rag said.

"Thank you," she said, taking the clipboard from one of them and signing the paperwork.

"That's two-hundred thirty-five dollars," the Browne in the Yankees cap said.

"Check okay?"

"Check's fine."

She went into the bedroom to fetch her checkbook, leaving her father staring at Durk, who smiled and waved at him.

"How's it goin' Mr. Ryan?" Durk said.

Del looked a bit confused, yet relieved to be anywhere other than in an institution.

"I'm on the job with Eileen," Durk yelled much too loud. Ryan could hear him from the bedroom. *He had a stroke he's not deaf, you drunkin' idiot*, she thought.

She returned with a check and forty dollars in cash as a tip. The Browne brothers thanked her profusely and wished her good luck with the baby and her father, while each one dropped a plastic shopping bag of Del's belongings on the ground. Assorted shirts, sox, and underwear spilled onto the floor.

I probably should've taken over some luggage, Ryan thought, *or a hamper. Damn, there's going to be a lot of laundry to do in this house once the baby comes along. I'll all for going green but since now I'll be washing my father's drawers, there's definitely, absolutely, without a doubt, no friggin' way I'm doing cloth diapers. Sorry, Mother Earth, but with two more asses to wipe, in addition to my own, this mother will be contributing lots of plastic diapers to landfills without a shred of guilt.*

Her father looked down at his belongings and around the newly decorated room and then up at Durk with a pained expression that seemed to ask, *Am I in the right house?*

"Daddy, this is Barry Durkin. Do you remember the Durkins? From East 242nd Street? Barry's a lieutenant."

Her father just stared blankly at Durk and then back at Eileen.

"Do you like the way I rearranged the furniture?"

He looked troubled.

"I thought this would be easier for you to navigate in the wheelchair."

No response. Blank, empty stare.

Shit, Ryan thought. *He's vapor locked. Did he have another stroke?*

"Dad? Are you okay?"

He grabbed the sides of his chair and pushed himself forward a bit before stopping again and looking around, as if trying to get his bearings.

He does know he's home, right?

"Dad? You okay?"

"I—have—to—go—to the—baffroom," he finally said.

Ryan grabbed hold of the handles of the chair and pushed him at a quick clip down the hallway past the kitchen toward the bathroom. Her initial attempt to get the chair over the inch high saddle was unsuccessful. She had to back up the chair in the narrow hallway, which was no easy task in her condition, angle it slightly, and vigorously push until it had enough momentum to clear the lip.

He didn't make any mention of the newly installed grab bars if he noticed them at all but he instantly put them to use. *Does he think they were there the whole time, or does he really have to go that badly?*

With a flick of his chin, he motioned for her to leave him alone. Fine with her. She'd be cleaning up enough bodily fluids that weren't her own soon enough. She stood outside listening and, once satisfied that he was okay, she returned to the kitchen to find Durk holding open the refrigerator door, his head cocked back, draining a Vitamin Water.

When he saw her, he stopped, bringing the bottle down from his mouth and wiping some errant drops from his chin. "Do you mind?" he asked.

"Not at all. You need it more than me."

"You got any Alka-Seltzer?"

"It's in the bathroom."

He started toward the bathroom and heard the strains of her father.

"Oh, ah, I'll just get some at the store, thanks."

"You're gonna leave?"

"Yeah, I should get going...I, ah...gotta pick up my daughter, I think...what day is today?"

"It's still Monday."

"Right."

"You don't have to pick up your daughter, do you?"

"No."

"But you're still going to leave, aren't you?"

"This isn't a good time, Ryan. You got a lot of shit going on and I got a lot of shit going on, and—"

"Just go."

"Call me if you need anything."

"Listen to the tape, if you can find your car."

He patted his shirt pocket.

She watched him through the window, squinting as he met the harsh sunlight. *A drunk should never be without sunglasses or a hat*, she thought. She had the sickening feeling in her gut that he wasn't going to find his car, that he would give up looking once he hit Katonah Avenue, and duck into the first dark bar he stumbled across. *Been there, done that.*

Vitamin Water was good, but it was no match for a little hair of the dog. Watching him in that condition convinced her that she wouldn't do that to herself or her child ever again. Goodbye, booze; goodbye, Vitamin Water; goodbye, Alka-Seltzer; goodbye, Vitamin Seltzer or Alka-Water; goodbye, Durk.

Chapter 67

Durk turned onto Katonah, bought a bottle of Pedialyte in a bodega, and chugged it while he looked over the box scores in *The Post*. He had watched the previous night's Yankees game in its entirety, yet had no recollection whatsoever who won, what the score was, or who pitched. There was a period of almost twenty years or so when all Yankees games had just blurred into one, and he could safely assume that Bernie Williams or a member of the Core Four—Derek Jeter, Mariano Rivera, Jorge Posada and Andy Pettitte—had somehow figured into its outcome and he'd be right, but now that they had all retired, it was a crapshoot. Getting old sucked. You needed to read reminders of what happened the day before.

He passed Gilligan's Aisle, saw too many people for his liking, and looked in the window of The Celtic Cross. Liam was now awake, sitting up in the middle of the bar with a fresh stein before him, and Jimmy was getting ready to end his shift. His tie was askew and his dark-rimmed glasses dangled at the tip of his nose while he counted out the register. He sensed Durk in the window and spun in his direction. With his arm outstretched, pointing toward McLean Avenue, he yelled, "Fuck off, Durk!"

Taken aback by the gesture, Durk quickly retreated and ambled across the street, to The Pot O'Gold. Two beers into nursing his hangover and watching the highlights of the previous night's Yankees game on the six o'clock news, it dawned on him that Declan McManus used to tend this bar. Whoever killed him may have sat on this very stool. Or maybe Ryan did. His head was foggy but he tried to piece together the events, based on what he knew about it. Ryan went out for a night on the town with her friend, probably on the prowl, maybe drank a little too much, flirted with some guys, ran into this hunk of an Irish bartender with sky blue eyes and the gift of the gab and the guy winds up dead. *Who's the culprit and what's the motive? Jilted wife? No, she's back in Ireland. Girlfriend? Ex-girlfriend? Another bartender? Boyfriend of another girl he hit on?*

In all his days on the job, he'd found that there were two kinds of murders. The premeditated, professional mob-style knock offs, and the spur of the moment crimes of passion fueled by jealousy, rage, alcohol or drugs, or some combination. Durk wondered if he'd always think like a cop. Did anyone ever really retire from this job? He swigged his Bass and looked up at the television. The previous news items didn't interest him—the robberies in midtown, the arson in Queens, the mother of four on the Island charged with DWI while driving her kids to school at eight o'clock in the morning. It was all background noise until the sports segment came on. Pieces of the game began coming back to him. CC Sabathia pitched. ARod struck out twice and stranded six runners. Ellsbury got injured. Some things you could still count on.

During one of the replays, when Teixeira fouled a pitch off his shin, Durk could see a police officer standing behind the backstop. A woman. She reminded him of Ryan. He remembered bumping into Ryan when she was patrolling the area around the Stadium. Damn, she was cute. He usually didn't go in for bottle blondes but Ryan wore it well. And she had that sparkle in her eyes, those dirty girl eyes. Like she would be hot in bed. Did Ryan really say she loved him? Did she mean it? He pushed away his pint glass and left five bucks on the bar.

He found himself standing in the alleyway of The Pot O'Gold, imagining how it went down. He pictured Slats, poor Slats, taking out the garbage and finding his friend or acquaintance or co-worker or whatever he considered him—

someone who talked to him cordially at least—with a broken bottle in his neck. Then he had a crazy thought. What if Ryan stuck him with the bottle? The rumors around the precinct were that the guy was nailing everyone he could, including Ryan. She was a tough broad with an Irish temper. What if McManus put the moves on her, promised her the world, and then she stumbled upon him with another woman? Or...what if Ryan were carrying his kid and he had no intention of providing for it?

Durk trudged up Katonah Avenue in search of his car, by-passing the other five bars, two pubs, and one tavern, four of which he had stopped into the previous night. Every single one of them had customers, at six-thirty on a Monday evening. There weren't many jobs being created during the recession, but it sure seemed to be creating more drinkers. With no sign of his car, he continued onto McLean Avenue, toward Paddy Doyle's, where he remembered stopping into last night. But there were parking meters all along the avenue, and he wasn't stupid enough to park there, was he? Maybe he did what a lot of the drinkers did and parked it along Van Cortlandt Park, on the dark strip of road where Alvarez had shot Hickey.

"Hey, Lieutenant," he heard a voice call.

He spun to see Slats exiting The Comfy Corner, a take-out carton in his hand, ubiquitous headphones on his head.

"Tommy!" he said, stunned that he remembered his proper name. "Tommy, come here for a second."

"Oh, no. The last time I spoke to you, I was in trouble."

"You're not in trouble, but I need your help."

Slats shuffled his feet, looked down at the ground.

"I need to borrow your Walkman," Durk said.

Chapter 68

Ryan wheeled her father into the bathroom and stood by his side. Despite his inability to use the toilet himself, he continued to try. She didn't mind cleaning the seat and the floor, and she probably wouldn't mind cleaning a backside with a flushable wipe—as if such a thing really existed, those moist conveniences were gumming up sewer systems everywhere and costing millions of dollars in repairs—either, provided it belonged to her baby, not her father. This, however, she couldn't get used to, and neither could he, which was why there was no longer an aide coming to the house.

He could wipe his own ass, thank you very much, he struggled to tell the last one, a beautiful Jamaican woman who listened to pulsating reggae on her iPod while she cleaned. Truth of the matter was, he really couldn't, and it was the one thing that really bothered him. He prided himself on being independent and capable and instilled in all his kids a desire to be self-sufficient, mostly out of fear that none of them would ever get married and have a spouse to rely on. Now that his independence was gone, along with his spouse, he was trying his best not to be a burden on his daughter. He never wanted that. Even though he swore he'd never spend the last days of his life waiting to die in a nursing home, he was willing to do that if it meant his little girl could live a somewhat normal life without the worries of having to care for an invalid father. What he didn't realize was that Eileen needed his company now as much as he needed her care.

Ryan would watch her failing, stubborn father struggle all day with the menial tasks—talking, walking, eating, pissing, shitting, farting, burping—and wonder why the hell he bothered. He was never going to get well, was he? Some days were better than others, but he would never get the urge to get off his wheelchair, open the door, and walk up to Katonah Avenue to buy coffee and the newspaper again. This was it. His best days now consisted of him rolling out Play-Doh on a tray and squeezing the shit out of a therapy ball that she could tell he wanted to throw at someone's head if only he could. Whose head she wasn't so sure, though she imagined he'd want to play a little chin music on her whenever she insisted on feeding him strawberry smoothies or beef stew that she pureed in a blender with skim milk so he wouldn't have to chew. This was his treat now, a beef shake. In the evening, she would give him a sponge bath against his will, but there were certain things she just wouldn't allow. If she were going to live in his house again, he was not going to sit in his own shit at night. A woman had to lay down the law, even in her old man's house.

She wanted to take him out but the choices were limited. Now she had to take into consideration wheelchair accessibility. She couldn't believe how many of the restaurants around town were ill equipped to handle handicapped people. There were few if any ramps, narrow doorways, small tables that were too low to the ground or countertops that were too high. Just to go out and have a cup of coffee and a yogurt was a major hassle, and it had the exact opposite effect of what she desired. He wasn't happy to get out. He was angry that he was fucking handicapped. And she was angry that she was caring for her handicapped father, basically on her own, while she was now seven months pregnant. There was only one cure: a trip to the firing range.

The Coyne Park Rifle and Pistol Range on McLean Avenue in Yonkers, just a stone's throw from a passel of pubs, was a place where she had taken out her frustrations over the years. Everyone needed an outlet. Some liked to run, lift weights, play tennis, go bowling, or whack golf balls. She liked to shoot. Pulling on a pair of safety goggles and industrial

strength headphones, hand cranking the targets, and squeezing
the triggers of her Glock and LadySmith made her feel alive.
What a rush. She'd never tried heroin or crack, but she imagined this must be what it felt like if it kept people coming back
to it. Heart racing, blood pumping, head clear, eyes wide, en-
dorphins releasing and tingling her extremities. It was the clos-
est thing to orgasm she'd ever experienced. She could do it
alone and without the guilt of masturbation. *Thanks again,
Catholic Church.*

Now that her trigger finger was broken from punching
Conor in the face and in a soft cast, she couldn't shoot but her
dad could. None of the friendly staff remembered Del, but they
recognized her and appreciated the efforts she made to get him
down to the underground range. Gun enthusiasts were a wel-
coming bunch. They knew there was strength in numbers. The
more the mightier. It made their voice stronger and cemented
their right to bear arms. There were only seven lanes but the
aisles and attitudes were more accommodating than most of
the area's restaurants. There was an elevator from the hallway
entrance down into the cellar, where mostly off-duty cops, the
majority of them rookies, were partaking in target practice. A
few of the old timers were there, too, either to keep sharp or to
get away from their wives or because they didn't know what to
do now that they had retired and didn't like to fish or play golf
and the Yankees had a night game. None of them were in a
hurry. They were just milling about, shooting the shit along
with the occasional target, and graciously let Del go ahead and
pick a lane.

She wheeled Del up to a post, outfitted him with the requisite headgear and eyewear, cranked a target, and offered him a
choice of her LadySmith or Accu-Tek Model AT-32, which
weighed a super low sixteen ounces and was made of combat
rubber. She thought they would be easier and safer for him to
manage, but he was having none of that. He demanded that she
put his Smith & Wesson M&P in his good hand. He caressed
the nickel-plated handle for a while, as if ruminating on whom
to shoot first. Who was to blame for his condition? Why was
he in this situation and who should pay for it? When the

vengeful feelings subsided, he focused on the target before him.

He slowly lifted his good hand, bringing the gun up to his sightline, and slid his left hand into his lap, steadying his right elbow. He extended his right hand and squeezed the trigger. An immediate rush of adrenaline warmed his body. *God, that felt good.* It had been years since he shot a gun.

The last time was probably that hunting trip he took with a few old cop buddies, when he sat in a tree stand drinking warm cans of Schaeffer until he finally spotted a white tail and pumped it with a single shot from a Remington rifle. The recoil caused him to kick the cans and nearly fall out of the tree. There was no recoil with the Smith & Wesson M&P. This, he could manage.

Somehow, he felt like he had regained a piece of his manhood by proving that he was still capable of taking the life of another man, as evidenced by the bullet hole in the forehead of the character outline on the target. True, he had been aiming for the shoulder of the trigger hand, but a shot between the eyes would disarm the assailant just the same. It might kill him, too, but when it was a matter of self-defense, that would be considered collateral damage. If faced with kill or be killed, Del Ryan would kill every time. "Better to be judged by twelve than carried by six," as they used to say on the job. *Still got it,* he thought, raising his right hand and squeezing off five more rounds, peppering the target from the waist up to the face. *We may not all be able to play centerfield for the Yankees, but at least we can all pretend to be Charles Bronson once in a while.*

Mission accomplished, Ryan thought, seeing the joy in her father's face for the first time in years. She hadn't seen him smile like that since the Benny Hill and Morton Downey Jr. shows went off the air. He was exhausted, too. As much as a thrill as it was, it was tiring. He just wanted to shower and go to sleep.

Chapter 69

Durk had played the cassette over many times and had only come to the conclusion that Hickey was a little nuts. He knew the guy had some issues and that nobody on the force was particularly fond of him, but over a couple beers at a 9/11 memorial service, Durk had a long conversation with him because nobody else would. Hickey's heart was in the right place most of the time. Whatever shit they found in his locker, it was hardly incriminating. So, the guy had some hang-ups and fetishes but they were harmless. About the worst of it was the fact that Ryan was creeped out by him and rightfully so. Had Hickey been dusting down Durkin's car and hording lockets of his hair, maybe he'd feel a little different.

But Hickey was a good cop, took the job seriously, and did it well. He was very thorough in his investigations and often led detectives to consider alternative motives and suspects. He was up on all the new technologies and was innovative in putting them to use. In his spare time, he volunteered at area animal shelters and took the initiative to begin swabbing the mouths of abandoned pit bulls, starting a DNA database of abused dogs that eventually led to the arrests of thirteen people involved in an interstate dogfighting ring. Now that he was dead, the FBI would be taking all the credit, of course, but without Hickey that program never would've gotten off the ground.

So, as flaky as the guy seemed at times, there might be

something buried in that cassette, after all, but damned if Durk could find it.

Simultaneously watching highlights of baseball on the flat-screen television in the corner of The Pot O'Gold and reading the scrawl across the bottom of it detailing more baseball minutiae, Durk decided that he would refer to his drinking as "hitting" from now on, as in, "Durk is in the midst of an eleven-game hitting streak," or "Durk has now hit safely in twenty-seven of the past thirty games." Had a nice ring to it, sounded as if he were partaking in an active sport, rewarding skill and commitment. This way, he wouldn't feel guilty about being sedentary and pissing his life away. If life were indeed a game, then he would treat each day as if it were the championship, and he was going to hit like a fuckin' All-Star. He drained his glass of suds and motioned for another.

As Durk pored over old newspaper clippings he had downloaded from the Internet and printed at the library, he poured a Smithwick's into his pint glass. He had been coming to The Pot O'Gold regularly for the last month and liked the atmosphere. Crowds had kept away since Declan McManus had been murdered, and that was the way Durk liked it. He'd duck in for a couple pops late in the afternoon, sometimes staying well into the night, watching baseball games and reading over old cases, particularly the ones Hickey had outlined on the cassette. The voice haunted him, as if he were summoning a ghost at a séance. In the middle of the night, he'd bolt upright, sweating, hearing Hickey's eerie rasp.

'*These prints were also found at two other locations within the last sixteen months where crimes were committed, one in the men's bathroom of an after-hours joint on the Lower East Side of Manhattan, where a woman was assaulted and raped at approximately five-fifteen in the morning, and the other took place in Prospect Park in Brooklyn...*'

The assault and the rape occurred at The Stumble Inn, a speakeasy with no markings on a non-descript metal door on the street level in the alley of a fourth floor walk-up. Patrons would receive a text message by three-fifteen if it were going to be open. Durk had a hunch a police officer may have been involved, not only in the bar's operation but also in the crime. Foot patrol had been beefed up in that area years ago, and with Operation Prohibition launched in the Bloomberg/Kelly years, nobody was operating illegal after-hours joints unless palms were being greased. The victim in this case, a nineteen-year-old Columbia student, texted a group message to seven of her contacts at five-forty-five, telling them that she had been raped and assaulted and was bleeding while locked in the bathroom, but was afraid to call nine-one-one, fearing her assailant would kill her. The case sparked national media attention and was responsible for municipalities across the country allowing text messages to nine-one-one. New York City still wasn't equipped to handle that possibility, fearing that a million nuts a night would be texting nine-one-one because they were locked out of their apartments or couldn't find their cats.

Police hadn't arrived on the scene of the rape until after 7:15 a.m. Surely one of her contacts would've notified police immediately. The only reason for a delay of that length would be 1) the night shift didn't want to put in the OT, which was highly unlikely; 2) the owner of the speakeasy was paying off the police or was a member of the force; 3) the suspect was on the job and the vaunted blue shield allowed time to protect a member of the brotherhood. Or, 4) most likely, her friends were asleep at that hour and didn't call nine-one-one until they woke up.

Durk didn't hear the door open nor notice anyone enter the bar until Keegan sidled up next to him.

"'Sup, Durk?"

"Hey, Keegs, what brings you around?"

"Just looking for a quiet drink."

"Same here."

"This your local now?"

"I wouldn't say I'm a regular, but—" Durk shuffled some of the newspaper articles before him and motioned toward the flat-screen television that was now airing a soccer game from God knew where. "—good place to see a game."

"Who's playing?"

"Not sure."

"How long you been here?"

"Couple beers."

"What's this?" Keegan asked, grabbing some of the papers. "The Columbia student? They never solved this?"

"No."

"Prospect Park?" Keegan said, before ordering a Heineken and motioning to the young Irish bartender to back up Durk with another Smithwick's. "Why do you give a shit about a murder in Brooklyn? Didn't you retire, Durk?"

"Didn't you?"

"Yeah. I leave for Tampa next week."

Durk had been hearing about Keegan's Tampa plan for so long, he had come to the conclusion that the guy would never make it. There'd always be some excuse why he hadn't yet taken off, but he'd be sitting in Bronx bars till he was ninety, telling everyone within earshot that he was fed up with life and heading for the Sunshine State, to wither up and die without a care in the world.

"Let me ask you something, Keegs. Can you honestly say that you can read about unsolved murders and rapes and it doesn't bother you?"

"I put my time in, Durk. Saw more than I ever wanted to see on the job. I'm ready to leave it all behind."

Durk drained the last of his beer and the barkeep popped him a fresh one.

"It's on him," the bartender said.

"Thanks, Keegs," Durk said.

"No, thank you, Durk."

"For what?"

"For not being a dick of a boss."

"Thanks...I guess," Durk said. "How come I don't believe you?"

"What? You weren't a dick."

"I meant about leaving the job behind."

"Don't get me wrong. I'm haunted by a lot of things, and I still miss some parts of the job, but it's not like I'm leaving behind any unsolved cases."

They drank in silence, pretending to look at the soccer match.

"You ever listen to that cassette Hickey made?" Durk finally asked. "Honestly?"

"No."

"Let's take a ride."

Durk didn't wait for an answer. He left his beer and his money on the bar and walked toward the door, knowing that Keegan would follow him. This time his car was right in front of the bar where he had parked it. Durk got behind the wheel and Keegan sat in the passenger seat, shoving Taco Bell and White Castle wrappers to the ground, as they rolled down Katonah Avenue. When they got beyond the humming of the idling number thirty-four buses, they made a left onto Van Cortlandt Park East. Durk circled East 240th and East 241st until they had listened to the tape four times through without saying a word. Finally, Durk pulled over across from St. Sebastian's Church and hit eject.

Across the street, a figure emerged from the shadows of the side door of the rectory. Father McLanahan, with his Yankees cap pulled down tight over his square, black rimmed glasses, hands jammed into his Members Only windbreaker, was making his way toward McLean Avenue. They watched him walk toward the beckoning neon lights of the saloons, disappearing around the corner.

"He kinda looks like Joe Maddon, the Chicago Cubs manager who used to manage the Tampa Bay Devil Rays," Durk said.

"Thanks for that image," Keegan said, squinting at McLanahan. "I'm about to take a job working security for the Devil Rays and that's all I'm gonna think about when I see Maddon now."

Yeah, good luck with that, Durk thought.

"This guy looks a little more sinister," Keegan said. "Like a stalker out on the prowl, looking for a kill. You ever see those *Death Wish* movies? With Charles Bronson?"

"Of course."

"That's what this guy reminds me of."

Durk waved the cassette in front of Keegan's face. "What do you think?" he asked.

"I think Hickey was an asshole, a bit of a freak," Keegan said. "All caught up in his image, thought he was Don Johnson and Baretta and Mike Hammer and The Equalizer wrapped into one—"

"Yeah, but—"

Keegan sighed. "Honestly? I think I'd be worried right now if I were Ryan."

Durk pulled out his cell phone and scrolled for her number.

Chapter 70

Ryan was slicing pound cake in the kitchen when she thought she heard fists pounding on a door. She hurried to the bathroom and called out, "Dad? You okay?"

She opened the door and peaked behind the shower curtain, relieved to see Del holding the shower massage handle above his head, eyes closed with a smile on his face. Quietly backing out and closing the door behind her, she still heard the banging.

She looked out the small rectangular window of the front door but didn't see anyone. No one at the neighbors' doors across the street either. But there it was again. This time like a battering ram. She marched toward the back door to investigate when she heard her cell phone ringing. She hesitated, then ducked back into the kitchen, and grabbed her phone and the knife off the counter.

Pressing the talk button with her left thumb, she brought the phone to her ear and slid the curtain across the glass door with the knife.

"Hello?" she said.

She never saw the Timberland boot that smashed the window and shattered her nose.

Chapter 71

*W*hy did I bring the knife instead of a gun?

Ryan had never practiced stabbing anyone before but she had logged hundreds of hours shooting at targets. Now, the first time she really wanted to put a bullet in someone's head, she couldn't. She tried stabbing him in the heart but he was too quick and too strong.

He blocked her first attempt, which put a sizeable gash in his left palm and rained down blood on her white blouse, then squeezed her right wrist with such force the knife fell from her fingers.

As he pushed her toward the bedroom, she upset a side table, knocking a lamp and some unread books to the floor, and backed into the framed photographs on the wall. Pictures of her and Karen with varying lengths and volumes of hair crashed to the floor, along with snapshots of her brothers and sister frolicking in an upstate lake, and Christmas card photos of her nieces and nephews through the years. Landing on top of the debris, she grabbed a glass shard and aimed for his jugular but missed. She stuck another piece in his cheek but he was undeterred.

Fuck it, he thought. He'd just do it here. Her dumping him at the train station with nary a thought or a call and giving him a fake phone number had stirred a fury in him that he didn't know existed. It consumed his thoughts, drowned out the other voices in his head. Maybe because she was an authority figure, a cop, she made him feel powerless. But not anymore.

He always had the upper hand. Nobody slighted or jilted him. She was about to find that out his way.

Once he had her subdued beneath him, he reached into a pocket of his navy blue Adidas sweatpants with the white racing stripes and pulled out a roll of blue duct tape. Grabbing her hair, he lifted her head and wrapped the tape around her mouth to drown out her cries of "Stop it! Stop! Help! Help! Danny, please!"

The color of the tape matched her eyes, he thought, as they welled with tears. He tore her blood-covered blouse and pulled her stretchy paneled jeans down to her ankles, deftly deflecting her kicks with his Timberlands.

This is not going to happen, Ryan thought.

She balled her fists despite her broken trigger finger and punched repeatedly, so fueled with adrenaline she didn't even feel the pain. Rapidly flailing with both arms, as if struggling to swim through a riptide, she pummeled his face. She could feel the baby kicking and punching, too, like the mixed martial artist Conor McGregor defending his Ultimate Fighting Championship, but Danny Boy just wouldn't be deterred.

Chapter 72

All the physical therapy Del did with his right hand kept it powerful enough so that he could hoist himself from his chair onto the transfer bench in the shower by pulling on the grab bars. Once Ryan got the water temperature right and lathered up his hair, he'd give her a wave of his one good hand, indicating that he wanted her to leave, and she'd give him the hand-held shower massage. She'd leave him alone for a few minutes, let some decaf Earl Grey tea steep for both of them, and come back to finish the job.

He had pretty much lost all sense of time—what was the difference when it was mostly misery?—but knew he had been left alone a little too long when the hot water ran out. Eileen never let that happen. The water turned lukewarm, tepid, and finally, frigid. He attempted to call out to her to no avail. Maybe she was doing laundry in the basement or running the dishwasher, both of which would effectively drain the hot water and render his cries inaudible. He placed the shower massage over the faucet, turned off the water, and pulled down the towel from the shower rod, attempting to dry himself and ward off a chill. The sound of shattering glass startled him.

He heard a thud, followed by the unmistakable sound of flesh on flesh and bone crunching bone, along with some gasps and muffled cries. A piece of furniture hit the floor. More glass shattered. The mirror? A picture frame? He slid across the transfer bench and swung his feet over the side of the tub.

With his right foot he steadied his wheelchair against the

wall, then reached with his right hand for the grab bar next to the toilet and pulled his naked, dripping body onto the chair. He wheeled to the vanity, opened it, reached under the sink, and grabbed his shaving kit.

The Smith & Wesson Military and Police Model Ten four-inch K frame was right where he had placed it the day he retired from the police force. Hadn't been used since, as far as he knew. Not unless Eileen had gotten her hands on it. He couldn't hide anything in this house—extra cash, Christmas or birthday presents—without his wife or one of the kids finding it. His shaving kit was the only place none of them would think to look. He had made a point of always buying the boys their own electric razors and the girls those pink Lady Bics that stuck to the wall with suction cups. Now that the boys had kids of their own, this was probably a stupid place to hide a gun, down where they could find it, but they never came to visit anyway. He unlocked the safety and placed the gun in his lap, covering it with the towel.

Swiftly but gently he turned the handle and opened the door. He grabbed the pistol and steadied it. Nobody there. He attempted to roll out into the hallway but he needed a hearty spin of the wheel in order to get the chair over the saddle between the bathroom and the hall. The moaning was getting more desperate. Fuckin' saddle. Nearly every day he lived in this house he'd thought that someday he'd level off that doorway so nobody would trip over it. He never thought it'd be a matter of life or death.

His mother's voice echoed through his head. *'Why put off till tomorrow what you can do today?'* She was only referring to the homework he hadn't done, of course, so why the hell was he thinking about this now? Wasn't your whole life supposed to flash before your eyes at these moments, not one snippet from the hen-pecking mother of an adolescent boy? Placing the gun back in his lap, he grabbed tight on the steel rim of the wheel and pushed. It rolled into the door. Fuck. He backed it up again and wheeled. Not enough power to clear the inch-high saddle between the bathroom and the hallway. He backed the chair to the tub and took a deep breath, pushing off with his good leg and good hand. The momentum lurched him over the saddle, into the hallway, and against the wall. The gun slipped off of his lap, between his legs and tumbled onto the hardwood. He heard grunts and muffled screams coming from the living room and turned to look.

Eileen was on the ground with bruises on her face, her blouse in tatters, and jeans pulled down to her ankles. Duct tape was wrapped around her mouth. On top of her was a thrusting man, his white ass peaking over a pair of partially pulled down sweats. The kitchen knife was beside them, with blood on its point.

Del reached down for the gun but it was out of his grasp. He needed his tool, the grab stick. Without it he couldn't put on his shoes, pull up his sox or grab the box of oatmeal from on top of the fridge. He had spent three weeks of physical therapy at Browne Rehabilitation perfecting the use of the grab stick. Nobody had ever taught him how to pick up a gun with it but he was sure he could manage, if only he could reach it. He reached around, feeling the basket of the wheelchair but the stick eluded him. Backing up the chair, he banged into the wall with a thud, hoping it would jar the stick loose where he could reach it.

The man on top of Eileen turned to see what the noise was. He dismounted her, grabbed the knife, and pulled up his sweats. As he stood above her with the knife in his hand she began to squirm toward the kitchen. He placed the knife against her neck and she froze. Then he made a run for her father.

Ryan ripped the tape off of her mouth and screamed, "Danny, no!"

Danny Boy hesitated.

Ryan's father lurched forward, falling from his wheelchair onto the floor.

"No!" Ryan screamed. "Don't!"

Danny Boy pointed the knife at her and put a finger to his lips, demanding that she be silent. He intermittently pointed the knife at Eileen and spun around toward her father. Would he have to kill them both? Or could he make the old man's death look like an accident? He'd have to kill Ryan now, not that he wanted to. He just wanted her to love him. But she never did and there was no way she ever could now. He'd certainly go to jail. He'd have to kill them both.

Danny Boy stood above the old man, looking down at him.

"Leave him alone!" Ryan screamed.

Del wasn't moving. Maybe he had a heart attack. Perhaps he was already dead. Danny Boy crouched down to check for a pulse, keeping the knife pointed at the old man's neck.

Looking for life in the old man's eyes, he never saw the pistol in his right hand. His good hand. The old man squeezed the trigger the way he'd been squeezing that little blue therapy ball for the past six weeks. The first bullet pierced Danny Boy's testicles. The second one ripped through his heart. And the third one shattered his skull.

Eileen cried as blood and flesh splattered the walls and soaked the hardwood floors, then let out a wild scream.

Her father called out to her. "Ei-neen! Ei-neen!" he yelled.

Her face was buried in her hands. She could feel the baby inside her kicking; she thought she heard him crying, too. And why not? The poor thing wasn't even safe in the womb.

Chapter 73

There was a loud bang at the front door and then a second one that sent it flying off its hinges. Keegan rolled to the floor and popped up behind the radiator in the hallway, holding Durk's service revolver. Durk stood in the doorway in a three-point stance, clutching a .38, surveying the scene. Then he ran to Ryan's side to check on her.

"You okay?" he asked.

She nodded through her tears. Durk brushed them away and helped her to her feet. There were scratches on her face and wrists, and her arms looked like bruised fruit. There was blood on her belly but he couldn't tell whose. He placed a hand on her stomach and waited. He hadn't put his hand on a pregnant woman's stomach since his wife was expecting their daughter. *C'mon, kick,* he thought to himself. *Goddamnit, kick!* He felt a heave but realized it was just Ryan, crying. *C'mon, you little bastard, kick!*

Keegan helped Del Ryan back into his wheelchair and pushed him into the bathroom, where his clean clothes had been laid out on top of the hamper. Del pushed him away with his grab stick, insisting that he could manage on his own. Keegan grabbed a sheet from the bedroom and placed it over the dead body.

Police sirens were in the distance, about three minutes away.

"You staying, Durk?" Keegan asked.

Durk, looking down at Ryan's face in his hands, nodded.

"I'm outta here," Keegan said.

With his luck he'd be brought in for questioning in this murder, too. He handed Durk the service revolver, wished them luck, then calmly walked out the front door, taking one last look back at the scene. Maybe this would finally get him to Tampa, where he wouldn't be nostalgic for the job at all.

"You sure you're okay?" Durk asked.

Ryan shook her head. She wasn't sure of anything anymore. Other than life surely sucked sometimes.

"I think you should go down to the hospital, make sure everything's okay," Durk said.

"No," she cried. "No—I can't."

"You have to," Durk said. "For the baby's sake."

"I'm fine," she said. "The baby's fine."

He knew she was a tough Irish broad, but the baby didn't know how to be tough yet. Or so he thought. Just as he moved his hand a little lower than her belly button, hoping to feel any sign of life, a kick worthy of a World Cup soccer player landed in his palm.

Son of a bitch, he thought. *I might end up watching this kid on television in The Pot O'Gold someday, kicking or whacking a ball.*

Chapter 74

Ryan took Cleary up on the offer of therapy sessions. As much as she wanted to just block it out of her mind, she couldn't. She needed to understand how and why it all went down. Through relaxation and meditation and the power of suggestion, she was able to coax together some of what happened the night Declan McManus was murdered.

Durk managed to strong arm Conor into coughing up everything he recalled from that night, too, threatening him with deportation if he didn't. Though he was no longer officially a police officer, he wasn't above placing a phone call to immigration. The rest was purely conjecture, as some of the best police work was, but it was therapeutic nonetheless. It provided some closure, though there would always be doubts and cracks, but this was the version Ryan chose to live with, allowing for further amendments depending on her mood, because a woman reserved the right to change her mind as well as her hair color.

After singing her lungs out with Danny Boy at The Shamrock, they did the pub crawl along McLean Avenue, stopping at The Turntable, the karaoke bar on top of the bar that used to be a bowling alley she frequented as a kid. In the early '90s the business was sold. Since it already had a bar area, the geniuses who bought the place decided to turn the bowling alley into a dance floor. Each night a DJ would spin records and patrons would drink and dance and, if the noise level got too loud, there was a quiet pub downstairs, O'Shea's, where they could talk or watch sporting events on television. No doubt some payoffs factored into the equation. How could you place a bar above another bar, with staircases at either side where drunks could stumble down and hurt themselves and sue the owners and the city? Never made sense to Ryan. But, she didn't care. Yonkers wasn't her jurisdiction and she wasn't much of a dancer. She didn't like the thumping bass lines or rap music that permeated those places and didn't spend much time in the area anymore. But something about this night brought out a wild side in her. Karen had already paired off, and Ryan was determined to find a man for herself. When the DJ gave way to the karaoke machine, Ryan suddenly found herself doing a serviceable cover version of a Taylor Swift song and then launched into a Shakira imitation, which consisted of shaking her hips at breakneck speed. The men in attendance slipped into football fan mentality, egging her on and calling out for her to show her tits but she only did that once at Mardi Gras on a dare from Karen.

She went through the whole repertoire of karaoke songs while Danny Boy waited in the wings, quieting seething as the crowd whistled at her seductive posing and teasing. When she finally announced she had to pee and got off the stage, there was a mini mob scene of men following her, including Conor. She found him cute, and Danny Boy more classically hand-some, but either one would do. She hadn't yet decided which would be her conquest. They continued down the Katonah strip of bars, sang aloud to whatever decent song was on the Finian's Rainbow jukebox, and eventually landed at The Pot O'Gold, where Ryan now turned her attention to Declan. While she was in the ladies room, Danny Boy dropped some gamma-hydroxybutyric acid, the date rape drug, into her healthy cocktail. Then he stepped outside for a smoke, bring-ing his Coors Light bottle with him. And that's when Declan confronted him.

"You can't bring that bottle outside," Declan said to Danny, who kept walking towards the alleyway.

"Says who?" Danny said, nonchalantly checking his cell phone for text messages.

"That's the law. No smoking inside, no drinking outside."

"Yeah? Well, that law don't apply to me tonight."

"Why's that?"

"'Cause I'm about to fuck a cop."

"What makes you so sure?"

"Works every time."

Declan wanted to punch his smug face in. It dawned on him that Ryan had left her drink unattended when she went into the bathroom, and Danny was hovering over it.

"You put something in her drink?" Declan said.

"What's it to you?" Danny said, clicking off his phone.

"You piece of shit. Get the fuck out of here before I call the cops."

"Didn't you hear me? I'm fucking a cop tonight."

Declan reared back and swung a wild roundhouse at his head. Danny ducked just in time, smashed his bottle against the wall, and lunged. When Declan turned back to face him, the bottle lodged cleanly into his neck. He raised his hands to pull it out, but Danny grabbed them, pulling them down, and instinctively resorted to his signature high school wrestling move, the half nelson. With one hand clasped firmly behind Declan's neck, and the other on his wrist, keeping both arms outstretched, Danny watched the blood spill to the sidewalk. The gasping and choking sounds gave way to gurgling noises that gradually subsided as Danny pulled Declan's body toward the Dumpster. There was no way he could lift his big, limp body without getting blood all over him. He heard the creaking of the heavy oak front door and the saxophone solo from Van Morrison's "Wild Night" escaping from the jukebox, and dropped the body.

"Danny?" Ryan called out.

He checked his hands. They were clean. No, shit. There was blood along the side of his palms. He wiped them vigorously under the crotch of his Adidas sweatpants, out of plain sight, and walked back up the alley.

"Danny?" Ryan called out again, taking another sip from her healthy cocktail.

He stepped out of the alley and saw her looking up the avenue. She spun around and spied him.

"Oh—are you okay?"

Fuck, Danny thought. *There's blood on my face.*

"Danny?"

"What?"

"Are you okay? I thought you went out for a smoke."

"Yeah," he said. "You—want—some?"

He reached into his pocket and produced a small pipe.

"Weed?" Ryan said. "No. Don't smoke."

Danny grabbed her by the arms and pulled her into the dark alley. She tried fighting him but damn it he was strong. He pushed her up against the brick wall, not far from where he broke his beer bottle, and kissed her hard on the mouth. At first she resisted but then felt herself melting into him. She dropped her cocktail and it shattered on the ground as she grabbed his waist. He pushed into her with his chest, held her tighter across her back. She could feel his heart racing against hers, as if he were running a marathon.

He wanted to thrust his pelvis into her but remembered the blood on his pants. Pulling back from her and looking into her eyes he said, "Let's go."

They hailed a cab, went back to her apartment, made fast and furious love, and went to sleep. She woke to the news from Durk that Declan McManus was dead and dropped Danny Boy at the train station before going in to work.

One mystery satisfied, or at least rationalized away, but now she wondered, who is the father of my child? Was he a philandering, lying, drug addict, and gambler? A serial rapist and murderer? Did my father kill him? Some mysteries were best left unsolved.

Epilogue

Ryan considered retiring with three-quarters pay, citing post-traumatic stress disorder, maybe heading down south with her old man, but he was never one for the beach. He took her to see *Jaws 3-D* when she was a kid and swore he got sunburned. She'd never be able to wheel his chair over the sand, anyway, unless they got one of those special chairs that looked like they could roam the moon but that wasn't her father's style. There'd be no wasting away in Margaritaville for her, spending early mornings working on her tan, afternoons enjoying happy hours in Key West, and evenings under palm trees in the arms of independently wealthy, age-defying men. *Ah, well. We can't all play centerfield for the Yankees.*

At least she could still watch them on the flat-screen television with her father and newborn Little Del, maybe even take in a couple games in the expanded handicapped section at the stadium. She still had some connections down there, and a place where she could park the new, custom, wheelchair-accessible van. She donated the Jeep—too many horrible memories associated with it.

Maternity leave granted her eight weeks and the family medical leave act provided another six months to fully take stock of the situation and plan for their future. She couldn't foresee the police force being a part of it. Then again, her old man probably never saw it being in her future, either. She already hoped, like her father before her, that Little Del wouldn't follow in their footsteps. Maybe they'd just lie to the kid, tell him they came from a long line of shoemakers or butchers instead.

Cleary continued to reach out, offered his services and some prescriptions, but she never filled the scripts nor found the time to talk with him anymore. She had enough to keep her mind and body occupied now. Those last few pregnancy pounds were tough to lose, but she found an unexpected workout partner in Lisa Durkin, who offered to show her how to use the elliptical machine at the gym. They looked familiar to one another and finally put it together over coffee how they knew each other and shared a laugh at the thought of Durk having an affair. Poor bastard barely had the energy to pull his pants on in the morning. There was no way he was expending whatever energy the job hadn't sapped out of him by sneaking around to have sex in the middle of the night. He needed all the energy he could muster up just to pop a few caps off his beer bottles during Monday Night Football.

Durk came crawling back to Lisa in the middle of the night, with half a bag on and a fistful of tiger lilies he had pilfered from an Italian neighbor's lawn, begging her to take him back. Her fling with the fire hydrant, as Durk called him, was brief and officially over, as he was now behind bars for dealing steroids. Fingerprints, wiretaps, and surveillance video sealed his fate. Turned out Hickey had been following a hunch about HGH and anabolic steroid trafficking at a series of Goomba's gyms in The Bronx and over the county line in Yonkers, leaving behind a series of incriminating evidence on a hard drive in the forensics office. Unfortunately, Lisa Durkin turned up on the tapes, too, canoodling with the fire hydrant, but she had no knowledge of or involvement with the drugs and escaped the predicament with only her reputation taking a hit.

As for Ryan, she was going to stay put, in the same house where her old man raised her, and raise Little Del. It was the only house the old man had ever lived in, and though she had lived in a series of apartments before settling into her bachelorette pad in Riverdale, it was the only house she had ever lived in as well. She knew where everything was and how it worked and whatever needed updating had already been done—the kitchen, the plumbing, the electric, the roof—except for that damn saddle between the hallway and the bathroom door. For now it would serve as a barrier, preventing Little Del from scooting into the bathroom in his walker but once he was old enough to raise it over the lip and get at the roll of toilet paper or the vanity, she'd have it replaced. Plus, it was already paid for. Money ordinarily earmarked for rent or a mortgage could be put aside for college instead, because her child was going to college and would not become a cop.

She'd entertain the thought of home schooling but eventually decide against it, and she'd consider the public school on Katonah Avenue before sending him to St. Sebastian's, just like her mother did with all four of her children. It was good for a kid to have a solid foundation in something to rebel against later in life. The thought of lining McLanahan's pockets with her tuition money made her hesitant, but she wasn't above buying his forgiveness. He was no angel, but he wasn't quite the monster she had made him out to be, either.

The neighborhood had changed but change was inevitable, wasn't it? Change was good. At least that was what the conductor on the Metro-North railroad used to say when it rolled into 125th Street. *Change here for the four, five or six train...Change is good.*

They weren't the traditional family unit but they'd make do. They'd conquer their fears and overcome their challenges. They'd splurge on a motorized wheelchair and bring in a full-time aide. They'd fully vet her, of course, do a background check, and ask for references, the same way they did for the part-time babysitter who allowed Ryan to get out to the gym.

Sheila's sister had just come over from Ireland, where she was a nanny, and could use the extra cash while she worked toward a nursing degree. They wouldn't let just anyone into the house anymore. Maybe they'd get a dog, too—a German shepherd or a Doberman. And they'd always make sure there was a fully loaded Smith & Wesson M&P in the shaving kit, with the safety on, but they'd put it up in the medicine cabinet away from where Little Del might get his hands on it, and maybe put a LadySmith in the night table by the bed, too, just in case.

THE END

About the Author

Shaun Coen is an award-winning playwright, columnist, and feature writer. *The Pot O'Gold Murder* is his first novel.

Made in the USA
Middletown, DE
15 April 2020

89193977R00175